LEAVE NO STONE

A FAITH MCCLELLAN NOVEL

LYNDEE WALKER

First edition November 2019.

Severn River Publishing
www.SevernRiverBooks.com

ISBN: 978-1-64875-464-7 (Paperback)

ALSO BY LYNDEE WALKER

The Faith McClellan Series

Fear No Truth

Leave No Stone

No Sin Unpunished

Nowhere to Hide

No Love Lost

Tell No Lies

The Nichelle Clarke Series

Front Page Fatality

Buried Leads

Small Town Spin

Devil in the Deadline

Cover Shot

Lethal Lifestyles

Deadly Politics

Hidden Victims

To find out more about LynDee Walker and her books, visit

severnriverbooks.com/authors/lyndee-walker

For Dad and Pam, with my eternal thanks for your love and support.

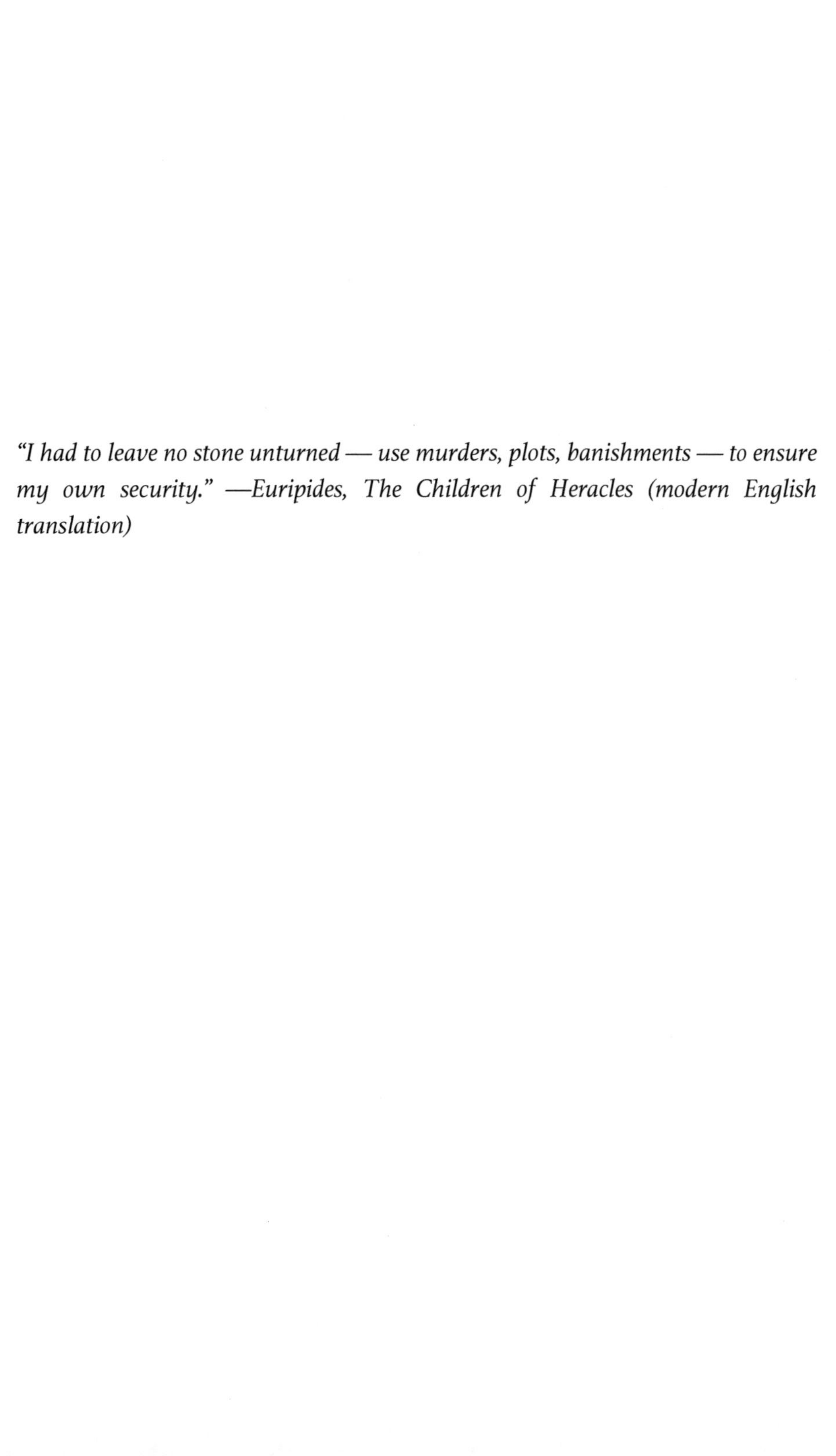

"I had to leave no stone unturned — use murders, plots, banishments — to ensure my own security." —Euripides, The Children of Heracles (modern English translation)

PROLOGUE

Seven hundred and thirty-one days without sunlight is long enough to forget everything about it.

The warmth sinking deep into her skin, the way shadows stretched long across the land, the impossible cornflower blue of a Texas sky—one by one they disappeared from memory, easier lost than longed for.

The dark was lonely, most of the time. She preferred it that way, when she wasn't being selfish.

Now that she had light again, it was harsh—bright, beating hot, and relentless—this glow she'd tried so hard to hold onto, craved even when she didn't know what she wanted anymore.

It hurt.

Her feet, moving from yellow line to yellow line, tingled and stung for fifteen thousand and seven steps, but now she couldn't really feel them anymore. Her eyes, pointed at black ground, only managed to open a sliver. Still, they leaked warm tears from each corner. Her skin felt scorched and tight, like the light was shrinking it on her bones mile by flat, empty mile.

Walk.

Twenty-four thousand three hundred nine. Twenty-four thousand three hundred ten.

Yellow line. Yellow line. Yellow line.

No matter how tired her legs got, no matter how unforgiving the sun she'd missed more than fresh air and good food and hot showers.

She had to keep walking.

He would come for her.

Her hand tightened around the steel of the rail tie she'd carried since before the sun came up. Before the yellow lines.

He would come.

But she had found the sun. Blisters and burns and tears couldn't sway her love of being in the light. She was good at tuning out pain. Ignoring screams.

He'd taught her that.

And if He found her, she would make Him regret it.

1

"Get...the hell...off me," I huffed, struggling to bring my arms up to defend myself.

What kind of bullshit was this? Hours upon hours in the weight room, and I couldn't manage to move even a little. I wriggled my shoulders. His eyes went to my chest.

Not what I was going for.

I forced air out of my lungs in a *whoosh*, letting every muscle relax for a twelve count. Tried the arms again.

Nope. Pinned securely over my head. And the large man straddling my sternum had the actual nerve to smile at me. Asshole.

"That the best you've got, ma'am? Fight harder." He leaned in, the stench of chili and onion following the words out, making my nose wrinkle, my head pressing back into the sticky blue vinyl mat.

I fought to fill my lungs when his weight shifted forward, his face coming even closer to mine.

I crunched my abs and shot my neck upward, my forehead connecting with his dimpled chin and sending his bottom teeth grinding against his top ones with a high-pitched scraping screech that stood every hair in the room on end. His grip loosened enough for me to wrench my arms down, and I shoved the rock-hard center of his chest with both hands. Scrambling to my feet, I flipped my half-fallen ponytail out of my eyes. My legs settled into a wide punching stance as my hands came up, catcalls and whoops flying from the edges of the room.

Bolton rose slowly, one wide paw cradling his lower jaw, the other curling into a fist so large it belonged in a comic book. He bent his knees and lunged to his left. I moved right. And so the dance resumed.

"Thought you had her, rookie." I didn't have to move my gaze from Bolton's flat, angry glare to know that quip came from Graham Hardin. I could see my old partner's moss green eyes dancing with a proud laugh without looking at him. "I mean, she is just a girl..."

I couldn't help the tiny smile as I stepped across my right foot with my left, keeping my circling speed even with the kid's, not daring even a blink.

Bolton's hand dropped, revealing the deep, angry, purple-red bruise already obvious on his chin. Not my fault. He was the one who said he didn't need gear to spar with a girl. He slid his foot back a quarter-second before he lunged left and brought a fist up in a wide arc.

I dodged the punch, darting behind him when the momentum of all that force not connecting sent him sprawling forward. Grabbing his left forearm with both hands, I twisted and pulled up in one lightning motion, putting a sharp elbow into his kidney and dropping to one knee as he hit the mat on his face.

I tightened my grip on his arm, but I didn't need to pull harder. He was still trying to reach me, wrenching his own shoulder more with every desperate flail. I knelt next to the side I had immobilized and waited for him to figure out he was hurting himself by moving.

"You give, rookie?" Graham stepped onto the front corner of the mat.

I flicked my gaze up, shaking my head. "No need to be mean, Commander."

"I'm not mean. He's cocky. And—I hope—learning his lesson." Graham rolled his eyes when Bolton snarled and flung his right side backward again, groping blindly for me with an arm that was bigger than my thigh. "Kid, you're just going to fuck up your shoulder. Give."

"No." It was muffled by the mat, but we heard it.

The steel edge in the word said that was about more than taking a loss in hand-to-hand. My temper flared and I shifted, bracing my knee against his elbow and pushing up.

Bolton screamed. Went still.

"Was that a conces—" Graham didn't get the rest of the word out before a sharp bark came from the doorway.

"McClellan! Time to send your playmates home for the weekend. You have actual work to do."

I didn't let go of Bolton, twisting my neck until I could see Lieutenant Boone out of the corner of one eye. "I turned in the arrest report on the Henning case this morning. It's in the green folder on your desk. The only thing missing is a straight-out confession, but he can howl not guilty until the coyotes come for him—he absolutely is."

My hundred and twenty-first career homicide case was also the easiest I'd ever worked, with a dead guy who'd been running a back-door gambling operation out of his grandmother's Italian restaurant and a regular player who'd lost too much to the house. Lots of blood, lots of brain matter splattered over the tasteful ivory jacquard-covered walls—and three eyewitnesses putting Mr. Losing Streak outside the murder scene. Follow that up with gas station video placing his car a block away ten minutes before shots fired and three minutes after, plus his prints all over the ballistics-matched gun that was registered to his cousin and had gone missing days before the murder.

The local PD sent an SOS our way on Monday when they ran across the betting operation, and I was the only free field agent. Thursday, I dropped the killer at county in time to meet Graham for happy hour, where he requested my help with an attitude adjustment for his ultra-macho rookie.

Boone shook his squarish head, which fit his stout body and nearly nonexistent neck. "Not Henning. You ever work an MP? Because we just got a call I think might interest you, in particular."

Hot damn. Missing persons meant I might get there before there was a murder scene to comb for clues. Meant my scary-specific memory could actually save someone.

Hell to the yes.

I dropped Bolton's arm. He whimpered, curling into a fetal knot around the injury before he squirmed into a tougher prone pose, rubbing his shoulder. The rookie forgotten, I hurried to the locker room with Graham on my heels.

Pausing in the doorway, I smiled at my lieutenant. "Thank you, sir."

"Never thank a man for something you earned, McClellan," he replied. "I'll be in my office when you're ready."

Graham held the door open for me and I ducked into the second row of lockers, which the rest of F Company kept clear for me, as the only woman in the ranks. Yanking on my starched Wranglers and blue button-down, I replayed Boone's words.

Why me "in particular"?

I stuffed my feet into my black leather ropers and stood up to go find out. Graham met me at the door.

"Thanks for your help," he said. "It's one thing when I lecture them about being misogynistic asses, but..." He let the sentence trail like he wasn't sure how to finish it inoffensively.

"But another when a woman puts them on their actual asses?"

"Something like that, yeah."

"Happy to do my part for female empowerment." I gestured to the hallway and he fell into step beside me.

"Sounds like you're about to get busy again," he said.

"I'll take it." I patted his arm and turned toward Boone's office when I spotted Deputy Bolton in the lobby. "Take him and his bruised ego on home and I'll call you later. Y'all drive safely."

Graham snorted, closing his long fingers over mine and squeezing. "I definitely think the mental anguish outweighs the physical pain, but it's good for the boy. He has a few things to learn yet, and I'd be hard pressed to find a better teacher than my favorite Texas Ranger."

I didn't miss the affection cloaking those last words, and a small smile still played around the corners of my lips as I walked into Boone's office. It faded when I saw the image on his desk of a towheaded boy sitting in a woman's lap.

"Amber alert?" I asked, picking up the photo, a color printout on plain office paper. There wasn't a file. A kid? I blew out a slow breath.

"Not the boy, McClellan," Boone said. "His mother."

2

"Lindsey Anne Decker, twenty-six, single mother of one." Boone waved me to the empty chair across from his. I took it, my eyes still on Lindsey's face.

"She was last seen leaving Lone Star Joe at Southpoint Mall in the Dallas exurbs after closing on May twelfth. When she hadn't come to pick up her son and wasn't answering her phone the morning of the thirteenth, a friend called the local PD—which one I can't say for sure, since this home address and the coffee shop are in two different jurisdictions."

"But the PD blew them off." I didn't bother with the inflection a question would give the end of the sentence. A pretty, young, single mom who stayed out all night wouldn't raise your average cop's eyebrow. Hell, most days I wouldn't be fazed by that; hot date, car accident, misunderstanding with the sitter—there are a thousand reasons she wouldn't have shown up that didn't require police involvement. Which department caught the call didn't really make a difference.

"That has continued for twelve days now, and about twenty minutes ago, a friend of Lindsey's called us. B Company is spread too thin, so they called me for help." Boone plucked a small blue sheet of paper from the basket on the corner of his desk. "Friend says she's tired of the 'keystone cops' dismissing her friend as an irresponsible jezebel and she wants 'real police' to help this little boy here see his mother again."

"Knows how to tug at your heartstrings, doesn't she?" I sighed.

"If I had any, I'm sure they'd be properly tightened," Boone chuckled. I blinked. The lieutenant made a joke. To me.

Before I could look around for Rod Serling, I realized Boone wanted me on this case because I had ovaries and therefore would be moved by the kid wanting his mother back. Not because my career clearance rate was the highest in the building. But, whatever. I wanted me on the case, too—the idea of finding this young woman before I needed someone to identify her corpse was damn appealing. At least Boone wasn't still treating me like a file courier.

"There won't be any evidence if nobody did an investigation, sir. She's been missing for nearly two weeks."

"I don't know who did what; all I have is a phone message." He glanced at the little blue missed-call slip. "If you want to head up there and see what you can find out, I have this address." He scribbled on a yellow Post-it note. "It's the MP's house, I believe, and this is the babysitter's cell number." He pulled the note free from the pad and held it and the original phone message up.

I took them, along with the photo printout. "Thank you, sir."

"Thought you might like one where nobody's dead—yet, anyway," he said. "Depressing, homicide."

I managed to keep my brow from furrowing at the kindness the words floated on. Boone wasn't ever nice to much of anyone, let alone me. I knew better than to question it.

"Her friend seriously believes somebody took her?" I asked.

"Dispatcher said this woman was adamant that Miss Decker wouldn't have abandoned the kid."

I squashed the whispers that I might be heading into a murder after all, because believing Lindsey was still alive lent a sense of urgency to this that exceeded even a hot trail in a homicide investigation.

I grabbed an empty folder off my desk on the way to the door and jogged to my truck.

GPS said an hour and a half without traffic, but it was Friday, and Memorial Day weekend to boot. There would be traffic.

Tick tock.

* * *

Lindsey's house could've been lifted straight off a *Saturday Evening Post* cover from 1956: white picket fence, low flowering shrubs, fat blades of well-hydrated St. Augustine, all fronting a gray brick home with black shutters and a scarlet front door sporting windows of rainbow stained glass.

I parked at the curb an hour and fifty-seven minutes from when I left F Company. Grabbing a notebook and my phone before I hopped down, I let myself through a charming little gate and jogged up the walk to the entry alcove.

The doorbell chimed a hymn I recalled from a childhood full of all-day-church Sundays. A dog barked, just once, and footsteps approached the door from the other side.

"Roscoe, back!" The voice belonged to the woman I'd reached on the phone while I was driving out of Waco. She'd thanked me a dozen times in a three-minute call, and I had a feeling that wouldn't be the end of her gratitude. I touched the silver star pinned over my heart, then my sister's charm bracelet. Something in the not-yet-oppressively-hot summer afternoon—maybe the door chime, maybe the picture of the kid, maybe the desperation that practically dripped into my ear during the short chat—called up a silent prayer that I'd be able to do some good here. More good than I was used to doing for the living.

The door cracked open. A fifty-something blonde woman used her wide, soft hips to restrain a golden retriever who just knew I was there to play with him.

Rose Poway was the kind of faded pretty that whispered of how stunning she'd once been—I'd spent my childhood smiling down that brand of beauty from a thousand pageant stages and could spot it at a hundred paces. But her eyes were where my gaze stuck. Large, liquid amber pools floated in a sea of red, anguish and worry as plain to read as the sign on the wall behind her proclaiming *Other things may come and go, but we start and end with family.*

I stuck my hand out for her to shake, my lips tipping up into a sympathetic, self-assured half-smile I perfected long ago in front of a bathroom mirror. The look that said *Trust me. Tell me your secrets. I will find you an answer.*

"Faith McClellan, ma'am."

She yanked me into the house, slamming the door and engulfing me in a cloud of pillowy arms, sprayed-stiff hair, and a few too many spritzes of Chanel No. 5. "Thank you for coming. For caring about poor, dear Lindsey. I swear that girl wouldn't have any luck at all if it weren't for lousy luck."

She stepped back, her hands knotting together in front of her diaphragm, and turned her head to look down the hallway. "Do you mind coming out on the patio? Jake is asleep on the couch, and while I'm sure this boy could sleep through a tornado, I'd rather not disturb him if I don't have to."

I swept one arm out for her to lead the way. "Whatever works for you, ma'am."

She stepped into the hallway and Roscoe saw his opportunity to make a new friend. As strong as he was energetic, he landed his front paws squarely in the center of my chest and almost knocked me on my ass.

"Hey there, buddy." Thankful for my TRX classes, I ruffled the silky fur behind his ears. He licked my chin.

"Roscoe!" He froze at the loud whisper as Rose whirled and hustled back. "No jumping!"

"He's not bothering me, Mrs. Poway." Squatting so I could get on his level, I cupped my hands around his face and massaged his head. He sat on the cool tile and stared at me, his breathing slowing.

"Good boy." I stood. He nudged my fingertips with the top of his head and trotted deeper into the house, looking back at us at the end of the hall. Rose shook her head.

"He's barely left Jake in more than a week, except to check the front windows for her car at nine-thirty every night," she said, leading me through the living room and nodding at the still child curled into a tight ball on the long, worn, beige sectional. The dog sniffed the boy's head and then turned to lie on the floor in front of him. "Child Protection came on Wednesday. They took my driver's license and fingerprints and did a computer check and agreed to leave him since I said I could keep him mostly at home, but he misses his mommy. That's why we need your help."

She tugged the sliding glass door open and turned on a ceiling fan. Taking a seat in a red slingback deck chair, she pointed me to the matching one opposite it. I obliged, crossing my legs and leaning forward to retrieve the notebook and pen from my hip pocket.

Opening it to a blank page, I looked up. “Tell me what happened.”

She laced and unlaced her fingers three times, her mouth twisting to one side before she spoke. “Poor little Lindsey. They moved into this house when she was six, and half the time I can still turn from my garden expecting to see the little girl in pigtails who liked to smell my gardenias.”

I scribbled a star and wrote *sympathy* next to it, also noting Mrs. Poway’s fidgeting. She felt like she was betraying something, or about to. A hundred questions clamored to escape my lips first, but I swallowed them. Best to let her talk for now.

“After her folks died, she took on raising her little brother on her own.” She answered my most pressing question without me asking. “I don’t think she was quite eighteen yet, just out of high school, and she gave up her plans for school and got a job as a secretary somewhere and tried to take care of Adam. Never missed a teacher meeting or a track meet, that girl. But he was already in junior high when their folks died. It’s not her fault he turned out the way he did.”

Noted. Parents died young. Troubled brother. I kept my eyes on hers while I wrote.

She fell quiet for a full minute and I grasped her small, sun-spot-speckled hand. “Mrs. Poway, anything you can tell me about Lindsey and her life could help me figure out what happened to her. And nothing you can say is going to shock me—I’ve been in this job long enough to see just about everything.”

Her chest and shoulders rose with a deep breath as she nodded.

“You said Lindsey has a brother? Does he live here? Could he know where she is?”

She shook her head. “Lord, no. She wouldn’t let him anywhere near Jake. Lindsey loves that baby more than anything I ever saw. Adam hasn’t been welcome here since Jake was born.”

Huh. Lindsey kept a plaque inscribed with a sentiment about family being paramount just inside her front door. But she didn’t allow her brother into her house? Troubled and disowned are two very different things.

"Why is that?" I kept the pen moving across the paper while I held her gaze. Not having a recording is a pain in the ass sometimes, but generally speaking, people can ignore me taking notes a lot easier than they ignore a voice recorder.

"It's not my place to judge a boy who's been through so much," she said. "Adam wouldn't know where Lindsey has gotten off to, and he certainly wouldn't hurt her. Whatever has happened here, he didn't have anything to do with it."

I wasn't near as sure about that as she seemed, but steely resolve crept into her faded brown eyes and wrapped around the words, telling me pressing it would shut her right up. Subject change.

"Gotten off to? Do you think there's a possibility she didn't come home of her own accord, ma'am?" Boone said she was convinced Lindsey wouldn't run out on the kid, but her words suggested otherwise. With missing adults, a runner is the more common road. While Mrs. Poway's description of Lindsey's love for her son didn't jibe with her ditching him, I couldn't take anything for granted.

Rose's lower lip disappeared between her teeth. "When her friend came over and knocked on my door last Monday, I didn't know what to think. Lindsey is very careful about who is allowed to see Jake. She never brings dates home. But she's young, and sometimes she does get carried away, and she stays out...awfully late." Her eyes flicked away from mine. Read: all night. Got it. "But she's never been gone near so long before, and the more time that goes by, the more scared I get." She turned wide, pleading eyes back on me. "Do you think something could have happened to her? I mean, Jake is so little. And I don't mind helping out with him, he's such a love, but I have either forgotten how much work a toddler can be, or I've gotten old since my boys were babies. He's flat wearing me out."

"I can imagine. Can you tell me anything about the coffee shop where Lindsey worked? If it's in the mall, it closed at six on Sunday, right?"

"Yes. I think she usually had Sundays off. Seems unfair to have her work on Mother's Day, but I guess it's pretty busy at food-type places. My boys took me to lunch that day, and Maggie was here with Jake when I got home. I saw her car in the driveway."

"Do you know how to get in touch with Maggie?" I asked.

"They work together. Got close quick after Lindsey started there a year or so ago. She wanted to go back to school and study social work, and the coffee place has benefits even when you don't work full time."

"What about Jake's father?"

Her eyes dropped again, her thumbs twisting around one another. "I don't know."

"You've never met him?"

"Lindsey won't say who he is." Her lips pressed into a tight, disapproving line, but she fought through it. "As far as I know, Jake's never met him, and I think Lindsey aims to keep it that way."

I scribbled notes as fast as my fingers would move, trying to formulate a follow-up question that wouldn't sound critical.

Before I got one out, she sat forward in the chair and froze. "Did you hear something?"

I shook my head. She stood anyway. "Would you like something to drink? I'm afraid the offerings here are limited to water and juice boxes, but the social worker lady thought it would be better for Jake to spend as much time as he could in his own house."

"Water sounds lovely, thank you."

She disappeared into the house, and I tapped my pen on my pad, flipping back through my notes. I needed to find Lindsey's brother, find out if she had a boyfriend, and—the biggest question mark—locate the little boy's father.

I turned my head slowly, surveying the well-manicured yard surrounding the patio. A hulking wooden playground took up the left side of the space, a flower bed of black-eyed Susans, daisies, and lilies all in full bloom lined the back fence.

The patio door whispered back in the metal track and I stood.

Roscoe bounded onto the patio, making a beeline for the playset and hiking his leg on three of the four posts. A small blond head poked around the doorframe behind the dog. Big, round blue eyes stared above the pink lips pursed around a barely visible thumb. I waved.

Jake Decker popped the thumb free and gripped the door, carefully lowering one chubby foot to the shaded concrete patio. Pausing, he raised his eyes to mine again.

"Hi there," I said softly.

Planting his other foot on the patio, he let go of the door and swiveled his head between me and the playset.

"Would you like to swing?" I asked.

He nodded, a smile creeping up the bottom of his face, not quite reaching his eyes.

I followed his unsteady steps to the edge of the porch, putting out a hand when he looked around for help. He closed small, sweaty fingers around my three middle ones and stepped down to the grass, pulling me to the yellow plastic swing and raising his arms for me to pick him up.

I hadn't ever spent much time around small humans. I lifted him, perching him on the seat. He gripped the plastic-encased chain and wriggled his bottom into a more comfortable position, turning his face up and nodding.

"Here we go." I pulled the swing up a few inches and let go, a smile touching my lips when he giggled. "You're Jake, right?" I asked.

His little head bobbed again.

"I'm Faith," I said. "Nice to meet you."

Two blinks.

Huh. Was he not talking to me because I was a stranger? Or did he not talk?

I laid my fingers on the plastic seat on either side of his legs and pushed again.

His tiny hands choked up on the chain and he leaned back, a long, infectious giggle erupting from his throat. I pushed more, he giggled again. We went on like that for a good three or four minutes before Rose Poway reappeared. She opened the sliding door and paused half out of the house, too far away and too shadowed by the patio roof for me to see her face. It was all smiles as she crossed the grass a moment later, though.

"I hope he wasn't bothering you," she said. "He loves that thing to distraction."

I shook my head, pushing the swing when it rose back to my hands.

"He's not a bother at all. Mrs. Poway, did the local police tell you anything about Lindsey's case?" It was a crapshoot of a question. Some departments, some cops, are good with loved ones, keeping them enough in the loop. Others share nothing, but might be doing ten times the work of the more personable outfits. She'd called us because she was unhappy with something, but if anyone had actually been working this case day and night for two weeks, a Rangers badge wouldn't be a welcome sight around their station, and I wanted to know what I was about to walk into.

She shook her head. "They haven't told anyone else anything, either," she said. "And when I called over to the news station the other day, they told me they would need an official police contact and report to put a story on TV about Lindsey. Nobody will help us." She tickled Jake's foot as he leaned back, hanging onto the chains and closing his eyes. "Except you, I hope."

I stared at the little boy. He locked eyes with me as he sat up, his crossing before he shut them while he waited for the world to right itself again.

Boone was right to send me here. Maybe it was my gender, maybe it was my stubborn streak—but if seeing his mother come home would make this kid's smile light up his eyes again, I would bring her back if I had to turn every rock from Dallas to Toronto to Mexico City and back again.

I smiled at Rose. "Would you mind taking over for me, ma'am? I'd like to have a look around Lindsey's room before I head out."

"Of course." She circled the swings, waving a *go ahead* in the direction of the house. "Last door on the left off the hallway," she said.

I patted Jake's back and went inside, the cool air blissful after standing in the sun awhile. Lindsey Decker kept a neat house. Sure, maybe her neighbor had straightened up, but the rooms were on the sparse side to begin with—no knickknacks, no candles, just a couple of painted ceramic tiles with sayings about finding joy in small things hanging on the living room walls. Save for a red plastic tub of toys in one corner, there wasn't much to make a mess with.

Bare ecru walls lined the hallway. Behind a white six-panel door at the end, Lindsey's room was tidy but worn, the furniture I'd bet had once belonged to her parents showing its age. The beige carpet under my boots had thinned over time. Lilac walls framed a queen-size bed, table, and half-full blue hamper at the end of the long oak dresser. Not so much as a discarded tissue out of place. I crossed to the small nightstand, lifting a cool metal frame by the edges, staring at a younger Lindsey, her blonde hair back in a ponytail, posing in front of the oil derrick at Six Flags with one arm around the thin shoulders of a young man in black shorts and a black T-shirt, his face half-hidden behind stringy, unkempt, chin-length hair.

"Hello, Adam." I poked my nose an inch from the image of his, studying his sullen expression. Teenage angst on steroids poured from the memory, but according to Mrs. Poway, the story wasn't that simple. Pulling my phone from my pocket, I clicked up the camera and snapped a clear shot of the photo before I returned it to the nightstand and flipped the sketchbook open.

Holy hell, Lindsey Decker could draw—the sketch of her son on the first page was gallery-quality. I turned pages. Three more of Jake—laughing, then smiling, then sleeping. A self-portrait. A few of Mrs. Poway's flowers. One more page and pay dirt—the last sketch was a guy. Strong jaw, straight nose, thick eyebrows and lips.

I let my eyes roam every line, raising my phone to get a picture of that, too. Was there a handsome mystery man in Lindsey's life? Rose said she never brought men into her house, but maybe this one was stuck in her head. Could she have taken off with him?

It was too soon to tell, with too many conflicting variables for me to know what I was looking at yet. This guy could be a boyfriend. He could also be a favorite soap opera actor.

I closed the sketchbook and took a pass through her closet—mostly black pants and white button-down shirts, coffeehouse standard uniform. A few pairs of jeans lay folded on a shelf next to a pair of black leather flats and two pair of Laredo ropers: one black and one saddle-leather brown.

I turned to the rack and reached into every pants pocket. Not so much as a big piece of lint. Strike one.

Along the back wall, four fitted minidresses dangled from hangers, two black, one silver, and one red. All size four, all from the juniors' section at Target. A woman's closet can be a powerful reflection of who she is, and this one said Lindsey Decker had two modes: work and play.

The dresser held shorts, T-shirts, socks, and underwear, the latter divided into piles of white cotton and black lace. Nothing hid in the bottoms or corners of the drawers, and I was careful not to disturb the neat stacks of clean clothes as I searched.

Damn. Strike two.

A small jewelry box sat alone atop the center of the dresser. I raised the lid and found a class ring from 2008 with a blue stone, a small pair of pearl earrings, and a silver cross pendant on a thick chain.

Next up, the hamper. I moved clothes side to side until I could see the bottom, and a crumpled paper fell from the pile to the plastic bottom of the basket. I reached for it, smoothing it as I flipped it over.

A card, the kind that comes with flowers. Two hearts and a spray of roses in one corner, black ink in bold strokes across the center.

Can't stop thinking about you. Love, Me.

That was coming with me.

I clicked the flashlight on my phone and checked under the bed, because I always feel like I should even though I've never once found anything important there.

In the bathroom, I borrowed the lone toothbrush in the holder just in case I needed baseline DNA to match.

On to Jake's room.

Similar story: clothes hung or stacked neatly, diaper table stocked with Pampers, wipes, and cream. A rocking chair with a blue cotton blanket draped over it in the corner, chocolate-colored wooden letters on the blue wall spelling "Jacob." This little boy was well cared for.

I spotted a stuffed owl and a blue pacifier in the crib. Touching the plastic edge of the paci, I turned back to his dresser to verify that there were two spares in a basket on one end.

Nobody knew who this child's father was, and now his mother was missing. I snagged the empty plastic grocery sack lining the wastebasket and dropped the card, the toothbrush, and the binky in. Twisting air out of the sack, I tied it shut before I slid it into my hip pocket. Strictly speaking, I shouldn't test Jake's DNA without his mother's permission. And the results might not get me anywhere—but I had to try on the off chance that they might lead me to Lindsey.

I stuck my head back outside and smiled at Mrs. Poway, sitting on the deck with both Jake and a picture book in her lap. Jake had his thumb back in his mouth.

"Thank you for your help, ma'am. I'm not sure what's happening here, but I'm glad you called us, and I will be in touch." I pulled a card from my pocket and held it out to her.

"Thank you for coming." She smoothed Jake's hair.

I squatted to meet his solemn little stare with one of my own. I smiled. He did the same. I touched my index finger to the tip of his nose. "It was nice to meet you, Jake," I said. "You be a good boy, and keep swinging and giggling, okay?"

If I couldn't find his mother, that would be a tough go for him. I knew more about losing the biggest force in your world than I'd ever wish on anyone. And I would do my damndest to make sure this kid didn't have to learn it before he knew his ABC's.

3

The suburbs are tricky business, law enforcement-wise. It seemed Lindsey lived nine miles and two jurisdictions from the mall where she worked, which meant my questions at the station closest to her house had been met with a lot of blank stares.

Back in my truck, with the right jurisdiction in my GPS, I stopped at a yellow light, pulled my phone out, and touched Archie Baxter's name in my favorites. He picked up on the second ring.

"Now, I know you have better things to be doing on a Friday night than talking to an old man. And if you don't, I'm afraid I can't help you," he said by way of hello.

Archie was a grizzled old cop who'd seen every kind of shit this job will throw at you, given his life to public service up to and including guarding the Governor of Texas, and traded his chance at a family for protecting his fellow man. And me. Because that former governor was my father.

"I've got a week without a single cigarette to brag about, and a spare pack I'd bet that you're still sitting at your desk as you lecture me about my work-life balance."

"So you want to be like me, now?" He laughed. "You need a new role model. And good on you, girl. I'm proud of you."

In less than six months, I'd graduated from "new girl" back to "girl," which he'd been calling me since he was slipping me bubble gum during some speech back in the day. Not too shabby for a former beauty queen who had never been expected to become anything more than some aspiring politician's trophy wife.

"I caught a new case today," I said. "Trying to run down leads in the Dallas suburbs and wondering if you know anyone at any of these departments. And if you know why the hell they don't talk to each other. If my jurisdiction was the size of a gnat's ass, I'd be nosy about what was going on with the flea next door, you know?"

He grunted agreement. "What're you working on?"

"Young single mom who disappeared thirteen days ago. Lindsey Decker, twenty-six, last seen leaving Southpoint Mall in Lake Whitney where she worked at a coffee shop, never showed up back home to relieve the babysitter."

Tap. Tap. Tap. Archie's index finger hit the back of the phone in a slow rhythm. I could practically see him as I steered the truck through Friday night traffic. He'd lean back in his gray mesh desk chair and cross one ankle over the opposite knee, his long, sun-leathered face wrinkling with concentration.

"I haven't heard her name," he said finally. "You said she's been missing more than a week?"

"Yes, though I'm not at all sure whether it's by choice or by force yet. Her neighbor called our office today, looking for help. She contends the local cops don't care that Lindsey is gone. I'm trying to figure out who was supposed to be investigating it and if they're not, why not. But from the blank stares I got at the department that's closest to her house, I'm wondering if it's inaction or just ineptitude."

"Often a toss-up," he said. "You said you're in the suburbs?"

"Lake Whitney," I said. "That's where I'm headed, anyway. The shopping center she disappeared from is two minutes from their headquarters, according to Google."

"Huh. Billy Roundtree is the chief up there, and he's an old friend of mine from my days as a trooper. He's a good cop. I can't imagine he runs a shitty department."

"Maybe they're just not talking because she doesn't have true family for them to talk to." I turned into the station parking lot. "Mind if I drop your name at the desk?"

"Drop away, for all the good it'll do you," he said. "Missing, but not dead, huh? That's different for you."

"I'm feeling the pressure to find her. The kid has these huge eyes that don't light up when he smiles. I've been on this a whole three hours including drive time. But I like it. At least, I like it as long as I pull it off."

"Give Billy my best, and call me if you need me," he said.

"Thanks, Arch." I clicked the red *End* circle as I pulled into a spot in front of the doors. Checking my teeth for lip gloss before I jumped down, I tucked the phone and a notebook into my hip pocket and took a deep breath as I ambled to the doors. Friendly smile. Easy tone. I wasn't here to bigfoot their investigation; I just wanted to help. And everything about me had to say that, or anyone Archie called a decent cop would show me the door before I got an eyeball on one word of their file.

A young desk officer with a crew cut wearing a starched polo with a department logo over his heart looked up when I walked into the brown-brick and dark-tile lobby.

His green eyes went from my ponytail to my boots and back, lingering both times on my badge. "Texas Rangers? My my. To what do we owe the pleasure?"

Did they have more than one thing happen here in a year that we might be interested in? Ignoring his derisive tone, I kept mine friendly. "I'm Faith McClellan. Looking for some information on the disappearance of a Lindsey Decker," I said. "Thirteen days ago, from the mall down the road a piece." Literally—it was six blocks up and across the street.

He plucked a pen from the cup on his desk and see-sawed it between his thumb and index finger. "I'm afraid the detective assigned to that case isn't in this late," he said.

I swallowed the *Why the hell not?* that threatened to pop out of my mouth. The sun wasn't even down yet. Policework isn't an eight-to-five gig. Especially not when someone's life might hang in the balance.

Maybe they knew things I didn't. Nearly two weeks in, I sure hoped so, anyway.

"Is Chief Roundtree still in, by any chance?" I asked.

His eyes narrowed. The pen stopped. "I'm not sure."

That was it. Didn't move to pick up a phone or stand to go look. I gave him five slow blinks and tipped my head in the direction of the thick, locked door to my left. "Might you be able to check for me?" I did my best to coat the words in sugar, but they definitely came out more pickled than sweet.

His jaw flexed, the little vein next to his eye popping to attention, as he reached for the phone.

Damn. Some folks were more receptive to help from the Rangers than others, sure, but nothing warranted this level of surliness.

I folded my hands behind my back and rocked up on my toes.

He put the phone to his ear and pressed three buttons. Paused. "Sir? There's a Miss McClellan from the Rangers out here asking to see you. Asking about that Decker woman. Should I—?"

He stopped, rolling his eyes, when I put one hand up. "Can you please tell him Archie Baxter told me to ask for him?" The tight smile I managed didn't make the words bright, exactly, but it stopped them from being outright hostile.

"She says Archie Baker told her to ask for you."

"Baxter," I murmured.

He sucked his cheeks into a fish face, nodding. "Yes, sir."

Replacing the receiver, he stood up slowly, leading me to the security door and entering a code before he pulled it open.

Five steps down the hallway, a short, round man in khakis and a green Polo pushed his wire-rimmed glasses up his nose and waved.

"Miss McClellan, a pleasure," he said when I stopped in front of him and shook his hand. "I'd apologize for you having to contend with Baxter, but I'm afraid I can't take all the responsibility for him anymore."

"I try my best to keep an eye on him these days." I winked, pulling my notebook from my back pocket. "I'm so glad I caught you, sir. Thank you for seeing me."

He ushered me into a plain box of an office—metal desk, three chairs, and a lone bookshelf on the back wall. Taking the seat behind the desk, he waved me to one of the chrome and white office chairs on my side and opened the file on the blotter. "We don't get much in the way of missing persons up here," he said. "When we do, it's usually some smartass kid who didn't listen to momma and busted curfew. With three quarters of my personnel working overtime every day trying to keep teenagers from overdosing on opiates, we don't have much time for runaways, and it seems to me that Miss Decker doesn't want to be found. So I thank you for making the drive out to us." He pushed the folder across the desk. "All yours."

I reached for the file. His manner and words were so far from what I'd expected walking in, my brain had trouble making the gear switch. To hear him tell it, he might've called Boone himself if he'd thought of it first.

"Thank you, sir." I laid the folder across my knees—it weighed next to nothing—and flipped it open. Two sheets of a report, dotted with plenty of whitespace.

Initial call from Maggie Anderson at 7:27 a.m. May 13, officer arrived at the mall at 8:30 to meet with security and interview Miss Anderson. Video footage showed Lindsey leaving by a rear door in an alcove on her way to drop trash into a dumpster. The camera outside the door had been hit with a hailstone in an April storm and wasn't yet repaired. The second page was a contact sheet of photos of the alcove in the daylight, including the dumpster.

"This is a fairly secluded area," I said. "So even in the daylight, someone might have been able to take her away from here with no witnesses?"

"It is far more likely that Miss Decker grew weary of all her responsibilities and took off." Roundtree rolled his chair backward and leaned down to open a drawer, hefting three folders onto his desk. "A quick search of the name in our files produced these." He thumped the fattest file down. "Her father, who had four PIs and two DUIs before the crash that killed him and his wife just up the road." He dropped a thinner one on top of it. "Her brother, who's on his third strike for both possession and dealing." And the third, not any thicker than the file I held. "And Miss Decker herself, who was a witness in a human trafficking bust two years ago, though not even a shrink could get her to admit she'd ever turned a trick."

My eyes wide, I felt my lips moving silently as I hunted words.

"I—what? Trafficking?"

Oh Lord. Is that why she wouldn't tell anyone who the baby's father was?

"Guy was running a slick little setup, using video of teenage girls having sex he bought off their boyfriends to blackmail them into turning tricks after school. Threatened to show their parents and teachers. Lindsey Decker knew an awful lot about the major players to be uninvolved, but she claimed they had nothing on her, and we didn't find evidence to the contrary."

"May I?" I reached for the file. Maybe his job wasn't as mundane as I'd thought.

Pages and pages of photos of pretty girls.

Roundtree flipped the other folders open. "That's a lot of family history in a police file room, Miss McClellan. Baxter is a good man, and I'm sure he'll tell you the same thing I'm about to: odds are almost a sure thing that this young woman is blowing off steam somewhere. Her car is gone. Nobody saw or heard anything around the mall, and we have video evidence that nobody followed her outside. Honestly, the only crime I see evidence of here is child abandonment. I can have a warrant for Miss Decker's arrest on that charge in a hot minute if you'd like, but given the dying teenagers we've had stacking up every day for a year, I'm still willing to give her a pass if you can get her to come on home."

I surveyed the files on his desk. An alcoholic father didn't exactly spark thoughts of a happy, stable childhood. Damn. I shook my head. I'd walked in here hoping to find an answer or two, and this just stirred up more questions. Did she run? An hour ago I would've almost staked my badge that she hadn't, because psychology says that people who experience a major loss early in life will do everything in their power to protect those they love from similar pain, and Lindsey loved little Jake. But if her dad's death maybe hadn't been a total tragedy for her, then what? A lot of drunks, particularly repeat DUI offenders, are mean drunks. Some kids who are abused grow up to shelter others from it, and some continue a pattern of it. And I didn't know enough yet about Lindsey Decker to so much as offer an educated guess about which camp she'd fall into.

"May I get copies of all these, sir?" I asked, returning the trafficking file to the desk. There were about a dozen rocks to chase down and turn just in those pages, and I was getting a late start.

He reached for his phone and pressed two buttons. "I need copies of some files for Miss McClellan, please."

"Yes, sir." Surly Desk Officer sounded just as surly talking to his boss on the speaker phone.

Roundtree looked back at me. "He'll be in at his earliest convenience, I suppose. Which could be a while." The words were so dry they could've crumbled and blown away. I was glad it wasn't just me, but beyond that his personnel issues were not my circus.

"Have you talked to the press?" I couldn't quite believe the words were coming out of my mouth even as they did.

"Find me a reporter who gives two damns about a missing woman who may or may not have run out on her kid," he said. "I haven't notified them because they won't put the kid on TV without a release signed by a relative, which we have a shortage of, and without the kid, there's not a story in it for them. With the kid, Miss Decker doesn't come off so great. I didn't see a reason to waste my time."

I shook my head, a lifetime of up-close-and-personal with political media spin doctors finally coming in handy. "It's all in your presentation, sir," I said. "For all we know, someone is walking around with cell phone footage in their pocket of exactly what happened after Lindsey left that building. We just have to ask the right way."

"Be my guest. I'll bet bending reporters to your will runs in your blood if I'm right about your last name."

"Has to be useful every once in a while. But I'm afraid I don't know the Dallas market. Who's your most annoying TV reporter?"

Somebody around here had to have a copycat Skye Morrow, and as much as I loathed every line on her botox-expressionless face, she was damned good at getting results.

"Chip Johnson at Channel Seven." Roundtree didn't hesitate. "Boy would worry a dog right off a bone."

Fuck. The only thing that might be more irritating than Skye herself was Skye with some testosterone pumping through her.

But, if Chip was the worst they had to offer, it meant every other reporter around here watched him and followed what he was working, so he'd be the only one of the bunch I'd have to talk to. I stood. "I appreciate it, sir."

He rose and gestured a *ladies first* to the door, stabbing the button on his desk phone a second time. "Simms? Come make me a copy of these files for Ranger McClellan."

Five beats, and the door at the end of the hallway clicked. Crew Cut from the front desk didn't look any happier as he picked up the file folders and disappeared.

"Don't mind him," Roundtree said, shaking his head. "Wife left him a week ago Saturday. For his brother. He doesn't hate you; he hates the whole world right now."

I pulled a card from my pocket. "Call me if you get anything new?"

"Sure thing." He dropped it on his desk. "Tell that old bastard Baxter I'm still prettier than he is, and let me know if I can help you." His grin revealed a row of straight, small white teeth.

Simms reappeared with eight folders, handed one stack to each of us, and turned back for his post without a word. Roundtree sighed. "I'm trying to give that boy some lead, but he's about to get pulled up shorter than is going to be comfortable."

I tried to cough over the laugh, but it didn't work. I liked the chief. He reminded me of Archie, with his ease and sense of humor. "Nice to meet you, sir. I sure hope you crack your opiate case. And thanks again."

"I have a feeling by the time all is said and done I may be thanking you, Miss McClellan. I've read about you. And Baxter has a good eye. Best of luck to you." He sighed. "These kids...too much money and too little supervision. It's the same story all across the country, I'm afraid. But we're giving it everything we've got."

He walked me to the door and waved as I climbed into my truck. I pulled my phone out and clicked the screen, swiping to ignore three missed calls from Graham. Eight-thirty. Chip Johnson shouldn't be in makeup just yet.

Lord help me, I was going to the TV station.

4

It took twice as long to get to Chip as it did to get to the police chief, and the TV station's lobby was lined with bulletproof glass the PD lacked. I didn't stop to think too hard about what that said about the world we live in, because it would just piss me off, and right then I needed to be on my game.

I didn't want to underestimate this guy. That became difficult when he finally materialized—he was maybe five-four and looked like Doogie Howser, action reporter.

His eyes widened so briefly when he saw my badge I would've missed it with half a blink. He strode into the lobby with a wide smile, his right hand extended. "Chip Johnson, what can I help you with?"

I shook his hand as I gestured to the door behind him with my free one. "I know it's almost time for your evening broadcast, but I'm wondering if there's a quiet place we can discuss a missing person." I offered a suitably somber frown.

His head started bobbing before I got the last word out, and he yanked the door open and waved me through. "Right this way."

Down a short hallway, he flipped on the lights in a small conference room, a round table for eight taking up all but a few inches of the floor space. He pulled out the closest chair for me before he closed the door and took the seat two over from mine.

"I monitor the scanner app on my phone pretty much around the clock and I haven't seen anything about a missing kid," he said.

I shook my head. "I didn't say it was a kid."

"I see." He sat back. "Can I be straight with you?"

"Please." I tried to ignore the dimples that showed even when he wasn't smiling. They made it damned near impossible to avoid giggling at his "tough guy" demeanor.

"Missing adults are a hard sell." He laced his fingers behind his head, exposing pale yellowish stains under the arms of his white button-down. "The stories don't get as many clicks, so the producers and the ad people don't love them, and management is always afraid the person in question will turn up later in a bad light, making us look stupid. So I'm not sure how much help I can be, Ranger...?" He raised his eyebrows as he trailed off and I leaned forward, resting both elbows on the cool laminate tabletop.

"McClellan." He was young, it might take a minute.

It did not. "As in...?"

I nodded.

He sat up straight. "Tell me what you need. I'm happy to see what I can do."

Once upon a long-ago time, I would've felt skeevy about using the governor's name to make inroads, especially with a reporter. I didn't even like being reminded that I was related to Chuck McClellan, much less reminding others about it. But right then, any tool in my box that might get Lindsey Decker back quickly and still breathing was fair game until I wore it out.

I pulled up her picture on my phone and held it out. Not for him to take, which he seemed to sense, but for him to see. "Lindsey Decker is twenty-six years old. Single mother of one son. Disappeared nearly two weeks ago between when she left work and her house, not even ten miles west of her place of employment. The local police investigation has run aground." I didn't even bat an eye at the paper-thin stretch to the truth, because opioid crisis be damned, Bill Roundtree wasn't doing his job to the fullest of his ability, and he was lucky I didn't tell this kid that instead. "We need a public appeal for information. If there's any way you can help with that, I'd consider it a personal favor."

I studied his face while he looked at Lindsey's. He didn't need to know that my father wouldn't give half a hairy rat's ass who had done me a personal favor. Ambition gleamed so bright in his eyes it was almost hard to look directly into them.

He drummed his fingers on the table, his head starting to nod. I pulled my phone back.

"I can get this on the air. Can I get a copy of that photo, and maybe one of her kid? Heart-wrenching is the angle here—I bet we'll get the same views as a missing kid, even, because she has a kid. Plus, she's not hard on the eyes." He produced a notebook from under the table and clicked a pen. "Spell her name for me?"

I obliged, my brain racing on the photo angle. I had only snapped a quick shot of the grainy printout image of Lindsey's face, which wouldn't do him any good. I swiped out of the photos and clicked my Facebook app open. Search. Lindsey Decker. Go.

Bam. Her profile picture was one of her and the baby. I touched it, saved it, and looked up at Chip. "Your email address?"

He reeled it off. "What else can you tell me about her?" He tapped his pen on the notebook.

"She worked at a coffee shop at the Southpoint Mall in Lake Whitney," I said. "She's on video leaving the mall by the back door on Mother's Day, but she never got home to relieve her babysitter. No accidents reported, no trace of her vehicle."

He clicked his pen in and out. "Did you just say she disappeared on Mother's Day? And you suspect foul play?" Of course. That was a story angle.

"This is a missing persons investigation until we have irrefutable evidence that the status should change, Mr. Johnson. And I'll remind you that her loved ones will likely be watching your broadcast."

I actually had no idea if anyone Lindsey knew watched the news or what channel, but odds were good someone would post a clip, and I wanted him to stay on message. If he veered into even a hint of a suspicion of murder, we could lose leads. Maybe the important ones. People can be reluctant to get involved in a violent crime, even by something as small as an anonymous tip.

He tipped his head to one side. “I wasn’t insinuating that the woman is dead, Ms. McClellan. Just that I’m correct if I include in my report that the Texas Rangers suspect she didn’t take off of her own accord.”

Oh. Oops.

I pulled in a deep breath. “Forgive me, it’s been a long day. And I’ve just taken over this case, so I’m not sure what happened to Miss Decker yet. What I do know is that with every second that ticks by, people’s memories fade, so I don’t have the luxury of waiting before I ask for your help. Even something as simple as a witness who saw her leave the mall and could share a time or a direction could be important.”

He scribbled shorthand I couldn’t have read even if it wasn’t upside down, his eyes narrowing as they traveled over my face and hair in a way that reminded me of long-ago swimsuit competitions. I returned the gaze with a smirk I wouldn’t have dared in front of a pageant judge until after my sister died—because once the person whose opinion mattered most wasn’t there, I didn’t give a damn about anyone else’s for a long time, it had turned out.

“Would you be willing to go on camera?” he asked.

Oh hell. I should’ve seen that coming.

Not even the faintest glimmer of interest. But, interested and willing are two different things. I’ve crawled through swamps and dark, narrow caves and even a landfill once en route to a collar. A TV camera at least smelled better.

“If that’s what it takes,” I said. “But not live.”

I wasn’t stupid. This guy might look like a baby, but Roundtree’s words hadn’t left my head altogether. A live interview gave Chip here way too much power.

His face sagged for a beat, but he recovered quickly, checking his watch.

“Let me grab my producer and a photographer, and we can just sit in here. I might be able to throw it into the last segment of the broadcast if it’s an easy edit.” He excused himself, leaving his notebook on the table.

I eyed it.

I shouldn't. It was snooping. And it wasn't like I'd know if I saw anything, anyway, with the chicken scratch on the page in front of me.

But knowing what the most irritating reporter in a city is working on is never a bad thing when you have a case shaping up there. And if I'd made the same error, I had zero doubt Chip would take advantage of it in a heartbeat.

I used the edge of my phone to slide the notebook across the tabletop toward me, flipping a half-dozen or so pages back.

JMD, SA, BC, 3 vc

The second and fourth lines had stars by the letters, but it might as well have been braille for all I could make it out. I clicked up my camera and took a photo of the page, and the next one, just as I heard voices approaching in the hallway.

Shit. Last page. I found it and shoved the pad back across the table, dropping my phone to the surface.

"Ms.—um, Ranger? McClellan." Chip, who'd donned a perfectly tailored navy blazer, tipped his head to one side when I stood.

"Ranger is better for this application."

"More official," he said. "Got it." He turned to the large man filling the doorway behind him, a bulky box camera with a boom mic on the front dangling from one muscled arm. "This is Jeff. Jeff, Ranger McClellan."

"A pleasure, ma'am." Jeff's voice was deep and velvety, the kind of smooth baritone that always brought good blues music to mind. He raised his hands, the camera in one and a folded tripod in the other.

"Jeff, why don't you set up in that corner"—Chip pointed to the back of the room—"and tell us where you need us to sit for you to get the best shots."

* * *

Jeff gave a high sign and Chip turned on the charm like ordinary people flip a light switch. I had to tighten my abs to keep from recoiling from the waves of charisma. A lifetime spent around politicians and murderers—both groups tend to score off the charts for charisma—will do that to a person.

"News Seven thanks Texas Ranger Faith McClellan for joining us to bring you this heartbreaking story," he intoned, a solemn stare focused on the camera. "Ranger McClellan, how did the Rangers come to be involved in Miss Decker's case?"

My eyes jumped between the camera and Chip's face before a lifetime of the governor in the background of my earshot took over and I leaned my forearms on the table. I steepled my fingers together, focusing on Chip. "We were notified of the disappearance by a friend of the victim today," I said. "If anyone has information that might lead to Lindsey's safe return home, please call your local crime stoppers office or reach out to me directly at (254) 333-6874."

"Miss Decker has a young son," Chip said. "Do authorities believe the child to be in any danger?"

I paused.

No?

"There is no evidence at this time that the child is a target in this case," I said, not a drop of uncertainty in my voice or a flicker of it on my face. "But we would like to return his mother home as quickly as possible."

"And Miss Decker disappeared from Southpoint Mall in Lake Whitney?"

"Yes, she was last seen leaving the center around six-forty in the evening on May 12," I said. "Anyone who was in the vicinity of the mall that evening and in possession of photos or video, please call. Something you don't notice in the background of your shot may just help give this little boy his mother back."

My skin crawled right up my arms, cold sweat leaking out of every pore. I was laying it on thick. Dramatic.

Chip gave Jeff a cut sign and aimed an I-want-my-Emmy smile at me. "Thank you, that was great. Good if I put that phone number you gave on the screen?"

I stood. "Yes, please."

Jeff waved. "Nice to meet you, ma'am."

"You too."

Chip hustled to the door, already flipping through his notebook. "Thank you, Ms. McClellan. Keep in touch. I'm going to run up and get this ready."

"Thank you for your help." He was gone by the time I got the last word out.

I checked my watch. Five after nine.

In my truck, I flipped open the moderately thick police jacket on Adam Decker. Punched his last known address into my GPS. It was more than a year old, but all I had to go on, and he was Lindsey's only family.

Google Maps said seventeen minutes. I drove, watching the clean, well-kept boulevards of the suburbs narrow into pothole-riddled four-lane roads with only double yellow lines down the center, the buildings lining them growing in both age and level of disrepair.

Following the robotic directions, I hung a left into a wide gravel parking lot surrounded by the kind of motel frequented by prostitutes and addicts. It fit with the description I had of Adam.

Room 136 was halfway down a wood-planked walkway on the far left of the lot. I stepped across a wide gap in the flooring and rapped on the door. Waited.

No light, no footsteps, no answer.

I tried again. "Adam Decker?" I called.

Thirty seconds. Forty. Sixty.

I looked around. Twenty-one doors. Two cars in the lot, one with actual duct tape holding the front fender in place. Four lit windows including the office. No people.

I knocked a third time. "Adam, I'm not here about you. Your sister is missing. Please open the door." I kept my voice even and non-threatening.

Still nothing.

I stepped back, careful to avoid the missing planks, and sighed.

Three strikes. Not a great way to start a case.

The door next to Adam's opened as I stepped past it. A skinny, dark-haired young woman in a threadbare T-shirt and purple cotton panties shot a hand out to tug on my sleeve. "Nobody's been in or out of there in two weeks," she said, deep craters under her wide eyes just as purple as her underwear. "Don't knock anymore, though, okay? You'll wake Robbie, and he's a real dick when somebody wakes him up." She jerked her head toward Adam's door, likely referring to his other neighbor. Noted.

"Nobody else has been here, either?" I asked.

She shook her head, unwashed hair falling around it in thick, sable-brown chunks. "He don't get much company. Weird to think he has a sister."

"Why is that?" I kept my tone pleasant and conversational, but her eyes narrowed, lighting on my badge.

She shook her head and shut the door, a chain lock scratching its way into place on the other side.

Damn.

I turned and strode to the office, where a lanky clerk with a buzz cut and bad case of acne glanced up from a paperback book and blinked three times when he saw me.

"Can I...uh...can I help you?" A pierced tongue flicked out to lick his lips. "I haven't seen anything."

I raised an eyebrow. "I haven't asked you a question yet."

He cleared his throat. "I just mean, I haven't seen anything weird. You know, anything... somebody like you might be asking about."

"I see." I pulled the door shut behind me, the tiny space hotter and danker than outside. A small metal fan whirred on the desk, pointed at the clerk.

"You work here every night?" I asked.

He nodded, closing the book and putting it on the counter. *Fahrenheit 451*. Not what I expected.

I pointed. "Enjoying that?"

"Yeah. It's crazy, to think the government would try to stop people from reading to make them dumber. Right?" He put one hand on the book, like I might try to snatch it away.

"I need to talk to Adam Decker," I said. "You know him?"

He flinched. "Haven't seen him in a good while, though. Couple weeks, at least. Quiet dude. Does his business, keeps to himself."

That made two for Adam disappearing right around when Lindsey had. Too weird to ignore.

I stepped to the counter, feeling good about this trail. "It's important. His sister is missing, and I need to know if she's tried to contact him. He's her only living blood relative."

His head bobbed fast, hands going up in a helpless gesture. "I would love to help you, miss." His eyes trailed from my hairline to my boots and back again. "And I bet Adam would, too. But I ain't seen him, honest. It's not like folks here give us emergency numbers or anything."

I pulled a card from my back pocket, picking up a pen from the counter and jotting my cell number on the back. "If he shows up, please ask him to call me at this number. Day or night." It wouldn't do any good to ask for this clerk's name—there are places and people where that's more of a hindrance than a help, and it wasn't a necessary complication here.

"Sure thing." He palmed the card. "And if you find him, tell him he better get his rent in before Roy gets pissed and changes his lock. It's an extra fifty to get your stuff back once he does that."

I promised I would, thanking him before I turned for the door. Sweat beaded under my bra strap, snaking a trail down my spine in the small, sticky room. Pausing with my hand on the knob, I looked back with practiced casual innocence. "Has anyone else been here looking for Adam?"

That was the million dollar question. And it got the reaction I needed even before his head started shaking. His thumb went to work fast-flipping the pages of the book, his gaze going from the wall behind me to the floor and back again.

"No ma'am." He cleared his throat again. "Not here."

Every liar has a tell, and his was textbook easy, with the fidgeting and throat clearing. I expected him to lie before he opened his mouth, though. It was the slightly breathless whisper of fear around the words that had my brain racing as I let myself out of the office.

Somebody who scared this kid more than my badge did was looking for Adam Decker.

That was a rock worth hunting down and turning.

I dialed Graham as I walked to my truck.

"I was beginning to think I'd been ghosted," he said when he picked up.

"Sorry. Chasing leads on a missing woman."

"That panned out?" His voice perked up. "Where? Details?"

Graham was the only person I knew who lived and breathed the job the same way Archie and I did.

"Feel like playing sounding board?" I asked. "As a bonus, you can make sure I don't fall asleep on the way home. I'm just now leaving Dallas."

"Anytime." His voice dropped a full octave, to nearly the same honey-velvet sexy as Jeff the cameraman. I didn't let myself wonder why, launching immediately into Lindsey's story and talking without a breath until I got to the light by the mall parking lot.

I paused, looking at the sprawling, empty building.

"Where'd you go?" Graham asked.

"Keep talking to me while I check out the lot where Lindsey was last seen," I said, parking in the fire lane when I saw a dumpster outline roughly matching the one in Bill Roundtree's file photo. I wanted to see if I could spot something they missed, and driving back up here over the holiday weekend sounded less fun than one of my mother's icy-fake formal cocktail parties.

"By yourself, after ten?" Graham sighed. "Put me on a headset and keep one hand on your sidearm, please."

"Of course." I pulled my earbuds from the console and plugged them into the base of the phone.

"Why the hell are empty public places so creepy?" I was talking to myself, fishing two small, black flashlights from the pocket in my door—one regular and one UV—but Graham answered anyway.

"Because they're the places teenagers get chopped up in horror flicks. Making the everyday terrifying is their game."

"Freddy Krueger I could handle all day," I said. "It's the flesh-and-blood bad guys who will actually run to catch me that I worry about." Odds that one was loitering in a mall parking lot long after everyone had gone home on the chance that a victim would swing through were pretty slim, but if there's one thing this job has taught me, it's that you really can never be too careful.

Sliding off the edge of my seat, I unsnapped the safety strap on my holster. "I won't be three minutes, I just want a look around her last known location. Local PD says the exterior camera took a beating in a storm, so they lost eyes on her when she stepped outside." I rounded the hood of my truck. "Hey—how's that rookie's arm?"

"If it wasn't okay, he would die before he'd admit it." Graham kept his voice low, so I could hear what was going on around me. Which was a whole lot of nothing. Towering light posts lit the parking lot every fifteen feet or so, and orange beams spilled from wall-mounted lights on the back of the building, stretching shadows long as I stepped to the mouth of the alcove.

I palmed the flashlight, clicking the button on the end and shining it in a slow arc around the space in front of me. The dumpster was the only visible hiding place, ten paces in and to my left. I closed the fingers of my free hand around the butt of my Sig and stepped forward, clearing my throat. "Texas Rangers. No need for alarm. If there's anyone here, please step into the light with your hands where I can see them. I'm not interested in processing anyone on possession charges tonight."

"Because a junkie loitering in a vacant parking lot is going to believe you?" Graham whispered.

I shushed him.

"What are you even looking for, anyway?" he asked.

I didn't know. But my gut said I needed to be in this space, to see where Lindsey had last been. I had a knack for noticing things other cops missed, even good cops.

I moved the light in a big rectangle all around the end of the dumpster closest to the parking lot. Standard issue commercial trash receptacle, dark blue, with a white label on the side listing the servicing company's phone number. When I pulled out my phone and took a snapshot of that, the camera flash lit up the wall behind the dumpster. Wait. Was that...? I raised the flashlight. Splatter. Of what, I couldn't tell with a regular light, but something had sprayed across this wall.

I cast an annoyed look over my shoulder at the orange wall lamp, sliding between it and the spots in question and pulling the UV light from my pocket. It wasn't a perfect science by any means, but it would tell me if this was bodily fluid or old coffee, at least.

Clicking the purple light beam on, I raised it to the wall.

The spots glowed like little drops of neon.

I moved the light around the side of the dumpster, stepping closer to an iridescent splotch running down the front corner in an upside-down teardrop shape. About shoulder height on me, as big as my palm at the widest point. Not every glowing spot is a bloody one—the vast majority aren't, in fact—but when a person has been a cop as long as I have, the reflex is to have a closer look at the very least.

Switching lights, I peered at the splotch, just dark enough over the blue paint for there to be a line, but not one I would have noticed in a cursory, sunlit inspection. True, my desperate desire to find something—anything—could make me see something that wasn't there. But it looked reddish-black to me under the white LED light. I pulled Roundtree's card from my hip pocket and scraped at the dumpster, keeping the light directed at the flakes coating the card's edge.

No question that right there was deep crimson against the card's eggshell background. Damn. I needed a baggie. Standing, I moved slowly around the perimeter of the dumpster, shining the light carefully over every inch, my eyes taking a methodical inventory.

"I can still hear you breathing, so I know you're alive," Graham said. "Anything?"

"I think blood on the corner of this dumpster and maybe the wall behind it."

"And the local cops would have missed that how? Especially if it was fresh?" He sounded skeptical. I didn't blame him. But I also wasn't really listening to him. I returned to the big stain.

Just to the left of the sliding door in the side of the dumpster. Where Lindsey might have stopped to put trash in on her way out of the coffee shop.

Huh. I glanced at my shoulder. Probably five and a half feet from it to the ground.

A head or nose bleed?

"Someone whacked something here. Hard enough to bleed."

"Faith." Graham's tone still held disbelief.

I got that. This was a long shot. But people had been fired for less irresponsibility than it would show if I walked away without trying to find out.

Loping back to my truck, I said a silent prayer. Something. Anything.

I grabbed a clean sandwich bag from the glove compartment and put the card inside, pulling my ice scraper and another bag out and walking back to the dumpster to scrape the drops on the wall.

Graham was right that the local cops should have caught bloodstains in their initial examination of the scene. But should have doesn't always mean did. The drops on the wall were tiny, the scene was cold by the time they got here, and it was a missing person they clearly thought was missing of her own accord. Plus, the photos in their file told me they'd checked this scene in daylight, when the spatter would be much harder to see.

Tucking the second sandwich bag into my back pocket, I stood and reached for the sliding door on the side of the dumpster. The sour smell of spoiled milk and rotting food was apparent, but not smack-me-in-the-face heavy. I shone the light on the collection of large, clear industrial garbage bags. Several were full of paper, shampoo bottles, and hair clippings from the quick-cut place just down from the coffeehouse. I reached into the dumpster and moved the top bags to one side, looking beneath. Coffee cups, food scraps, and wadded receipts.

The light caught something lower in the crevice between two bags—something not wrapped in plastic.

"Are you leaving yet?" Graham's low whisper held more than a tinge of annoyance.

"Almost," I said, leaning my top half into the dumpster and pushing the big, shapeless bags of trash apart. "There's something down here..."

My searching fingers sank into something spongy—and slimy. Scrunching up my face, I closed my fingers around it and pulled, raising my fist into the light.

"What?" Graham asked.

"It looks like...it used to be eggs. Scrambled eggs. Old, long-since-spoiled scrambled eggs." I shook my hand like the goo was battery acid, dragging my fingers across the plastic bags as I ducked out of the hole and straightened.

"So you found dirty concrete and spoiled food. In a dumpster. That's good detective work." Graham was laughing in my ear, but his tone was good-natured and sympathetic. It also wasn't the only thing I could hear.

I shushed him, backing up three steps, keeping the light pointed down as I took the last big step around the far end of the dumpster. I jumped backward and sucked in a sharp breath when the beam reflected off a large amber eyeball.

5

I kept my footing, lowering the angle of the beam to get a better look at whatever was snarling at me from the dark corner.

"Faith?" Graham's voice climbed two octaves too high.

"Shit." The word slid through my teeth, my eyes on the gangly-legged, svelte animal that had turned to face me, his feet planted, haunches coiled, teeth bared. "Shit, Graham, that's a coyote." I kept my voice low, slowly sliding my left foot out to a wider stance, my fingers so tight around the butt of my gun I couldn't feel them.

"Breathe." I had to struggle to hear his low murmur over the blood rushing in my ears.

"Trying." I huffed.

"Do not break eye contact with him," Graham coached. I snapped my mouth shut and forced a slow breath in through my nostrils. Graham grew up camping in the wilds of the Texas Hill Country. I nodded like he could see me.

"He's still growling." I tried not to move my lips or speak loudly, afraid to blink. "I thought they weren't supposed to attack people."

"He's just as afraid of you as you are of him," Graham said. I wanted to call bullshit. This creature in front of me did not look frightened. He looked pissed the hell off that I was bothering him.

"Slowly raise your arms away from your sides and stand up as straight as you can—no tiptoes, you might stumble. Make yourself big. But no sudden movements," Graham said. "Very small steps, back slowly toward your truck. Do not turn. Do not run."

I loved that he knew without asking that I didn't want to kill the animal.

I pulled the gun free from its holster, just in case, then moved backwards carefully, keeping my gaze locked with the coyote's. He snarled louder, a pink tongue flashing between the bared, yellowish teeth I was trying not to look at too hard.

"Faith, if he jumps at you, you're going to have to shoot him." Graham's tone was stern even in the low words. "And don't look away from him. I'm going to shut up now so you can listen in case he has friends."

Because coyotes travel in packs. Son of a bitch.

I slid my feet in tiny half steps that made for an odd, abbreviated moonwalk.

Slow breaths. In. Out. In. Out. My arm inched up more as I stretched my spine as long as it would go. "Stay, boy," I whispered. I'd only ever seen a coyote once, from the safety of my favorite mare on my granddaddy's ranch when I was in the seventh grade. Charity pointed him out as we were riding back up to the barn, the wide cerulean sky streaked with long indigo and raspberry wisps of encroaching twilight. That coyote had been smaller, and a hundred yards away near the fence line, but I still pulled Daisy up short and gasped.

"He won't hurt you, goober. He's a scout. It's the cattle he's after," Charity said, in her I'm-the-big-sister-and-I-know-everything-about-everything voice.

"Granddad said they've been picking the older cows off at night. Shouldn't we get someone?" I'd asked.

"What for? He's looking out for his family. They were here first. They have to eat, too, and it's not like we don't have plenty." With a shrug and a quick heel to her horse's ribs, she was off for the barn, calling for a race over her shoulder.

"No fair, you got a head start," I hollered, the coyote forgotten by the time I beat her back to the barn and hopped to the ground, grabbing Daisy a victory oat bag from the shelf inside the door.

Thirty years later, Charity was still right. The more sprawled our urban areas got, the less room for the animals who have roamed the Texas plains for centuries to hunt. And I didn't want any part of killing one for wandering into the concrete jungle—there wasn't supposed to be anyone out here this time of night, after all. "Stay," I whispered again, my parched eyes begging for a flick of the lids.

I didn't hear anything but the snarling huffs of the coyote, the soft friction of my boots on the pavement, and Graham trying not to breathe too hard in my ear.

An inch at a time, I had almost cleared the animal's line of sight when I heard the footfalls. Coming fast, they stopped probably ten feet behind me, replaced by a shaky command. "Drop that weapon and turn around slowly. Keep your hands where I can see them."

"Mall security?" Graham asked. I knew he meant, "Does he have a gun?" I didn't have an answer, which meant I had to assume he did.

Dammit. Talk, and risk irritating the coyote, or stay quiet and get myself shot by some guard getting paid peanuts to keep kids from trashing the flowerbeds with their skateboards.

Lowering my arms was out of the question. Hell would pick right up and relocate to Antarctica before I dropped my gun on this guy's orders in any normal moment, but I couldn't abandon my staring contest with the animal to check the guard's status, either. On balance, I was more afraid of a snarling predator than a kid who couldn't tell me to drop my Sig without his voice trembling.

Words, but soft ones. Slow. Clear.

"Texas Ranger Faith McClellan. Investigating a missing person, happened upon a pissed- off coyote. I can't move, because he can still see me." I got as loud as I dared before a snarl-snort from the coyote echoed off the walls and lowered my volume.

"I said drop that weapon!" His voice was high-pitched with excitement, and that was the familiar sound of a revolver cocking.

Son of a...the coyote spread his front legs wider, lowering his head, still growling.

Graham's breathing landed heavier in my ear.

Honestly, I liked my odds of surviving the bullet better—I've done that before. Twice. And with the shaky voice, who could even say this guy was a good shot?

"Texas. Rangers," I said again, putting more of a pause between the words than they required.

"Drop it now!" His last word came out in a long wail.

The coyote sprang.

I vaulted myself backward, landing sprawled on my ass on the pavement, clutching my sidearm. I raised it, locking both hands around the butt, my finger still outside the trigger guard when a shot ripped through the heavy night air.

"Faith?" Graham sounded more than a little panicked.

"I'm here," I muttered, taking quick stock of my person. No blood, no pain except my ass where it slid across the concrete.

Behind me, a clatter told me the guard dropped his gun. In front of me, the coyote's prone body told me why.

Dammit. I think I said it out loud when I stood, but I couldn't swear to it.

The security guard I rounded on probably had homework waiting for him, his horrified gape punctuated by a smattering of scraggly, pimple-dotted facial hair.

Tucking my weapon back into my holster, I held up my ID, pointing to my badge. "Texas Rangers. Didn't you hear me?"

He shook his head so hard he knocked his little cap askew, wide eyes flicking from me to the animal that wasn't nearly so terrifying sprawled whimpering over the asphalt.

I shook my head and bit my tongue. The kid was a kid, and a scared shitless one I wasn't convinced was old enough to have a permit for the gun he'd pointed at me. But he wasn't going anywhere; I could deal with him in a minute.

"Faith?" That was Graham.

"I'm okay. But the coyote isn't." I sighed, creeping in the animal's general direction in a wide arc, just in case he wasn't hurt as badly as he looked.

"Shot?" Graham asked.

"Yeah. Trigger Tony over here says he didn't hear me identifying myself. He screeched at me and the thing sprang. I'm not sure if he meant to shoot the coyote or me, but I was lucky enough to avoid the bullet."

The coyote was still breathing, its side rising and falling rapidly, wide eyes rolling around their sockets like glittering marbles. I could see the blackish blood puddle oozing outward over the dark asphalt, but damned if I could spot the source.

"Graham, I'm going to have to call you back," I said.

"Do not drive home if you're too tired."

"10-4." I touched the red *End* circle and then 911 on the keypad.

"This is Ranger Faith McClellan, DPS badge number 2984, in the south parking area at Southpoint Mall in Lake Whitney," I said into the phone. "I need an animal control officer and a local patrol unit."

"Animal control?" I knew that voice. Taut. Bored.

"Officer Simms?" I asked.

"Do I know you?"

"I was there meeting with Chief Roundtree a little while ago," I said. "Is he still in his office, by any chance?"

"Nope. And animal control works eight to five," he said.

Welcome to the suburbs.

Fine. I could figure it out.

"Can you send me a patrol unit, please?" I put so much ice in the words I should've been able to see my breath.

"I'll see if someone has time to do a drive by," he said.

I ended the call and turned back to the guard. "The local PD is less than cooperative this evening, and we are going to get this animal to a vet."

"What vet is going to operate on a coyote?" he asked.

"One with a heart, and most animal people have big ones." I spun for the parking lot as the coyote let out a piercing howl. Calling for his own backup? Shit.

"I'm going to get my truck." I took off at a dead run.

Jumping back down next to the guard a minute later, I unbuckled and pulled off my thick leather belt, my eyes on the coyote, silent again, but still breathing.

"We're going to slip this around his muzzle and hold it shut." The words sounded more confident than I felt, but it was the best option available sans animal control. I was mostly worried about the wound bleeding out if we tried to lift him. "We need a tarp or a big piece of plastic like a..." I jerked a bag from the dumpster and ripped it open. "Trash bag," I crowed, shaking the hair salon garbage back into the dumpster and spreading the bag on the ground.

The kid turned between me and the coyote, his eyes getting bigger with each swivel of his head. "This isn't what I signed up for," he stammered over the words.

"But walking around here with a .38 special like you're Dirty Harry, Mall Cop, is? Should I bother to ask to see a permit for that weapon?"

His prominent Adam's apple bobbed with a hard swallow, his nostrils flaring. "I don't want to touch some rabid coyote."

"I'm not asking you to." This was my idea, and I wasn't even convinced it was a good one. If someone was getting rabies shots over it, it'd be me. "Just come this way and stand there for a minute."

I walked a wide arc around the back of the animal's head, working the belt into a small loop. I had one shot here, probably. I'd never regretted not trying calf roping more in my life.

Pulling in a deep, steadying breath, I let the leather drop to the pavement in front of the coyote's thin muzzle. Off center.

Shit.

The animal flinched, but couldn't roll its eyes enough to see me. I waved the guard back, out of its sight line, and tried again.

Better. Holding my breath until my lungs burned, I pulled the belt slowly until the loop was near the coyote's nose.

Flicking my wrist, I landed the restraint, pulling gently to tighten the loop, but not too much. My waist being thicker than your average coyote snout, there wasn't a hole to secure it, so I rested the heavy sterling buckle in one palm and wrapped the leather around my fist.

The coyote let out a shuddering breath, but didn't move. I knelt. "It's going to be okay, boy."

I waved the kid over, looking for the entry wound.

"Pull that garbage bag to there." I pointed behind me. "And tell me if you see where he's bleeding from."

He obliged, shaking his head. "I must have hit his other side."

That's what I was afraid of. I didn't want to risk rolling the coyote if the bullet entry wasn't visible. "Straight up then," I said, the leather of the belt biting into my fingers when I flexed them around it. "You get back there by his tail and we'll lift on three."

He flinched, but did as I asked.

"Up over and down as quick as we can, as little lift as possible." I moved to the animal's head, spreading my feet apart, bending at my waist. I locked eyes with the coyote. "I'm trying to help. Don't bite me."

I counted. We lifted. Dark, thick blood gushed. We laid him on the plastic and moved wordlessly into position to use it as a stretcher. In two minutes, the coyote was in the bed of my truck.

"You think he'll be okay?" the kid asked.

I pulled the belt through a tie down on the truck bed and fastened it. "I hope so." I turned a stern look on him as I opened my door. "Don't point any more un-permitted guns at people. In fact, lose the gun altogether," I said. "Do you know how shitty it is to kill someone? Way not worth it for whatever you're making an hour."

He shook his head. "This place is going weird lately," he said. "That coffee girl disappeared like into thin air a couple weeks ago, and a couple days after, I saw somebody digging through that dumpster way after midnight."

He did?

Damn. This animal would absolutely bleed out in the back of my truck if I stood there long enough to get anything that made sense from the kid.

I eyed him. Slid behind the wheel and jerked my head to one side. "Get in. Sounds like you have a story to tell me, and I can't stay and listen right now."

* * *

Guiding people into sharing what they don't know they know is a vital skill in my line of work, and Sebastian the security guard knew plenty about Lindsey Decker. He just didn't deem any of it important—but in cases like this one, any little detail can be the key one.

The coyote was in surgery at a 24-hour animal hospital where the petite veterinarian hadn't batted a single auburn eyelash before she started barking orders at her staff for how to move him from the truck to a table. She said she knew a wildlife rescue that would pick up her bill and care for him while he recovered if he made it through. I thanked her and left a card and my cell number for her to call with an update. I then took Sebastian to a diner in south Dallas to get coffee because I couldn't drive home without it, and by the time we sat down in a cracked vinyl booth that made me thankful for the dim lighting, I was hoping some caffeine would jog his spotty memory.

"Tell me again what happened." I stirred sugar into the thick black liquid in front of me.

"I guess I've been keeping a close eye on that whole area since the coffee girl disappeared." His fingers laced and unlaced over the cracked Formica tabletop. "She told me a few weeks ago that the new manager there was creeping her out. I asked her if she wanted me to make a report and she said no, so I figured it must have just been nothing, you know?"

I put a star next to that, remembering the note in Lindsey's hamper. If I had a dollar for every time I've wished a victim would trust their gut, I could buy myself a nice vacation. But most people see murders or sexual assaults or kidnappings as something that happens to other folks, not them. So a prickly, skin-crawly feeling that should be heeded as their body's way of telling them a person or place is dangerous is pushed down, ignored, in the interest of manners. I got it, my mother is the queen of Southern hospitality. But it didn't make it less maddening when people—women in particular—turned up dead because they were more averse to making some deviant uncomfortable than they were interested in listening to their instincts.

"Tell me about this person you saw after Lindsey went missing," I prompted.

He shook his head. "I was just doing my regular lap of the parking lot and I saw this dude, in jeans and a black hoodie, creeping around the dumpster. I stopped because it was like ninety degrees out and I figured whoever was poking around in that getup was probably up to no good. But when I walked up on the guy, he took off. I tried to chase him, but he was fast."

I pulled out a notebook. “How big was he? Roughly.”

“Not too tall, less than six foot for sure. Not skinny, but not fat. I couldn’t see his face at all. And he sure could run.”

“Did you notify the local police?” I asked.

He shook his head. “I just put it in my incident log at the end of the night like we’re supposed to. People can’t steal from a dumpster, technically, right?” His voice trembled.

“Sebastian, are you under the impression that I’m upset with you?” I tipped my head to one side. Should I be?

“I mean, I was there, I was supposed to protect people. And I was working that night, on Mother’s Day.” His eyes dropped to his fingers, still busy moving in and out of lacing patterns. “What if something…you know…like really bad happened to her?” He didn’t look up.

“How old are you?” I asked.

“Nineteen. In July.” He said the words to the table.

“Say something bad has happened to her. You think you, eighteen years old and armed with a flashlight and some pepper spray, were supposed to stop a violent abduction?”

My head was still trying to spin through the possibilities for who and what and why, but I needed a whiteboard and possibly some bourbon for that, so I tried to focus on the boy in front of me, busy beating himself up for no good reason.

“Well sure. That’s my job, security,” he said. “So that’s why I had the gun when I saw you tonight. I wanted to be able to stop that guy if he came back. And then I thought you were trying to break in, or take some evidence, or something.”

“I’m pretty sure you’d get fired for carrying a piece, for what that’s worth.” I sipped the coffee. It tasted as chewy as it looked. More sugar. “I appreciate the protective instinct, believe me, but you do no one any good if you get yourself killed, or put in jail for shooting a human next time.”

“I just didn’t want to let anyone else get hurt,” he said. “And I do feel bad about the coyote. I hope he’s okay.”

“Have y’all had trouble with them often?”

He shrugged. “You see one around here and there, mostly by the lake, though. There was a complaint about a rabid dog that came in a couple weeks back..." His words trailed off.

"Yes?"

His fingers worked in overdrive. "I just...I think maybe that was right around the time the coffee girl disappeared. But I can't remember for sure."

A rabid dog. A city kid could confuse a coyote for a rabid dog. They're not supposed to be aggressive with people, but the one I'd seen tonight sure wasn't shy. But what was even the link there—that Lindsey was dragged off by animals? No way. I tried to ignore the thought that was crystallizing, hoping if I didn't look directly at it I'd get it in a minute. Something was off.

"Her car wasn't there. That night," he said. "I remember because when I heard that she was missing I thought about it and even checked my log. The car was gone."

Car.

That was it.

I looked up, putting my now-tepid motor oil coffee back on the table.

"Sebastian, did you see the car this mystery man in the sweatshirt took off in?" I kept my voice carefully even, my face blank. He was skittish anyway, I didn't need him getting the wrong idea. "Are there any other cameras on the outside of the building that might have gotten a shot of it?"

He shook his head. "It was small and sleek and dark, but that was all I saw. He went directly out of the lot on that east side of the building." He tapped one finger on the table. "All the TV shows say that the first few hours are vital to finding people. That's probably not good for her that nobody was looking, huh?"

I tipped my lips up in a quick smile. "I'm looking now. And I'm pretty good at finding things when I set out to." I stood. "Are you ready?" He asked if he could go to the restroom and I nodded, pulling out my notes and flipping back to a conversation with Mrs. Poway that felt like five years ago.

I was going to need a room for the night. But that would give me time to pick through those case files and see what else I could learn about Adam Decker—who was on the short side, from the photo I'd seen, and ran track in high school, according to his old neighbor.

* * *

Sebastian directed me to a back-forty lot on the north end of the mall, where he pointed to a blue Toyota pickup with white racing stripes and a fancy, empty rifle rack on the back window.

I handed him a card. "If you remember anything at all, give me a call," I said. "And seriously. No more guns for you."

"Thank you, ma'am. I hope you find whoever took her." He jumped out and slammed the truck door behind him. I watched him climb into his truck before I put mine in reverse.

Pulling in at a Whataburger up the street, I ordered some onion rings and a large Dr Pepper and parked the truck. Perusing Adam Decker's case file, I stuffed my face with fried batter and sweet onions and number five fancy ketchup. The lousy dashboard light lent an orange hue to Lindsey's brother's sallow skin.

Typical meth addict progression. In the first photo, dated six years ago, he looked like the all-American track star, dark blond hair slicked straight back from a pleasant face even with the mugshot scowl. By the most recent one, from September, he had a smattering of open sores on his face, his droopy eyes were dull, yellowed, and sunken, and the scraggly hairs growing out of his chin were starting to show premature gray.

I sighed, popping the last onion ring into my mouth. Could this dude have outrun young Sebastian?

Depended entirely on what kind of shape Sebastian was in, and how badly he wanted—or didn't want—to catch up.

So a maybe surrounded by a whole truckload of question marks.

I closed the file and clicked off the light, my eyelids heavy as the food settled in my stomach. I wanted a cigarette. But I'd promised Archie. And I don't break promises to Archie.

My phone buzzed in the console and I fished it out, knowing it was Graham before I looked at the screen. He worries.

"I'm okay. Getting food." I glanced at the clock on my dash and then the stack of files in my passenger seat. "And probably a room. I'm better than beat, and I'd like to get a look at the security footage at the mall for myself in the morning."

"Wise to stay up there," Graham said. "It's late and I don't like the idea of you driving home sleepy."

I put my pen down. We were starting to get maybe a little too settled in this odd little purgatory where neither of us was brave enough to make a move to take things further, but we talked to each other at least once a day and had grown equally comfortable with jokes, case brainstorming, and easy silence.

I might not be able to put a label on it, but it was a nice spot, and I was enjoying the hell out of it.

"It doesn't make sense if I'm just coming back tomorrow anyway. So much for a quiet Saturday."

"Let me know when you get back tomorrow night? Maybe we can grab a drink if you want a sounding board."

"Always in the market for a good sounding board. And a good cocktail."

"Sleep well, McClellan."

"You too, Graham."

I clicked the *End* circle and dropped the phone back into the cupholder, returning to Bill Roundtree's thin file on Lindsey Decker.

I had just enough information to know I didn't have enough information. The first seventy-two hours after a person disappears is vital to a positive outcome in the case, and I couldn't tell if anyone was even looking for anything in that window. But I had to do more than cross my fingers and wait for someone to call Chip Johnson with a magical cell phone video.

I pointed my truck toward the nearest DoubleTree, hoping a few hours' sleep and some daylight would help me see things a little more clearly.

6

A good imagination was the trick to surviving the darkness. When bad things came for her, she shut off her senses and escaped to a place where nobody could hurt her. It had been this way since she was a little girl. She had a puppy, black and white with gray-green eyes. She called him Kimbo, and her favorite thing was when he jumped up and planted warm, sloppy kisses on her nose and cheeks.

Kimbo was a good friend. Loyal. Sweet. Playful. And he was always a puppy, no matter how much time ticked by.

Kimbo would never hurt her. That was the problem with people—they always did, eventually. That had been a hard lesson when she was small, but one she'd learned over and over. People are evil. Even when they can be kind and have a clean, smiling face they show the world in the light, when the doors are all closed and the darkness settles in, the evil comes out.

The others never listened, never learned to shut it out. They screamed. They fought.

He fed on the fear like a demon straight from the fires of hell. She understood how it worked long before she opened her eyes to a dark so deep, so complete, it was three terrified, fitful sleeps before she was sure they were open at all.

She was always there. The one constant thing.

The first time she heard another voice, she touched her eyeball with a grimy finger to make sure it was open.

Not her imagination, then. Someone talking. Singing.

Jingle Bells, low and soft, but definitely not his voice.

High. Trembling. Scared.

She crawled closer, the cool concrete hard under her bony knees.

She'd been alone in the dark for sixty-eight sleeps then. He came every couple of awakes to prod her. After twenty He started asking why she wasn't afraid. Thirty-three was the first time He burned her.

She sat in a field with Kimbo, still in the sun then, and let the puppy lick her nose until He gave up. Again.

Jingle Bells had whispered a name, that first awake. Crystal.

Three sleeps that time before He came back.

Crystal screamed. He laughed—a low, menacing sound that grew tentacles, poking and tickling her ears until she found Kimbo.

Stop that, she wanted to say. But her silence, her escape, those were her shields in this thick, pressing darkness. She couldn't see Him coming unless He brought the burning stick—it glowed. But if she played with Kimbo and locked her jaw, He couldn't see her as easily. That's where the box came from. He grew weary of hunting her. One day He stabbed her arm with a needle and she woke up in her box. And that's where she'd stayed.

Crystal had a box of her own.

She lasted eight sleeps and she was gone.

Thirty-one more sleeps, and another scared voice, this time reciting a movie line on repeat.

Jack, he said when she asked for a name.

Jack's scream was high and long—a single, earsplitting note he could hold for a fifty count.

She tried to warn them. At first.

The needle. The knife. The burning stick. Always in that order. Nobody ever made it past the burning stick.

Except her.

The others disappeared into the darkness and never came back.

He talked to her, every time. Low. Hoarse.

Why didn't she scream?

Because it never did her any good.

So much easier to play with Kimbo.

He would break her, He said.

Go on and keep trying. We'll see. But she didn't say that, either.

She stopped asking their names after Jack. Nobody could see her, and when they heard her and tried to talk, she just petted Kimbo until they stopped.

Nine sleeps. That was the longest anyone lasted before. And it was easier to stand the screams if she didn't know them.

She wondered sometimes if she was evil, too. Did she have that, lurking inside her somewhere, some horror waiting to be unleashed on somebody weaker?

She didn't like to think so. But when the dark was at its darkest and there was no other voice floating out of it, when Kimbo was sleeping and her only distraction, her only fingertip hold on the edge of the madness cliff, was through folding into herself, she wondered. Deep, deep inside, she couldn't say no. Not for sure.

Because evil, the kind that allowed people to do terrible things, was about power. She knew that before she knew the words to explain it.

And she had never had power.

Frail, frightened girls are powerless. It's why nature is structured so bigger humans protect them.

Small comfort wrapped her when she realized Kimbo was her power—he lived and breathed because of her, and she could do whatever she wished to him, couldn't she? But all she ever wanted to do was throw his spotted ball for him and rub his silky ears while he licked her face. That had to mean she was a good girl. She had never felt like a bad girl.

Curled on the ragged, smelly blanket in the corner of her box, she wondered what she'd ever done to deserve this. Far back in her brain she could pull out snippets of a voice. Big, booming, strong. "*God blesses the pure of heart. Punishes evil.*"

It took seven hundred and nineteen sleeps for her to realize that the voice was exactly right.

It was just that the punishment part wasn't a lightning bolt from the sky.

It was her.

7

I knew the light would wake me up; that's why I didn't pull the blackout shades before I went to sleep.

Squinting into the unchecked sunshine pouring into the room, I stretched my legs and found them tangled in a wad of sheets. I kicked the covers to the carpet and sat up, shaking off a night of half-nightmares about Lindsey and Charity and a few dozen other young women I'd pored over photos of while I hunted killers for the past decade and a half.

Lindsey Decker, I still had a chance to find before she became that photo. Lindsey Decker, I could bring home.

"Coffee," I said to my tousled reflection, checking the clock. Seven-ten. I reached for my phone.

"Since when do you get up early on Saturday?" Archie asked when he picked up.

"Since I have a chance to find this woman before I have to tell a cute little boy with chubby baby feet that his mother is dead," I replied. Dramatic, yes—I wouldn't have to tell Jake his mom wasn't coming back, but I'd have to tell somebody, and saving them from that conversation was high enough on my priority list to drag me from bed. I padded barefoot to the coffee maker. "I'm still in Dallas. Your friend Roundtree said to give you his best."

"He did not."

"Okay, he said to give you a little hell. But I was trying to be polite."

"Any particular reason for the attempt at boosting my ego?"

"It was a weird night here." I dropped a coffee pod into the brewer. "I went by the mall after hours to check out the scene and tangled with a coyote and a teenage security guard who thinks he's auditioning for a *Bad Boys* reboot. By the time I had a chance to look over the case files I snagged from Roundtree, it was too far past my bedtime to brave 35."

I dropped to the floor while the coffee brewed, knocking out twenty pushups before the machine beeped.

"It's been over a week, Faith. The scene is more compromised than a diplomat with a foot fetish who owes the Russian mob a favor." I could practically hear Archie shaking his head. "Did you say a coyote?"

I moved to the sink to scrub the hotel carpet off my hands, remembering that I hadn't ever heard from that vet last night. "I did. But I can fill you in on him later. Here's the thing even a whole night of visits from the ghosts of victims past couldn't get me: how the hell does a woman get kidnapped from a public place in broad fucking daylight, and there are no witnesses? But my only alternative is that she took off and left her kid, and I can't buy that."

"Why not? People do it. You've seen it."

Sleep brought clarity to my perception of Lindsey and her family. "If she was going to run, she'd have done it a long time ago, when the kid brother she finished raising started doing dope, probably. She stuck it out. When you know that kind of pain, you either model the same behavior or you don't. Lindsey Decker seems to be a don't."

"Point taken. So if someone grabbed her, there is a witness. You just haven't met them yet," Archie said.

I shook two sugar packets before I ripped them open and poured them into my coffee, stirring with the little red straw before I took a sip. "I did go to the TV station and give an interview with her photo last night," I said. "Maybe that will turn something up."

"There you go. Now what?"

I sipped the coffee again, tapping my index finger against the side of the cup. The thing about homicide is, the urgency is all about catching the killer. I'm damned good at that. But in all my cases, the victim was already dead when I got there. Archie had worked a hundred missing persons in his long career. I wanted his advice.

"I don't know. Planning right now to go to the mall where she worked, find their head of security and get a look at the video footage from that day for myself. See if your friend's guys missed something. He says he's got an opioid problem at the high school and he's understaffed. Seemed happy to push this to me and be done with it. I probably ought to check in with the TV reporter at some point, too." My voice dragged and Archie snorted.

"Careful with all that enthusiasm," he said. "TV reporters often have fragile egos."

"Believe me, I know. I'm just afraid of following the wrong lead. What if I screw this up and she dies?" I sipped my coffee and plopped onto the edge of the rumpled bed.

"You're a good cop, Faith." Archie's voice sounded weird with no trace of sarcasm. His Faith voice. The one that said he knew my demons and loved me anyway. "I like to think I had a hand in making you a good cop. Trust your gut. Be thorough. This woman is damned lucky to have you on her case. Go find her."

I pulled a slow breath through my nose. He was right. I knew everything he said was true, even deep down in dark places where doubts like to hide.

"Thanks, Arch," I said. "You headed to the office?"

"I figure me not having a life is a small price to pay for all the good that gets done in the world because of it."

"Anything I can help with?"

He paused. Long enough to make me pull the phone away from my head to see if I'd lost him.

Still connected, according to the ticking call timer.

I waited.

"Nah, kiddo, you're busy," he said finally.

"Never too busy for you," I said.

"I'll keep it in mind," he said. "Holler if you need me, okay?"

I told him I would and turned to the file.

The mall didn't open until ten, which meant staff wouldn't be there for a couple of hours yet. The bakery on the corner had better coffee and free wifi. The thing I hadn't seen in the police file Chief Roundtree gave me last night, the thing I'd been too adrenaline-wracked and exhausted to notice was missing, was nestled in the laptop in my backpack out in my truck. Maybe a look into Lindsey Decker's online life would give me a few rocks to turn.

* * *

How a police detective could say they'd hit a wall in a missing person's case without pursuing online leads nearly two decades into the twenty-first century, I had not the first damned clue. Roundtree's department was small, but posh. It wasn't like I was dealing with a border town sheriff who had three guys covering four hundred square miles in a county so poor they were lucky to have a station shack with dial-up internet and a dot matrix printer.

Settled in a leather chair at the bakery with a looming 9:00 appointment to see the mall's security chief, I sipped my second coffee and flipped my computer open. "Maybe they just didn't know where to look," I muttered.

Facebook first, back to the profile I'd found the night before. Most everything she posted was set to "public," from what I could tell, even pictures of her son, which made the hair on my arms stand on end. Putting photos of a little one on social media for public consumption is two steps down from hosting a barbecue for your neighborhood's registered sex offenders. I wish on a regular basis that more young women took their online privacy seriously.

Nothing odd, threatening, or hinting at depression on her timeline, though that's not always an all-clear.

Groups, then. The page showed eleven: One Direction fan club, romance novel book club, and...something I could use. A local Mommy and Me playgroup. I went to the page, clicked the administrator's profile, and sent her a private message identifying myself and asking when she'd last seen Lindsey.

Watching the box in the bottom corner of my screen for a reply bubble, I went back to Lindsey's profile and clicked her "about" page. No relationship status, no family listed. New tab. I started simple, typing Lindsey's name and "Dallas" into the search engine.

Seventy-eight hits.

A birth announcement for Jake in a suburban neighborhood newspaper told me he was seventeen months old. I clicked back to Facebook and went back twenty-six months, looking for photos of Lindsey with a guy.

Not a one, but I found several of her dressed in one of the snug sheaths I'd seen in her closet, posed in red heels for a night-out selfie next to an olive-skinned young woman who had gorgeous hair and all the curves Lindsey lacked. Evie Mendoza, the tag read, except the link to her profile didn't work. It had been deleted. I saved a couple of the photos. Had Evie seen Jake's father? Scrolling up, I looked for more photos of her with Lindsey, but Evie disappeared about three months later, and there was a long gap—almost a year—between posts. Jake's chubby cheeks and wide eyes dominated after that. Like Lindsey had gone from one life to another. But the dresses still hung in her closet.

I jotted Evie's name down and returned to my original search results. Tinder profile. Instagram. Neither gave much away—Lindsey liked to post photos of beaches and flowers on Insta, and her Tinder photos were subdued and serious, her profile clear that she wanted a relationship, not a hookup.

Back to Facebook. No messages, and as far as I could tell, the playgroup admin hadn't seen mine. If Lindsey's life had become about the kid when she became a mom, maybe her mommy friends knew something I needed to know, too.

I clicked to their page. Chose events from the sidebar.

Hot damn. They were meeting at Montrose Park for a stroller walk. In twenty minutes.

I shut the computer, dropping it back into my bag, and grabbed my coffee on the way out.

* * *

Nothing in Lindsey Decker's online life pointed to her running out on her little boy. But I also wanted to know why everything I'd found was so...

bland. Was Lindsey actually the boring all-American single mom the internet would have folks believe? Maybe. It was possible that her lousy luck caught up with her again in the wrong place at the wrong time. But my gut said it wasn't so random. The audacity of someone snatching her from a public place in broad daylight pointed to an offender who wanted Lindsey specifically, and I hadn't found much that suggested who or why yet. What I had found was more questions. Was there a secret in Lindsey's outwardly boring life? If so, had she disappeared into it? Or had it devoured her?

* * *

Starbucks cups, designer workout clothes, spotless sneakers, and high-end jogging strollers: the moms' group, not a pound of actual body fat between the dozen of them, was easy to spot when I arrived at the park.

Not the crowd I would have picked for a single working mom with a sparse wardrobe beyond her coffee shop uniforms, but okay.

They were finishing their stretching when I got close enough to introduce myself. Every woman in the bunch reached protectively for the handle of her baby's stroller at the sight of my badge. "Facebook tells me Lindsey Decker was a member of your group," I said. "She's been missing for two weeks tomorrow, and I'm hoping one of you ladies might be able to tell me something that will help me figure out why."

Perfectly augmented lash extensions flicked down to hood every eye, their gazes going to their shoes or their neighbors as soon as I said Lindsey's name. They looked away. They whispered. But nobody gasped. Nobody expressed concern. Nobody asked me about Jake.

What the actual hell?

Of all the people I'd talked to about Lindsey, a manicured and nip-tucked suburban moms' group was the place I'd expected to see shock. Concern.

Instead, they all closed off the second I said her name.

I glanced at the one I'd messaged on Facebook—Darla was her name—the smirk playing around the corners of her lips as she closed her fingers around the handle of a bright yellow stroller telling me maybe she had seen my message and just chosen not to reply.

Nobody was talking. Nobody even asked for more information.

What were they so intent on protecting?

I stepped closer to a blonde woman who'd knelt to fiddle with her shoelace, squatting and leaning in. "I appreciate the instinct to avoid gossiping about your friend," I said. "But I have reason to believe Lindsey might be in danger. Whatever y'all know, maybe especially if it's not flattering, could help me find her."

She didn't move, save for breathing.

Given the part of town I was in, the grownup mean girls vibe didn't surprise me, but what I'd seen of Lindsey's life didn't fit this. She might live in the upscale burbs, but the world she moved in wasn't their world of fat diamond and platinum rings and upwardly mobile husbands.

My questions weren't flooding from the realization that Lindsey didn't belong. It was that she'd tried to in the first place.

The blonde untied and retied both of her magenta shoelaces. Twice. "Lindsey...isn't our friend." She shook her head. "If you want friends, you shouldn't sleep with other people's husbands." She kept her voice low, her words floating under the whispers flying among the rest of the group.

Oh.

"I see." I rose, looking at each well-made-up face in turn. They weren't protecting Lindsey, who would clearly be an outsider in this bunch.

They were protecting one of their own.

8

Pretending the blonde woman hadn't spoken as she tied her shoes, I raised my voice a touch. "Ladies, it's important that you share any information you might have that could help us get Lindsey home to her son safely."

Magenta shoelaces stood and looked around at her friends, getting a couple of glares in return. She shifted her weight from one foot to the other. "We haven't seen her in months," she said. "Since before Christmas."

"Has anyone tried the fifth ring of hell?" I couldn't see who muttered that, but a couple of the women giggled.

I cleared my throat. "I can get a judge to issue subpoenas, ladies, but I'd rather not waste the court's time or the taxpayers' money," I lied. I might be able to get a judge to compel them to talk if I had hard evidence that Lindsey was dead or in danger. Without it? I bluffed, and hoped nobody knew better.

"Do you have proof that Miss Decker is in danger?" A lithe redhead in the back arched one perfectly waxed brow.

Bluff called. Probably either a lawyer herself or married to one.

I met her gaze without blinking. "I'm still gathering evidence."

"Nobody is going to give you a subpoena without it." She folded her arms across her chest. "Like Cassie said, we haven't seen her in months. But if I were you I'd start with whoever she's hooking up with these days and go from there. Lindsey isn't terribly discriminating. And she doesn't like to sleep alone."

A little boy with dark eyes and pink cheeks wailed from a blue stroller.

Darla stepped to my right shoulder. "It's getting warm, and our little ones are getting bored. I'm afraid this conversation is over, Officer. But I wish you luck. Lindsey wasn't right for our group, but nobody here would hurt anyone."

I turned to leave, pulling a card from my pocket and pressing it into Cassie's palm as I stepped around her magenta running shoes.

She might talk, away from the rest of them.

And an affair with a married man meant my secret life theory might get some legs.

I could keep this bunch here all day and they wouldn't tell me how or with who. And I had an appointment to get to.

I hustled back to the truck, checking the clock as I started the engine. Twelve minutes, and I could get a look at the video feed from that day. Maybe it had another clue somebody had missed.

* * *

Randy Lassiter's baritone was as deep as his shoulders were wide, both filling the tiny closet where the monitors showing the building's security camera feeds were kept. He gestured me to a chair and stood behind me because there wasn't room for him to stand next to me.

"Our footage doesn't show anyone following her out," he said. "A full thirty minutes after she left, nobody else exited that door."

He pointed to the center monitor and pushed two buttons. Grainy, black and white Lindsey appeared, her long hair back in a ponytail, a black ball cap covering her head and shading her face as she neared the camera.

A small purse looped over her left shoulder, she carried a large, clear garbage bag with both hands, her arms flexed to keep it from dragging the ground. She struggled with the door, a wide triangle of sunlight washing out the bottom third of the screen when she got it open.

Nineteen seconds from when she entered the frame to when she stepped out the door, and there wasn't another person around.

I played it again. The shot was too grainy and far away to see her face well enough to guess if anything was bothering her.

"She took out the garbage and then she was just...gone," I said, thinking about the samples I'd scraped from the dumpster and wall the night before. I had to be careful not to assume they had anything to do with Lindsey until I had lab results. Besides, wouldn't someone have heard an attack that cost her that much blood? "She wouldn't have been alone in the building that time of the day, right?"

Lassiter shook his head. "We have store managers here until after eight on Sundays."

"And the local PD tells me the exterior camera is broken?"

"We lost three in that storm last month, and the landlord is fighting with the insurance company." He scratched his close-shorn head. "This is the only place our video had eyes on Miss Decker. She's perfectly fine when she leaves the building."

I pulled out my notebook. "And her car? Toyota Prius, blue, 2009, plate XWR426?"

He shook his head. "My security officer said she was parked on that same south side of the building. Our parking lot feed hasn't worked anywhere but the north bay in over a year."

"That's a long time for a widespread outage."

"When this place is less profitable every year, stuff like that gets less attention from the powers that be," he said. "Online shopping is going to put me out of a job before long."

I tapped a finger on the edge of the counter. "Is there any other exterior feed from that day I can look at? Anything at all from that end of the building?"

His forehead bunched. "I don't have any more video of Miss Decker. Believe me, when the PD came around asking, I went through it all."

"I'm sure you did a thorough job. But I'm not looking for Lindsey. I'm looking for someone who might have seen Lindsey."

His eyes popped wide. "Oh."

He flipped open a laptop on the corner of the counter and pecked at the keys with two fingers.

"We have three working cameras that cover broad areas of that side of the building," he said as the images on the three center screens changed. "Here, outside Macy's"—he pointed to the middle—"there, outside the movie theater"—he touched the screen on the left—"and here, at the main entrance. Now, I looked over them all to make sure nothing got an angle on that dumpster or caught a glimpse of her coming out, but that's all I was looking for."

I smiled. "I've done this a time or two."

He played the theater feed. Three birds and one dark pickup we couldn't zoom in far enough to get a plate number on. After the third run I shook my head. "That's no help. The description fits half the registered vehicles in the state." I looked at the timestamps. "And besides, that was three minutes before she opened the door. They wouldn't have seen her."

Next, we looked at the department store feed, from 6:38 to 6:43. Not even a car in that one, but the birds had a starring role.

Lassiter stood up and rolled his shoulders, clicking play on the main entry video. "This place clears out pretty damned quick at closing time, especially on Sunday night," he said. "It was a good idea, though."

I shook my head. "The only good ideas that matter in this line of work are the ones that get you somewhere."

The birds didn't even like the glass front doors. I watched five minutes of feed twice, and nothing moved.

Damn.

I hunched forward, staring at the center monitor like I could will it to show me something.

Lassiter cleared his throat. "I'm sorry I couldn't be more help."

I shook my head. Stopped.

Leaned closer to the screen.

I tapped his arm. "Rewind this, and play it again. Just the last minute or so."

Afraid to blink, I kept my eyes on the screen. He leaned over my shoulder close enough for me to feel his warm breath on my neck.

"Right there." My pinky finger pointed, tracing the long afternoon shadow poking out from under the huge concrete arch in front of the department store. It was hard to see on the low-resolution video, but it was there. We backed the feed up. The shadow appeared and receded four times, then slid from beneath the arch and stayed for a forty count—right after Lindsey would have opened the exterior door in the alcove.

Someone was out there. A woman, from the shape of the hair.

"Why is somebody just hanging out on the porch like that?" Lassiter asked.

I grinned, wishing for the third time in two days I had a cigarette. "Because they stepped out for a smoke, but it was hot out and they wanted the shade." I stood. "Can you see the dumpster from this archway?"

"You can, but not well. Depending on the angle, part of it would be obscured, and it's a good hundred and fifty, two hundred yards across there."

Far away and partial was better than nothing. I thanked him for his time and turned for the door. "Which way is that department store from here?"

He pointed. "That way and take a left. But isn't chasing a shadow we couldn't even see well kind of like looking for a needle in a haystack?"

"Entirely. But I have a knack for locating needles."

9

Was it worth my time to ask around about smoke breaks at the department store? Maybe not. But I had another forty-five minutes until the coffee shop would open, and possibly someone in this store who may not realize they saw something vital to cracking my case. The number of smokers has declined every year for nearly a decade—something I learned from the anti-smoking memes Archie likes to text me—narrowing my haystack a bit.

The glass doors were drawn and locked this early, but the lights were on, employees getting ready for the day. I rapped on the glass, a woman in an orange sundress and strappy yellow sandals turning from where she was arranging a beach hat on a faceless mannequin and tapping her wrist with one finger.

I pointed to my badge.

Her face scrunched up, but she walked toward the door.

She peered through the glass, first at my face, then at my badge and back again.

Pulling on a coiled plastic bracelet, she stuck a key in the door. The lock squealed free and she cracked the door open, her fingers tight on the handle. "We don't open for the police until ten, either." The eyes behind her no-nonsense rectangular black framed glasses were wide with skepticism, her free hand on her hip.

"I need to interview one—or maybe more—of your employees," I said, keeping my hands at my sides so she didn't think I was trying to force my way into the store. "I thought it might be easier if I came by before the store was open."

Her forehead scrunched into surprisingly deep lines. "Somebody steal some cattle or something? What do the Rangers even do these days, anyway?"

"At the moment, this one is investigating a missing person's case." I kept my tone even, smile in place.

Her eyes popped wide behind the glasses. "Oh, the girl from the coffee place, huh? I saw that on TV last night. How come y'all are just now asking about her?" She pushed the door open and let me inside. "I heard she took off with some dude. Been sending her flowers and stuff." She turned the key to lock the door behind me.

The card in Lindsey's hamper. Weird, for her to wad up a love note from a guy she would abandon her son to be with.

"Where did you hear that?"

"Bunch of people were talking about it in the break room the other day. Someone said the security people were getting hassled by a friend of hers, and someone else—I don't remember who—said she'd been getting flowers at the coffee shop. I figured she had a boyfriend and took off with him. I didn't know she had a kid until I saw you on TV."

So nobody told her Lindsey had a boyfriend, she inferred it.

"Were you here the day this happened?" I asked.

"Mother's Day is all hands on deck. People like to bring mom shopping, you know? I was working in cosmetics."

I followed her back to the table where a stack of bright-striped Polo shirts waited to be folded. "Do you remember what time you went home?"

She flicked the edges of a shirt expertly around a plastic form. "I had to leave right at six because I was meeting my mom for dinner downtown." The narrowed eyes that met mine through her thick lenses were shrewd. Better than most at reading faces, I'd bet, since mine was carefully blank. "You think someone hurt her?" she asked.

"I've been on this for about eighteen hours," I said. "I'm not sure what I think yet, except that I don't want to miss the lead that might help me bring her home. Do you know who was here late that day?"

"I can tell you for sure Marlena was. Because mostly it's the men who work late that day. The managers try to let the mothers go and be with their families." Her tone said Marlena was not her favorite person.

"Does she smoke, by any chance?" I asked.

"Like a freight train." She rolled her eyes. "Every ninety minutes, she's out front. You could set a watch by it."

Needle located. "Is she here this morning?"

"Men's shoes."

I pulled a card from my back pocket. "My cell number is on the back. Please call me if you think of anything or hear anything I need to know." I jotted my cell on the backs of the cards I carry in my pocket because the lieutenant didn't like for us to give personal numbers out, but in my experience, that was a mistake—a lot of the people I have to talk to in the course of a case would much rather call a cell number than one that rings into a law enforcement office. Less intimidating. And leads are way more important to me than protocol.

She tucked the card into her pocket. "I hope you find her."

"Thank you for your time and your help. Where might I find men's shoes?"

She pointed. I turned and strode in the direction of her finger, making a sharp left, then a right, where I spotted the shoe racks in the northeast corner of the building.

The only woman with a Macy's name tag also sported hair bigger than Lady Bird Johnson, a skintight Lycra dress that would be more at home in a nightclub, and four-inch heels.

I guessed, since I couldn't read her name from twenty paces. "Marlena?" I stepped off the tile and onto the carpet in the front corner of the department.

She looked up from the display table, wide brown eyes flicking from my face to my badge before she folded her arms across her cleavage. "What can I do for you, Officer?"

I stopped short—she was definitely a smoker. Two packs a day, I'd bet.

Funny how I couldn't smell that just a few weeks back. "Faith McClellan, Texas Rangers. I understand you closed up on Mother's Day?"

"You were on TV last night. Something about a missing woman." She tipped her head to one side. Her hair kept its straight-up angle.

Way more people still watched TV news than I would've thought.

"Lindsey Decker worked at the coffee shop around the way. She was last seen leaving by a back door that evening. Did you happen to step out for a cigarette after the store closed?"

"I didn't see nothing." She said it a little too fast.

I didn't flinch, leaning one hip on the wooden arm of a chair. "Might you have heard something? Or noticed a car, maybe in a big hurry to get out of here?"

She plucked a tasseled loafer from a plastic stand and scrubbed at an imaginary smudge with her index finger. Not raising her eyes, she muttered, "Where I come from, if the cops come asking about something, people who didn't see anything live longer."

My breath sped and I concentrated on slowing it. That didn't mean she knew something. It only meant she was afraid to know anything. One step at a time.

"I'm just trying to find out what happened to her," I said. "She has a little boy at home who misses her."

She blew out a slow breath. "I saw his picture on the TV last night." She replaced the shoe on a display. "I didn't see much of anything. I was looking at my phone, swiping through losers on Tinder, the whole time I was out there. I heard a..." She stopped. Looked around. Leaned in. "Not so much a scream, you know. But like a squeal. Dumpster is over there. I figured somebody saw a rat, and like, started to scream and thought better of it."

Holy hell. Or maybe Lindsey started to scream and somebody slammed her head into the dumpster?

"I walked down to the arch and looked, and all I saw was a little blue car zipping off like a bat out of hell."

"You didn't get a look at the plate?"

She shook her head. "I didn't hardly get a good look at the car. If I had blinked I'd have missed it."

“But it was a car?” I pulled out a notepad and pen. “Not a truck or van?”

“Yeah, definitely a car. I couldn’t tell you if it had two or four doors or who made it. I was only under the roof in the shade because it’s getting hot outside, you know. All spring and winter, I get my smokes over in that alley where I can get some sun, too. Do you think somebody took her? Like right from here?” She pressed one hand to her heart, long scarlet nails glinting in the overhead fluorescent light. “Never thought I’d see the day I’d be grateful for this damned heat. If not for the beating sun, that might’ve been me.”

Somehow I didn’t think so. Objectively, I knew I still didn’t have shit that would hold up enough to even get me a warrant, if I knew what I needed one for. This woman hadn’t seen Lindsey, the camera was busted, and she also hadn’t seen anyone else. The car—small and blue—could have been Lindsey’s Prius. So, the idea that she’d spotted a rat—or maybe even a coyote, given my adventure in that same alcove the night before—and hightailed it the hell out of Dodge held water.

It made more sense than the whispers in the back of my mind that someone surprised her, knocked her out, and stuffed her in her own vehicle before they took off with her.

But my gut said the easier answer here was the wrong one. I just needed to keep digging until I found proof it was right.

* * *

By the time I left Marlena shining wingtips, the coffeehouse was bumping. A line twenty deep snaked through the smallish space. Five people worked at a frantic pace behind the counter, shouting at each other about light roast and shots and whip as they brewed fancy coffee-infused concoctions in front of a chic chocolate and teal backdrop.

I found a spot in the front corner near the windows, waiting for a lull while I sized up Lindsey’s workplace.

Rectangular main room, about thirty by forty feet, shelves lining the right side wall housing books, magazines, and coffee mugs and tumblers for sale. Three cameras: one on the door, one on the register, and one in the back corner I assumed was aimed at a hallway leading to the restrooms.

A dozen tables were scattered around the space, plus four cushy velour armchairs clustered around a coffee table in the middle of the slate floor. The crowd was mostly teenagers. Boys with scruffy chins and Tom-Petty-artfully-shaggy long hair in white Abercrombie T-shirts and khaki shorts shared drinks and tables with lithe, tan girls modeling carefully messy buns, bikini tops, booty shorts, and colorful Laredo cowboy boots. Every last one looked like they'd walked out of a Vogue shoot on a Texas sailboat to get coffee before they headed to the lake for the weekend.

Behind the counter, the staff rushed to keep the caffeine coming. The young woman at the register sported two sparkly nose studs and a septum ring, royal blue highlights shining against her bobbed black hair. The bushy-bearded guy with the blond dreads working the espresso machine had full sleeve tattoos up both arms. Was he the manager? I watched the way he interacted with his female coworkers closely and didn't get a skeevy vibe once.

My eyes skipped over the rest of the staff, Sebastian's words running through my head on a loop. My creep radar isn't perfect, but it's pretty damned close. Tattoo guy wasn't my guy.

The door to the back room swung outward and my eyes locked on the young man who slouched through.

There.

No more than 5'10", black shirt under his purple and yellow apron, round, wire-rimmed glasses, skin that probably hadn't seen the sun in months—I watched for five full minutes, and I didn't see him meet eyes with a single person. Not staff, not customer. He kept his gaze on the floor, the ceiling, or the food he was pulling from the bakery case and heating in a countertop convection oven before he handed it wordlessly to the next person in the pick-up line.

Plenty of people are uncomfortable looking other folks in the eye for a myriad of reasons, but they will do it for a second or two, exchange a smile, and interact politely.

This guy was different.

Off, in a way that twisted hot and sharp in my gut. My foot moved his direction all by itself, no small amount of self-control pulling it back.

My stare should've burned the ends off of his floppy brown bowl cut by the time the line cleared and the staff had a minute to breathe. The register girl made herself a cup of coffee. Tattoo dude headed for the john. My guy? Pulled out his phone and turned his back to everyone in the room.

Was this the source of Lindsey's mystery flowers?

I pushed off the wall and strolled to the counter.

Blue highlights sipped her coffee and stashed the cup under the counter, revealing a row of straight, bright white teeth with a quick smile. "What can we get for you?"

"A manager." I touched my badge. "I have some questions about Lindsey Decker."

She reached across the counter and grabbed a hand I hadn't offered, pumping it hard enough to rattle my shoulder in its socket. "Thank God. I've called the police to try to check in every day, and they won't tell me anything. Do you think she's alive?"

I extracted my fingers. "I have no reason to believe otherwise at this time." I dislike police double-talk, which is what that amounts to, but it's tricky, getting people to understand urgency without giving them false hope. "You must be Maggie."

She nodded. "She was being so weird that day, I knew something wasn't right with her. Rushed off out of the house when I got there without even kissing Jake goodbye. That wasn't like her at all. God, if she was in some kind of trouble, I wish she would've just said so. We could have figured something out."

"You two are friends, I understand?" I asked.

"Closest thing to best friends we've got. I help her out with Jake when I can, she listens to me bitch about my love life. We're there for each other."

"But you don't listen to her complain about her love life?"

She snorted, wriggling the studs in her nose. "What love life? Far as I can tell, except for when she got knocked up, she's pretty much a nun."

Huh. Not according to Mrs. Poway. Or the mommy and me ladies. And more than ninety percent of kidnappings are perpetrated by someone the victim knows. For grown women, a significant other or ex is almost always the culprit, when it's not a stalker. Maggie's worried eyes and earnest face earned my trust. She wasn't lying to me that I could tell, and my human polygraph abilities are legendary. Was Lindsey keeping secrets even from her bestie? Because when a person keeps the dark parts of their life hidden even from those they love most, those parts can prove pretty damned hard to wrestle into the light.

"What makes you think she was in trouble?" I asked.

"I don't know. Lindsey had the biggest heart of anyone I know—she was too nice, sometimes, and got herself into awkward situations. Hell, she's been feeding a freaking coyote our outdated deli sandwiches for a month now. A coyote. I kept half expecting her to get herself mauled." Oh hell. So that poor animal was hanging out by the dumpster waiting for Lindsey to come back with food?

Maggie shrugged. "I mean, I guess it's easier to think she got herself in over her head, you know? Better than assuming some rando grabbed her and is doing God knows what to her, isn't it? I work here too. I take out the trash sometimes. I wouldn't be able to make myself come in if I thought that might happen to me."

Astute. And brutally honest—it's a psychological phenomenon that happens without people recognizing it most of the time. When terrible things happen, humans look for a reason to blame the victim. It takes extraordinary empathy to avoid that trap, not because most people are assholes, but because they want to keep right on moving through the world in their bubble where horrors touch other lives, but not their own. If there's a reason—any reason—that points back at the victim, the people whose lives intersect with theirs on my whiteboards can still feel safe. Sympathetic and maybe slightly judgmental, but safe.

It makes my job easier in some ways because I have to ask those questions, given the probability that the offender in each case was someone the victim knew. But more than 120 homicide investigations have taught me two things about that: it's never the victim's fault, and no one is as safe as they like to think.

"You said there was nobody special in her life, but I heard she was getting flowers, here at work," I said. "Do you know who was sending them?"

Before Maggie got an answer out, a woman walked up and stopped so close her arm touched mine with every breath. I slid to the side, waving a "go ahead." She ordered a caramel latte and side-eyed me as she moved to the pick-up line before I stepped back to the register.

Maggie pulled her coffee from under the counter and sipped it.

"Flowers?" I asked when she didn't say anything.

Maggie shook her head. "I don't want to get anyone in trouble, you know? I mean, we didn't ever find out for sure what the deal was with that." She put the cup down. Twisted a fat silver ring around and around her left thumb. "I don't think I should tell you stuff I'm not sure is right."

So an admirer Lindsey didn't necessarily want. The note was crumpled in the laundry basket.

The set of Maggie's jaw told me I needed to tread carefully. Just facts, then.

"How often did the flowers come?"

"Once a week, at least." She looked up at me through thick, glittery blue lashes. "I thought it was weird, but it didn't seem to bother her much. She just kept wadding up the cards and then passing out roses to anyone who came in."

"She gave them away?" I folded my lips between my teeth, my eyes going to the skinny guy in the corner. "To people here?" If whoever was sending them worked here, that probably wouldn't go over well.

Another customer approached the counter before she could answer that, and I stepped aside again. Tall teenager in board shorts and a rash guard ordered a frozen coffee. Maggie gave him the total and he reached into a pocket before his eyes went wide. He patted his shorts, looking around. "Damn, I think I left my wallet in the car," he said.

I dug a ten out of my jeans pocket and handed it to her. "No worries," I said, smiling when the kid tripped over himself thanking me. "Just be careful out on the water today and we'll call it even."

His eyes flicked over my badge and he nodded solemnly as Maggie passed my change back across the counter. "Yes, ma'am. Thank you again."

"No worries." I wanted him to move so I could keep talking to Maggie, but I couldn't find a polite phrase to convey it.

"Pick-up is right down there," Maggie said, pointing.

That'd work.

She turned back to me. "I'm due for break in five if you want to hang around and talk somewhere quiet." She studied me. "You really do think you can find her, don't you?"

"I think I have a shot at it. I'm trying to work fast."

"Five minutes." She turned her attention to a group of young women pointing at items in the bakery case and arguing over calorie content.

I retreated to the corner nearest the counter, almost tripping over the little guy with the phone addiction. He managed to keep ahold of a brim-full garbage bag, his gaze not moving from the floor. "Sorry."

"No, I'm sorry. I wasn't looking where I was going."

"Why are you asking about Lindsey?" he muttered to the trash.

That was all the opening I needed.

"I was just assigned to this case, so today I'm playing catch up. Do you know her well?"

His shoulders lifted, his face still angled down. "She works here."

"So I understand. Were you working with her the evening of May 12?"

He shook his head. Shuffled his feet. Didn't look up or speak.

Not at work meant no alibi. Yet, anyway.

I stuck out one hand, making sure it made his field of vision. "I'm Faith McClellan."

He half-shook it, his palm clammy and his grip almost nonexistent. "Nice to meet you."

I waited three beats. "And you are?"

"Alvin. I'm Alvin."

"Nice to meet you, Alvin. Do you remember the last time you saw Lindsey?"

"May ninth, 9:07 p.m.," he said. "She was wearing black pants and a gray shirt and her purple apron that had her name on it."

Textbook stalker, but why the hell would he admit it, to me of all people?

"How long have you worked here?" I asked.

"Three years, two months, six days."

I took a step back. Looked him over with fresh eyes.

Without seeing his face up close, I couldn't venture a guess on age. But the mannerisms and speech suddenly looked a lot more like the autism spectrum than a stalker to me. Before I could formulate a polite way to ask, Maggie tapped my shoulder. "I'm good when you are."

"I'm good. Nice to meet you, Alvin. You have yourself a good day." I stepped out of his path and he continued toward the back of the coffeehouse, holding the big trash bag awkwardly aloft as he shuffled to the door.

"Is there a quiet place to talk here?" I asked.

Maggie turned, waving for me to follow. "The office."

She opened a locked metal door tucked between two shelves on the back wall and we walked through a storage and break room, into a teeny cluttered closet that passed as an office only because someone wedged a desk into one corner. Maggie perched on the corner of the desk and gestured to the lone chair. "You can shut the door if you want, up to you," she said.

I nudged it with my boot until I heard it click. "Something different in her life—anything you can think of. Anything that might have been bothering her."

"I was thinking about that while I got their drinks. The only thing she didn't talk about was her school stuff. Like ever. She was super quiet about it."

"But she didn't say why?" I was pretty sure I knew the answer before I asked the question, but I had to ask anyway. The more I learned about Lindsey, the more it seemed she was good at keeping things to herself. She wasn't the type to give a reason for avoiding a subject.

"No, I just learned to stop asking about it because she never would answer me," Maggie said. "Honestly, I've never been able to figure out how she was paying for it in the first place. It's not like we make that much here. I guess she has savings or whatever."

"What is she studying?"

"She was working on her psych degree when she got pregnant with Jake," she said. "So that, I guess. She wanted to be a social worker. Help kids like the ones she met at the shelter where she used to do volunteer work."

"What shelter?"

"The Harbor House, I think it's called? Lindsey spent every minute she could there for the longest time. Until she started taking classes again. She talked about making the world a better place. Stopping human trafficking."

My head bobbed slowly. Had Roundtree's men seriously not looked deeply enough into this young woman's life to know she had information to share on traffickers because she helped their victims? Then again, a human trafficking shelter isn't your average community service choice. People arrive in places like that broken, untrusting, sometimes even nonverbal. Lindsey Decker was looking to help people polite society had thrown away and forgotten. Those who profit off them want to make sure it stays that way.

And traffickers aren't usually the sort of people you want to piss off. I made a note of the shelter's name. Definitely worth checking out.

"Thanks, Maggie." I had to try one more time. "The thing with the flowers—if they were bothering Lindsey, or someone was giving her the creeps, it would be a big help to know that."

Her shoulders heaved with a deep breath. "Look, I can't prove anything, but the guard, the one on the night shift—Lindsey was nice to everyone, but she would freeze right up when that guy was around. Something was weird there. I asked her once and she said he watched her. In a way that made her, you know, uncomfortable."

"Do you remember if that was before or after the flowers started?"

"I think before?" Maggie bit her lip.

"When you say the night guard—skinny kid, acne issues, kind of skittish?"

A worried crease appeared between her eyebrows. "She didn't say he did anything. She hadn't even mentioned him in a while. You don't think he did something to her, do you?"

I hadn't before she said that. But I had missed something. Sebastian had called Lindsey "that coffee girl" twice that I could remember. Like he didn't know her. But it was the last thing he said to me that came back in a haunting whisper right then—*I hope you find whoever took her*. He also told me it was the coffeehouse manager who had been bothering Lindsey.

I put one hand on Maggie's arm. "It's too soon for me to know which rabbit trail to follow here, but good leads are never a bad thing to have. Thank you for your help."

She stood. "I have to get back to work." She opened the door and waved me out, following me to the counter before she tapped my shoulder. I turned, holding out a card.

"Find her," Maggie said, taking it.

"I will give it everything I've got. Hey, who's the new manager here? Is he working today? I'd like to get a copy of the surveillance footage from the two-week window surrounding Lindsey's disappearance."

"Sure thing. The manager will be happy to help you with that." Maggie beamed with pride. "Which I can say for sure because the manager is me."

10

I managed to get the video footage and leave the mall without my head exploding, though I'm not sure exactly how. Somebody was lying. And whoever it was, they were better at it than the average criminal.

Charts.

I needed whiteboards, markers, lots of coffee, and Graham. Maybe not in that order, but my thoughts were zooming by so fast it was damned near impossible to keep up, let alone organize them.

I pulled my phone from my hip pocket and hit the speed dial for my old partner as I jogged to my truck.

"Morning." He sounded far away, like maybe I woke him.

"Hey, what are you doing today? I have another stop up here and then I'm on my way home with a conflicting mess of a case to untangle and a ticking clock. You feel like volunteering for the cause? I can even come to Austin, meet you at headquarters."

"No." The word was a touch too sharp, stopping me short at my door as I reached into my pocket for the keys.

"I mean, no, you don't need to come all the way down here. I can meet you in Waco, especially if you're driving from Dallas." Graham's voice was gentler, and someone who didn't know him as well as I did would miss the strain in it.

"What's going on?" Breezy. Light. Just a hint of inquisitive.

"Nothing. Just trying to be helpful." He sounded almost nervous. I heard a soft click in the background. A door closing? A woman's low voice, kind of familiar but not one I could place offhand.

Oh.

OH.

"If you have company there, I can text you my ETA in a bit." Harder to keep the easy tone that time, but I think I pulled it off.

He paused. "Yeah, okay. Let me know when you're going to be in, I'll meet you up there as soon as I can get away."

I unlocked the truck and slid behind the wheel. "Sure thing. Thanks, Graham."

End call. Dropping the phone in the cupholder, I let my head fall back against the warm leather of the seat.

Graham Hardin was a grown man who could keep whatever company he wanted.

I knew every word of that was true, but it didn't squelch the bitter bubble of jealousy rising in my throat. I let my eyes fall shut and swallowed hard, stabbing the key into the ignition and cranking the engine.

"Not my place," I muttered, turning my head to look out the back window as I shifted the truck into reverse. "And I do not have time to worry about Graham and women today."

That last part was downright gospel. I turned my attention back to Lindsey as I drove toward my hotel.

Back in the room, I opened my laptop and searched for Harbor House.

Problem: nuclear secrets are easier to uncover than the address for a shelter serving abuse victims. Not a bad thing, just a damned frustrating one.

Chief Roundtree didn't answer his cell phone. Google's only help was a news article, more than a year old. I clicked the link and found a color photo of Lindsey, folding a blanket and looking beatifically at something off camera to the left. The story was a feel-good feature about saving young people who'd been through unspeakable things, Lindsey identified by her first name only, as a volunteer who was passionate about the cause.

Yep. I needed to talk to the people in charge of this place. And absent a handy area police contact, I was left hanging my hopes on a reporter. For the second time in two days. The universe has a twisted sense of humor.

It took me longer to get Shannon Tillis from the *Morning Telegram* to answer her cell phone than it did to find the number, and five minutes of begging for her help got me jack shit.

“Even if I had driven myself and I still had the address, I couldn’t give it to you,” she half-snapped. “I signed an agreement with them. I can’t tell anyone where the shelter is located, they can sue me if I do.”

“The young woman in your photo is missing,” I said, keeping my voice even.

“I didn’t take the photo. I told you, the photographer took me to the place. I don’t remember talking to a blonde volunteer. Did I quote her?”

Deep breath. Flat voice. I have dealt with way more frustrating uncooperative people. Just none more annoying that I could think of right then. Different tactic.

“No, the only person quoted in the article was the woman who runs the shelter, but you only used her first name. Do you remember her last name? Maybe I could get in touch with her.”

“Yeah. Marland. And I am not trying to get the paper tangled up in a court battle with the Marland family by talking to you about this.”

Damn. There were only a handful of family names in Texas with the kind of punch my own packed, and that was one of them. The Marlands were legendary Texas oil money—my parents used to say the TV show *Dallas* was based on them.

I heard a cabinet door slam followed by three seconds of silence before a coffeemaker started burbling. “Look, no disrespect, but I have seen some screwy shit in my time,” she said. “How do I know you don’t have a brother or a husband who’s a pimp? How do I know you aren’t one? Anybody can say they’re a cop on the phone.”

That was fair. Irritating and obstructive, but fair.

“How did I get your cell number?” I asked. “The phone number in your tagline on your story is your desk phone, which went straight to voicemail. So I pulled your DPS records, betting that the number you used there would be a cell.”

"Phone numbers aren't part of public DPS records," she said. "How did you get this, come to think of it?"

I sighed. "Phone numbers aren't part of the public DPS record. For law enforcement, they are visible. I'm telling you, that's how I got it. I'm a Texas Ranger, this woman is missing, and if she caught the attention of some scumbag through her work with this shelter, I need to know it right now." I couldn't keep the frustration from creeping around the edges of the words by the end, but I didn't shout.

"What did you say your name is?" she asked.

"Faith McClellan."

"McClellan, like Governor Chuck McClellan?"

My eyes rolled up on reflex when people said the governor's name with that borderline-reverent tone, but I kept my voice bright. "Yep."

Computer keys tapped in the background.

"What was your sister's name?"

"Charity." I swallowed hard.

"When is your mother's birthday?"

"September seventh."

"Name of the victim in your last case?"

"Tony Amorici. Am I looking for a lead or trying to get access to my bank account?" I paused, wishing I could suck that back in and swallow it. I settled for a deep breath. "Sorry. This case has me on edge."

"Just making sure you're you. As sure as I can, anyway. I'll call you back at this number in a few minutes, okay?" She hung up before I got the "thank you" out.

I looked back at my notes.

The mommy group.

Growing up on the pageant circuit, I knew a thing or two about mean girls—the smirk on Darla's face and the way the rest had closed ranks against Lindsey was familiar. I clicked to Darla Worthington's Facebook profile.

Three photos in, I spotted the mystery man from Lindsey's sketchbook.

Hot damn.

He wasn't in Lindsey's friends list—and neither was Darla, or any of the other moms from the group. I put a big star next to Darla's name before I closed my laptop and cleared the desk, laying out everything I had so far. A blue plastic pacifier, flakes of something that might very well be blood, the card from Lindsey's hamper, her toothbrush, and a black thumb drive with two weeks of video footage from the coffeehouse, because it was as far back as Maggie said she could go. I'd only get a couple of Lindsey's shifts, but the last one should be there, and maybe it would tell me something.

Jake's pacifier might be a long shot, but with whispers of a secret relationship—maybe even of an affair with a married man—seemingly everywhere I turned, if there was a ghost of a chance I could find the kid's father, I had to take it.

I reached for my phone and texted my favorite coroner.

I know, I know, DNA isn't your department. But I can't keep up with all the personnel changes at the lab and I need a superspeed run. Any help you can offer? Send.

I laid the phone back on the desk and picked up the scrapings from the dumpster. The shoe clerk's description of the shortened scream and racing car was too coincidental to be unrelated to Lindsey's disappearance.

Back to the phone. *Make that two.* I sent that to Jim just as the reply bubble came up.

You know I would if I could, but I don't even know any of these new kids. Budget cuts are some serious bullshit when some of these big companies aren't paying a dime in state taxes, you know that? I'd go over there for you, but we're in Houston for another 23 days. Sorry.

I smiled, thumbs flying.

Don't be. How's she doing?

Jim's wife had a rare form of cancer. I'd asked my father to call in a favor to get her into a drug trial at Anderson three weeks ago, and she'd already been there ten days. The governor is an abject bastard on many fronts, but showing off his power never bores him.

The bubble came up almost immediately. *She's tired. But this morning's scans showed progress. The doctor said cautious optimism.*

I let my eyes fall shut. Thank God. *You take care of her and give her my love,* I typed. *I'll worry about the lab.*

Buzz. *I'll call around this afternoon and see if I can stir up any help. And don't tell me not to, because I'm going to anyway.*

Thanks, Jim. Send.

Buzz. *I'll let you know what I find out.*

I pulled the empty plastic bag from the ice bucket and stowed my precious pieces of possible evidence, flipping back through my notes.

Adam Decker, her brother.

Maggie Emmins, her best friend.

Sebastian Lowry, her stalker?

Darla Worthington, the scorned wife?

As suspect lists go, it didn't suck for how long I'd been looking for Lindsey. I just wished I knew for sure whether Foul Play Avenue was going to get me anywhere in this case. My gut was convinced, but my head cautioned that it was too early to dismiss anything without hard evidence.

A few background checks and a look at the coffeehouse video might turn up some.

I put the evidence bag into my backpack and grabbed my phone. I didn't get it into my pocket before it started buzzing.

A 214 number I didn't recognize.

I hit the green talk button.

"McClellan."

"Hi there, Officer—this is Dr. Avery from Rock Harbor Animal Clinic. I have an update on your injured coyote. I would have called sooner, but I just got back. Those night shifts are brutal."

"Did he make it?" I asked.

"He was a she, and I'm sorry to say we lost her despite our best efforts, but it wasn't the bullet wound that killed her."

I paused mid-stride. "I'm sorry?"

"That's what I wanted to talk with you about. The bullet did superficial muscular damage that was easy to repair, but her blood pressure didn't stabilize and my assistant noticed her abdomen was bloated, so we ran a scan and saw a foreign object. The intestinal damage was too severe by the time we managed to cut it out, and she lost too much blood in the surgery."

"Foreign object?"

"It was blocking her intestine and the tissues had started to die and decay. The toxicity in her system is probably what caused her to be aggressive with you. You told me that when you brought her in, right? That she was snarling at you?"

"Yes," I said. "I thought that wasn't normal behavior."

"Not at all. She should've just run when she heard you coming. They have intensely acute hearing. But she was in too much pain to run, and the poison feeding into her bloodstream from the gangrene had likely affected her brain. Please let the young man who shot her know this was not his fault."

"Of course." I couldn't keep it in anymore. "What was in her intestine?"

"A ring. Chunky. Gold. Still around what's left of someone's finger."

11

"No shit?" It slipped out, my fingers fumbling with my notebook. "Pardon my language. Doctor, do coyotes frequent areas where they've found food?"

"I thought this might be helpful to you," she said. "I assume you weren't looking into a dumpster at the mall that late at night for fun and profit. And yes, they do."

"So it's possible she bit someone? Near that dumpster, I mean?"

"It is. And I took the liberty of checking this morning because I was curious—no hospital in the Metroplex has had an ER visit with a missing finger via animal bite in the past three weeks, which is the maximum time this could have taken to cause the tissue death we observed."

"So whoever she bit didn't report it." I hurried out of the room to the elevator.

"Or they lied about their injury." Her voice jumped an octave with excitement. "I'm not a police officer, obviously, but I do love to read crime novels. I made you a list of all the missing finger injuries regardless of the reported cause. I don't have enough of a sample to be certain which finger we have, but I'm guessing ring or pinkie depending on the size of the...uh... previous owner."

And just like that I had a new favorite person. For this morning, anyway.

"Can I come see you and get that list, along with whatever you cut out of her intestines?"

"Sure thing. Happy to help. The thing is, it would take something out of the ordinary to provoke a coyote to attack a human that way. Particularly in a populated area."

Something like her food source being knocked out, maybe?

I pointed the truck toward the freeway and cranked the air conditioning. "Interesting. I'll talk with you soon. Thank you, Doctor," I said before I hung up, stomping my boot down on the gas pedal and merging into a crowd of vehicles any other city short of New York or LA would call ridiculous on a Saturday morning. Five months in Waco and I'd nearly forgotten what traffic looks like—as long as you avoid the university strip in the evening and steer clear of anything with the Gaines name on it, the only time you see tail lights is if there's a red light or a wreck.

Ten minutes later I walked into the clinic.

"Officer McClellan." Dr. Avery waited behind the desk when I walked in. "I have everything ready for you back in my office. Right this way."

"Thank you so much for your help."

"My pleasure. If we could have saved the animal, too, this would've been my best Friday night shift ever."

She pushed a thick powder blue door open to reveal a small, tidy office. Striding to the desk, she picked up a manila folder and a small metal box with a funky flip clip seal and a red biohazard label on the side, turning back to me. "I have to ask. Do you think she bit some horrible criminal?"

"God, I hope so. It'll make my job so much easier than usual if that"—I pointed to the box—"belongs to my kidnapper."

Her eyes popped wide. "Kidnapper? No kidding."

"Well. Maybe—a young single mother disappeared from the mall parking lot in Lake Whitney in broad daylight. It seems she'd been feeding a coyote in the weeks prior to her disappearance. Would that be enough to provoke the animal to attack someone?"

She snapped her fingers. "I saw that on the news last night! It ran right before you came in. That's why you looked so familiar. To answer your question, it just might. Every animal is different, of course, but this one was definitely on the lean side. If your single mom was a trusted source of food and the animal was waiting for her, and someone interfered with the coyote getting fed, she might have jumped at them."

I took the file and the box. "Thank you. For everything. Not many vets would take an injured coyote in the middle of the night."

"I got into this to care for animals. I don't figure it matters too much what breed they are if I can help them."

I liked this woman. "I owe you one, Doc. Call me if you ever need anything."

She winked, opening the door and waving me out. "No offense, but I hope I never have to take you up on that. I sent some samples to our lab for testing after we closed her up last night. I'll let you know if they find anything interesting."

"Please do." I stepped into the hallway and paused. "Do you need help covering the costs for disposing of the remains?"

She shook her head. "I appreciate the thought, but we have a deal with a place out in Terrell. They take our orphans and we send them business."

I moved back to the front door and tapped the box. "Is this going to make me sick if I open it?"

Her eyebrows waggled overtop of her glasses. "You squeamish?"

"I make it through an autopsy all right."

"Probably not, then," she said. "But fair warning...stomach acid doesn't play nice with that kind of tissue. The smell is pretty rank when you pop the seal on that."

"I'll just take it straight to my friend Jim at the morgue, then."

"I'd say that's the safest bet."

Back in my truck, I dropped the folder into the passenger seat on top of the case files from the Lake Whitney PD and set the box gingerly in the console. I don't have to transport body parts...well, ever. Definitely a weird footnote to this case. With a splash of gross.

I checked my phone. Still nothing from the newspaper reporter, and I couldn't wait around for the possibility of her doing me a favor.

I started the engine, opening a text to Graham: *Headed south. I have to drop something at Jim's office, so I'm going to Austin. Maybe see you at HQ this afternoon?* I tapped *Send* and dropped the phone into the cupholder, my mind on the case and eyes on the road. Graham would show up. What he did on his nights off might not be my business, but I knew him—the chance to help me return Lindsey to her son would pull him away from anything.

Somewhere, between the finger in the box and all these half-complete, intersecting reports, fell the truth of what happened to Lindsey Decker.

We just had to find the magic rock.

12

Government budget woes are the lamest reason any criminal has ever been allowed to walk free.

The desk clerk who logged the pacifier, toothbrush, and scrapings at the lab reminded me that they're closed to actual science from noon on Fridays to noon on Mondays until further notice. He drawled it, annoyed, like any cop anywhere could forget that. I disagree with most of the things my father did when he was governor, but he never had a budget stall for one day, let alone thirty-six.

I thanked the guy before I sped to the morgue, where I dropped the finger in the box with Jim's assistant, who I knew without calling would be at her desk on Saturday morning. She promised to let Jim know it was urgent as soon as he was back at work. Sometimes I think they both live at the office, but glass houses and stones and all that.

By the time I got to headquarters, the different elements of Lindsey's case were so snarled up in my head I wasn't sure I could untangle them. But that's why good cops have friends who are also good cops.

Archie sat behind his battered metal desk, head bent over a fat file of mostly photos.

"Anything interesting?" I asked, reaching into his star-shaped crystal dish for a peppermint.

"Hey there." His face spread into a grin when he looked up, but his eyes were tired. "Same old same old. New day, new dead people."

"Anything I could help with?"

He closed the folder. "I'm honestly not sure yet. This is a weird one, but it just landed on my desk day before yesterday. I'll keep the offer in mind, though. What brings you to town in the holiday traffic?"

I held up the folders from the Lake Whitney PD. "I had to take something to Jim, so I dropped my samples at the lab here. And I was kinda hoping you felt like talking through my MP with me."

Archie leaned back in his chair. "Anytime, kiddo. What've you got there?"

I gave him the rundown: alcoholic father, car crash, raising the brother who turned out to be an addict, kid—everything I had up to and including the body part I'd just dropped with Jim's secretary.

Archie ran one hand down his face when I stopped for a breath. "Damn. This girl has had a messy life."

"But I'm not sure which part of the mess needs to be under my microscope."

"From hearing that, I'm not either. I'll tell you what I am sure of, though. She didn't bolt."

I put the stack on the corner of his desk. "What makes you say that?"

"Because I'd bet you she's spent every day since the first time her kid brother got arrested thinking that if her mother hadn't died, her brother wouldn't be an addict. You know and I know there's no way to prove that. But somebody who spends years beating themselves up like that, they don't leave a little boy they love without his mama. No way."

It was an angle I hadn't quite noticed, but it fit with every other gut reaction I'd had to this case. And Archie was the best of the best—one of the most decorated lawmen in Texas history. When he gives his thoughts on a case around here, folks listen, and he's almost never wrong.

"I'm going to work it as an abduction until someone proves me wrong," I said. "I've played devil's advocate at every turn so far, trying to convince myself your friend up there is right and she took off, she'll come back. But I just can't make myself buy it."

"Bill is a good cop, but this one he blew." Archie shook his head.

"Nah. He didn't want to see it because then he'd feel bad that he doesn't have the staff to handle it." I unwrapped the peppermint and popped it into my mouth. "He's got himself an opioid wildfire at the high school and his men are stretched thin trying to prevent kids from dying. Moving resources from that to this with no hard evidence would be a tough call for anyone."

"And that's where we come in." Archie smiled. "So, she's sleeping with a married man?"

"Maybe? The other women in that group seemed to think so. And she's never told anyone who her son's father is. It's not even on his birth certificate. But her closest friend said she wasn't sleeping with anyone."

"Not exactly a situation most people brag about, though." Archie's lips twisted to one side. "If an affair came to an ultimatum and she's been gone two weeks, I don't like your shot at finding her alive." Archie is always honest. Even when it hurts.

Not that I didn't know that. I was just choosing to ignore it. "But we know this drill. Until we have a body, we assume she's not dead."

"Fair enough." He snagged his own peppermint from the dish. "So where are you on this?"

"I need to know more about my players," I said, pulling my laptop from my backpack and moving to the empty desk next to his. "Maybe something in someone's background will move them to the head of the list."

"Anything I can do to help you?"

"Play sounding board if I find anything. Feel free to return to your weird dead person in the meantime."

He winked. "Go get 'em, kiddo."

I plugged the LAN cable into the computer and typed in my access code. Running backgrounds may not be as exciting as car chases or shootouts, but it's safer and often more productive. I touched my sister's charm bracelet, always cool around my wrist no matter the weather, and sent up a tiny prayer for a break.

* * *

Adam Decker definitely had the longest record of anyone on my list. Not surprising, and from the looks of that motel he probably knew a dozen people he could trade his sister to for a fix or some cash. The question, then, was would he actually be capable of that? Having never set eyes on him, I couldn't venture a guess.

I leaned back in the chair, clasping my hands behind my head. "The brother has a thick jacket that extends beyond the suburbs—he was even arrested here last year, a PI at a concert in the park. He peed in the fountain."

Archie turned his chair to face me. "You think he sold her?"

"Hell if I know. I mean, that's quite a jump, from dealing and using to trafficking, and especially his own sister. Not just any sister, but the one who gave up college to keep him out of foster care when his folks died. There's nothing here that indicates he's into that scene. Not even a soliciting charge." I sighed. "But sometimes my biggest handicap is not wanting to see just how dark desperation can make a person go."

"Have you talked to this guy?"

I shook my head. "I tried his last known, but no sign of him. This says he's moved around a lot the last few years, though, and the place I checked was a flea hole motel, which fits the junkie profile. No phone number. License expired last October."

"It's not a good look, him being MIA right after his sister disappeared."

"The neighbor said they don't talk anymore. She doesn't want him around her kid."

"Yeah, but if he thought the kid was the problem, he'd have taken him, right? That would be easier," Archie said.

I nodded, putting my hands back on the keyboard. "He'd probably be able to get more for him, too. Adorable little towheaded boy, perfectly healthy? That'd buy a whole lot of meth. But it seems Lindsey had a knack for finding folks who aren't what you'd think, too." I sighed. "Every trail until it runs out, right?"

"Hasn't failed you yet."

I clicked back to the only violent offender I'd run: Mommy and Me queen bee Darla Worthington. I hadn't expected to find so much as a speeding ticket on her—she seemed the type to find run-ins with the law embarrassing. So my eyebrows went up when I got a hit: a domestic violence call to the Lake Whitney PD in October. Darla wasn't the victim, she was the perpetrator.

Her husband called 911 when—he alleged—she came at him with a knife. I couldn't see the report online, but they took her in, so they had to have seen something when they got there.

I picked up my phone and tried Roundtree's cell again. Left another voicemail. The department's phones were routed to a regional call center after midnight on Fridays, thanks to a particularly heinous marriage of technology and budget cuts.

Damn. Moving on.

I plugged the thumb drive with the coffeehouse video into the USB port and propped my chin on one fist.

There was Lindsey, making coffee and talking to Alvin. She didn't look a bit afraid of him, her smile relaxed and genuine. Tattoo sleeves strolled over, drying a shaker glass with a white rag, and leaned in with an interruption. Lindsey tensed, her head nodding. I wished for the three thousandth time in my career that surveillance video had volume. I hadn't gotten a creeper vibe from that guy, but now I was second-guessing myself. I clicked fast forward when she went back to her conversation, letting it run and watching for a change.

Two hours' worth of feed showing customers coming and going with Lindsey and the two guys zipping around making drinks sped by, but I didn't see anything out of the ordinary.

At two hours and four minutes, I saw someone I recognized. Emmett Worthington, every inch as handsome as the sketch on Lindsey's nightstand and the photos on his wife's Facebook page, walked in. I slowed the feed and sat up straight, checking the date.

This was the day before Lindsey disappeared.

Emmett barely glanced at Lindsey, making a beeline for the counter. He was tall, probably six-four or five, broad shouldered, with thick, dark hair and a physique that testified to hours spent in a gym every week.

He stopped at the counter. Said something. Tattoo sleeves turned and broke into a grin that could've lit up a small city. He moved to the counter. Turned to say something to Lindsey, who looked around the shop and shrugged. Tattoo sleeves pulled off his apron and waved Emmett toward the far wall, where they disappeared into the office.

Holy shit. Fast forward.

Seventeen minutes later they reappeared, slightly rumpled to a careful eye, but not obviously so.

Ah ha.

Emmett looked at Lindsey as he passed the counter. Paused and backtracked. Leaned in close and spoke to her.

She froze while he talked, everything about her face and body language screaming that she wanted away from him.

I clicked to the next day's file, scanning fast through the Mother's Day crowds for Emmett.

Over the next two hours, I ran the feed at high speed twice. He wasn't there. But I still needed to talk to him. I didn't give half a damn about this dude's personal life. It was the being in a room with Lindsey less than twenty-four hours before she vanished, and the look on her face when he spoke to her, that bothered me.

I clicked to DPS records and found the Worthingtons' address. Scribbling it on a Post-it, I stood.

"You've been quiet a while," Archie said. "Anything interesting?"

"I don't think Lindsey Decker was sleeping with her friend's husband, I think he told his wife she was so he didn't have to tell her he was sleeping with a guy Lindsey worked with," I said.

"Suburban intrigue at its finest," Archie said.

"Yeah, he whispered something to Lindsey the day before she went missing, though. Something that made her look...not scared, exactly, but... bothered. Looks like I'm headed back to Dallas Monday."

My phone buzzed on the corner of the desk. Text message. I touched the notification. From the newspaper reporter who'd done the feature on the shelter: *I can't give you the address, but I did get a phone number for Mrs. Marland.*

"Whoop de do, I did that myself," I muttered before I texted back a quick *thank you*.

"What's that?" Archie asked.

"Another trail. Miss Decker spent a lot of time volunteering at a shelter for survivors in the past few years. I wanted to talk with the folks there and called a news reporter hunting the address. She just sent me a phone number I looked up myself an hour ago." I dropped the phone on the desk. "Nobody is answering it today."

"Sounds like you're not sure where to go next," Archie said. "In my experience, this is when you really have to trust your gut. Pick the thing you know is off, but don't know why, and go run it down."

"What if she dies while I'm chasing the wrong thing?" I asked.

"What if she's already dead? What if you save her?" Archie stood and patted my shoulder. "If you let fear govern your investigation, you're going to lose for sure. Focus on one thing at a time, and just work the case. The clock is going to keep ticking whether you're watching it or not, Faith. It's a distraction." He stepped around the desk. "You want a Coke?"

"Dr Pepper if we have any, please."

"I have Diet," he said, laughing when I made a face.

"I'll take whatever's not. I could use the sugar rush." I looked back at the computer. "Hey, Arch? Thanks."

"Anytime, kiddo."

He disappeared, and I clicked back to the window on Maggie. She had a couple of small-time shoplifting charges and a DUI. Nothing serious, just enough to point out that she didn't necessarily mind breaking the law when she wanted something. So did Lindsey have something she wanted? Sebastian said Lindsey was complaining about the new manager, which was Maggie. But Maggie said Sebastian was creeping on Lindsey. The difference between the two of them on paper was that Sebastian didn't have a record. Not even a traffic violation. All ten prints were cataloged in the DPS database, and as far as the law was concerned, the kid was a boy scout.

But in person, I didn't completely trust either of them. Then there was Darla. And her husband.

Focus. Work the case.

Emmett Worthington was my front runner for the moment.

Archie rounded the corner cradling two cans in one large palm just as Graham appeared in the doorway. He stopped short when he saw me. "I thought you were going to Waco," he said.

"You should check your text messages." I wasn't trying to sound mad, but I'm pretty sure I did anyway, my eyes locked on Skye Morrow's pointy face peeking over Graham's shoulder.

* * *

At least he didn't have a girlfriend.

The voice in the background sounded familiar this morning because it was Skye. But she was twenty years too old and about a million levels too irritating for Graham. So what the hell was he doing with her on a Saturday? And why would he bring her here? On purpose?

"Sorry, I didn't see that." Graham tucked his phone back into his pocket.

Archie's head swiveled like he was watching a tennis match. Or maybe a bad reality show.

"Hardin. Skye. What...uh...what can we do for you?" he asked.

"I was hoping I could get a minute of your time." Graham kept his eyes on Archie. "Faith says you're always here, so I took a chance, and I spotted your car in the lot. I have a time- sensitive issue I'd like to speak with you about."

I was halfway to my feet when Graham's eyes flicked to me, then to the carpet. "In private."

My ass hit the chair hard enough to send pain shooting from my bruised tailbone.

Archie waved Graham toward the conference room. They went in and shut the door.

"That must sting," Skye said, her dancing blue eyes letting me know exactly how much she enjoyed the idea.

"Eh. Not as bad as losing that Emmy last month to someone less than half your age did, I'd bet." I wrapped a saccharine smile around the words, reaching for my computer. I might not be sure what to look at next, but I'd read the dictionary before I'd make small talk with Skye.

She walked to a whiteboard along one wall, trying to read the evidence trail scrawled on it in red and black marker.

I wasn't up on what they were working down here, but I wasn't too worried about Skye seeing something she could actually decipher. My eyes went to the closed conference room door. I was awfully worried about what was going on in there. Why would Graham shut me out of a conversation with Archie?

Skye strolled back across the room on her tottering black Louboutins, stealing a peppermint from Archie's dish.

I sighed. "What are you doing here?" Besides being proof that the universe hates me this weekend—but I didn't say that part out loud.

She mocked my syrupy tone. "Police business, you understand."

I rolled my eyes when she spouted one of my favorite deflections at me. Fine.

She held her smile until she was sure I'd stopped looking, stepping toward my desk with her eyes on the open folders. I flipped them all closed and stacked them up, setting my laptop over the stack to cover the tabs.

Skye smirked and dropped into Archie's chair.

The silence was so constricting it was almost painful. Ten thousand things I wanted to scream at her, and I couldn't utter a word because if I started, I wouldn't stop.

The conference room door clicked open after ten minutes that felt like ten hours, and I launched from the chair. "All done?" It came out way too chipper.

Archie's face folded into the most apologetic look I've ever seen. He shook his head at me before he turned to Skye. "Can you join us for a moment?"

I don't think I remembered to breathe as I watched the door close. Archie and Graham were just doing their jobs—I knew that. Without question. But what the hell business could Skye possibly have with Graham that wasn't hassling him about something?

The flat, dark wood of the closed door meant I wasn't getting an answer to that soon. And if I didn't find an answer to something, I was going to lose my shit.

Back to the computer. I flipped my notes open.

Roundtree said he'd put out an APB on Lindsey's car, and in all the running around and computer searches, I hadn't checked up on it.

I opened yet another new tab and entered the information.

Hot damn.

A Potter County sheriff's deputy found it in a stand of trees thirty miles outside Amarillo. Five hours ago.

I started stuffing things back in my bag and scribbled a note for Archie on a Post-it. Amarillo was more than seven hours away, and the sun was already sinking outside. But Lindsey's vehicle was the biggest clue anybody'd found in this case so far—literally and figuratively—and I needed to see it for myself.

13

Brutal. Beating. Relentless.

She'd never wondered before if it would feel better to die.

Yellow line. Yellow line. Yellow line.

Nobody stopped. Nobody asked if she needed help. The cars flew past on either side.

Kimbo. Kimbo had gotten her through the darkness. So she pretended she was walking him now. He danced around her ankles. Yipped at the cars as they flew by.

Thirty-one thousand six hundred twenty-eight. Thirty-one thousand six hundred twenty- nine.

She blinked hard, the yellow lines on the black pavement blurring, shimmering in the sun. No trees as far as she could see in any direction. Flat road, flat grass, black and brown. She'd rather be in the light where she could see Him if He was coming.

He always said He kept her safe, tucked away in the dark, where no one could hurt her. In a way, He had been right. But the dirty blanket, the cold floor, the cage, the others who came and went—nothing ever felt safe. He always said He didn't hurt them, but she wasn't sure. He said they were ready to go back. They screamed. They learned. But when she could hear the screams, smell the blood and the seared flesh…she didn't think they made it out alive.

Kimbo kept her safe.

She didn't scream. He couldn't beat her.

And now, here in the sun, He couldn't find her. Not to drag her back. Not again.

She kept walking, the sun sinking in the sky to her right. When dark came again, she would keep walking.

Kimbo skipped by her side. Slanted, orange rays still warmed her blistered skin.

Day seven hundred and thirty-five had been the best in a long time.

14

Amarillo was godawful sticky in the hazy lavender hour around sunrise. The heat was already oppressive, with the mercury creeping close to ninety before the sun was even up, and the air felt heavy, practically visible, and wet enough to make me wish I had gills instead of lungs.

By the time I ducked under the droopy yellow crime scene tape someone had half-ass strung between a couple of low, thorny mesquite trees, my not-so-crisp-anymore white button-down was plastered to me in three places.

I walked a hundred yards into the small thicket of mesquite, careful not to brush against any branches.

No car.

The report said just off the road, so I turned and headed west. Two hundred paces later I turned back. A hundred retraced steps led me to the sheriff.

"I thought I saw you disappear that way." Carl Benson reached to shake my hand. Google said he'd been the sheriff around here since the year before I was born, and the crevices lining his face said he wasn't a young man when he first won election.

"Thank you for coming out on a Sunday morning, sir."

He lifted his caramel felt Stetson off his head and ran his fingers through thick, sweaty gray hair. "Ain't nobody with a brain turning down a request from the Rangers—especially not when it comes from Chuck McClellan's little girl. But I gotta tell you little lady, I have no idea what it is you're after here. People run out of gas on this road every day. I expect your runaway mom will be by the station at some point today, whenever she comes back for the car and finds it gone."

Gone? I cleared my throat, mostly to try to remove irritation before I spoke. "You moved it?"

He slowed his speech like I was having a hard time following. "It's at the county impound yard. Why would we leave it here when there was an APB out on it?"

Because it might have been a crime scene? I wanted to feed that back in the same condescending tone, but it wasn't worth the time it would cost me to fan flames with this guy.

"I would have liked to have seen exactly where and how it was found. And your forensics team needs to process the interior as a crime scene." I settled for cold, and the ice in my voice would have frozen at least three rings of hell.

He put his hat back on. "The APB said this woman is of legal age and took off." His twang thickened when he was annoyed. "So you can stop looking at me like my men have done something wrong right now."

Deep breath. He was right. Roundtree set it up this way. "I understand that, Sheriff. I wasn't attacking your procedure. Just blowing off a little frustration with this entire situation. We have new information that suggests Miss Decker might not have left home of her own free will, and a forensic scope on the vehicle's interior will hopefully go a long way toward telling me if I'm right about that."

He grunted and reached for his phone. I think he woke the guy on the other end, but he gave the order and hung up, turning back to me. "You think somebody kidnapped a grown woman with a kid? In her own car? Why?"

I shook my head. "I don't know. Can you show me where the vehicle was actually found?"

He pointed back toward the road. "Right up here."

I followed him to a small clearing, where he pointed at the base of a taller mesquite tree. "Just there," he said. "My deputy spotted it on patrol and stopped to see if anyone needed aid. He found the vehicle, but no people around."

"Do you know how many people were out here? How many cars?" I stepped carefully over the still-visible lines in the parched grass.

"Taylor left his unit up at the road, called a tow truck after he ran the plates. As far as we know, that's the extent of who's been out here since. This isn't exactly a tourist attraction."

Excellent. I kept my eyes on the grass, following the tracks to the roadside. Back to the tree. Roadside. Tree.

On my seventh lap, the sheriff put a hand up. "What are you doing, sweetheart?"

I swallowed the reflexive "actual police work."

"See the tire tracks in this grass?" I pointed. "Here, the more defined, fatter ones, are from your tow truck. He backed in, pulled forward and to the left, and backed up again."

Benson bent forward, squinting at the grass. "Okay. So?"

I crouched next to the other, fainter set of tracks. Partly obscured by the fresh ones from the tow, there was still enough visible for me to know Lindsey Decker had not parked her car here.

"See this? Thick flat line, thin row of straight blades, thick flat line?" I pointed. "It's repeated eight times across. Lindsey Decker's 2009 Prius didn't do that. None of these marks match the wheel size. This was a big double dually pickup."

Benson dropped carefully to one knee in the grass and peered at the mashed-down blades. Pulled his hat off again. Scratched his head. "I'll be god-chicken-fried-damned, girl. That's a fine eye for detail you've got yourself, there."

"It's helpful on days like this."

He stayed down there, taking pictures with his phone and muttering under his breath, as I walked a wide arc around all the tracks I could see. I snapped several photos of my own on my way to the base of the tree where Benson said his man found Lindsey's car. I tiptoed close, eyes scanning the ground, and crouched when I spotted what I was looking for.

Four neat little craters in the earth, perfectly symmetrical, each a rounded half-moon. The two closer to the tree were deeper than the two in the front. I snapped pictures of both sets before I stuck my index finger into the back right one. Dry as church country on revival Sunday. I poked the mounded-up dirt next to the track, pretty sure it was not even before I touched it.

Yep. Damp, even in this heat. I looked up. "Sheriff Benson? When did it rain last?"

He raised his head from his phone, flicking fingers up one by one. "Thursday week," he said.

Ten days ago. Which meant Lindsey's car sat here unnoticed for nine after somebody hauled it out here and dumped it. His deputy had a good eye, too.

Benson got to his feet with a bit of difficulty and ambled my way. "Why?"

I stood, brushing damp soil off my fingers. "The back tires made deeper ruts because the vehicle was dropped ass-first off the pickup bed, a little clumsily, too. So all the weight of the whole car landed here"—I pointed to the craters—"while only half of it fell onto the front tires." I pointed to the ruts a few feet away. "The top layers of dirt under the tires are bone dry. The softer dirt around them is damp. Before last Thursday, it had been a while since y'all had a storm, I'm guessing."

"A month, almost."

I tapped nervous fingers on my thigh.

"Why d'you think anybody would go to all this trouble and then leave the car where somebody might see it from the road?" he asked.

"That is a damned good question, sir. I'm afraid I don't know."

"You really think somebody took—" He didn't finish that before his radio crackled to life.

Static, then a voice. "Sheriff? APD says superficial blood in the driver's seat and on the wheel of that car you asked about, and significant blood, plus some unidentified bodily fluid, in the passenger seat."

My eyes fell shut, my pulse taking off to the races. Science said all the nicotine was out of my bloodstream by now, but damned if I didn't want a cigarette worse than I maybe ever had.

"What about the trunk?" I whispered.

He relayed the question.

"I don't believe they're there yet, sir," the dispatcher said. Benson thanked her and told her to keep him updated.

"Y'all have a K-9 unit?" I asked when his radio fell silent.

"Blood and fluid." He shook his head. "How did you know?"

Because my gut said the scrapings from the dumpster were blood. Lindsey's blood. And if I waited for the lab to give me absolute proof before I chose the kidnapping trail, I might as well shoot Lindsey myself. "I hate being right about shit like this." I wasn't sure if I whispered the words or just thought them.

I was still in braces when Archie spent two long, tense days trying to get to my sister before she died. I wanted with everything in me to deliver Lindsey Decker back to her little boy like Archie hadn't been able to bring Charity back to me.

"Yeah. Yeah—I'll get the dogs out here," Benson said.

I surveyed the waist-high grass stretching as far as I could see beyond the trees.

Had I missed my chance before I got started? Was a hunter or a kid or a search party going to find Lindsey in this field?

I pulled out my phone to call the sector field office for search support.

* * *

I liked Carl Benson. Sure, he was cranky and country and grating with his condescending attitude at times, but he was also a decent cop who wasn't afraid to admit his guys missed something and was more than willing to try to make it right. The latter meant way more to me than the former.

Sheriff Benson had a dog and handler on scene in less than thirty minutes, and a dozen deputies walking a grid through an increasing radius surrounding the car. Our K-9 unit arrived at close to the hour mark, and I introduced the officer to Sheriff Benson before I left everyone with my cell number.

The way the car was dumped and the blood in it was all the evidence I needed that Lindsey Decker was kidnapped. Whether she was dead or alive, my job was to find out what happened to her. And the trail got colder every minute.

The sheriff promised to fast-track the DNA runs on the samples from Lindsey's car and send them to me as soon as he got them.

"If she's out here, we'll get to her," he said, pushing my door shut after he walked me back to my truck. "You consider yourself welcome anytime you need anything, Officer McClellan."

"No offense, sir, but I'm hoping y'all look all day in this heat and have nothing to show for it." I started the engine.

"Me too. Drive safe now."

I made it almost to the freeway when my phone binged a text message. From Bill Roundtree: *Fishing all weekend, just got your voicemail about that shelter. Here's the location. Run by the Marland family's anointed heir apparent and his wife, but they do good work. Help a lot of people. Heads up: their kind of money means they don't always have to follow rules.*

I skimmed the message and clicked on the address to open it in the map. I had called the number I found for Mrs. Marland nine times in sixty-five hours. Time to swing by. I clicked the *Go* button in the bottom of the screen, determined to make at least some progress on this case today.

* * *

Thanks to the nonexistent early Sunday traffic, I made it to Dallas in record time. I navigated through a section of the city where pawn shops were outnumbered only by liquor stores, into a tangle of switchback turns through a sprawling industrial park before I finally stopped at the address on my screen.

Um.

Was Roundtree right about this?

I stared at a large blue warehouse with a low-pitched, corrugated metal roof and an eight-foot security fence topped with large spirals of razor wire.

I had to give it to them, if this wasn't about to end up a wild goose chase, nobody would suspect that building housed anything related to sheltering humans. I'd been in jails that looked more homey and inviting.

I spotted a gate nestled low in the fence, with what looked like an intercom box next to it. My phone stayed in the console because no shelter I've ever visited allows them on the premises. Crossing the street, I noted cameras well-hidden along the building's roofline. They could probably monitor everything for at least a two-block radius from up there.

I pushed the button on the box and pulled out my ID.

Five seconds became thirty became a hundred and twenty.

I rocked up on the balls of my feet, fixing a smile on my face and pushing the button again, turning so the camera closest to me might pick up my badge. Geometry wasn't my best subject, but the sight line should be right if the camera had any kind of decent resolution.

Almost another minute ticked by. A speaker crackled to life.

"Can I help you?" It was a man's voice—probably not any older than Sebastian the security guard, and hesitant.

My brow furrowed. I was expecting a woman. Shit. Was this the wrong place? I couldn't give away what I was looking for until I was sure I'd found it. I glanced at the wire lining the fence and cleared my throat.

"Faith McClellan, Texas Rangers. Can you open the gate, please?"

The speaker went dead for five beats. Crackled again. "Can I see some identification, ma'am?"

"Of course." I turned to the camera and held up my DPS ID with one hand, pointing to my badge with the other.

More static. "What can I do for you?"

You can open the gate. But I couldn't say that.

"I'd like to talk to the person in charge," I said.

"Concerning?"

"I'm not sure you want me to stand out here and say that too loudly." The words came out before they fully registered in my head, but they were perfect: putting the responsibility back on him, while not tipping my cards even a little bit. Nearly twenty years of this police work stuff pays off at the damndest times, but I'm always thankful for it.

Silence. Static.

A new voice, a woman this time. Confident. Direct. "Are you under the impression that we've broken a law, Officer?"

"I am not. I am hoping you can help me find someone."

The speaker went dead. Stayed that way for five beats.

"Hello?" I asked.

Damn. I was a quarter of the way to my car when the same clear alto, sans the speaker distortion, stopped me in my tracks. "Officer?"

Bingo.

Jogging back to the gate, I slipped through when she opened it, following her wordless turn for the large metal door camouflaged in the side of the building. She punched in a code that slid it back, and stepped through Alice's looking glass—nothing and no one appearing what it seemed from the outside. The interior of the ordinary-looking warehouse was all soft blues and grays and shiplap and big, overstuffed furniture in neutral tones spotted with huge, fluffy pillows. Like Joanna Gaines magicked an impossibly large great room into feeling cozy.

I turned a slow circle as the woman from outside bolted the door with three locks and a wrought iron bar.

"Not what you expected?" she asked, her blue eyes bright. "I'm Emberly Marland. Welcome to Harbor House."

I put a hand out and she shook it before waving for me to follow her. We walked through another living area, past ping pong, pool, and foosball tables, and I spotted a large industrial kitchen at the far end of the building.

She unlocked a deep mahogany stained door and held it open for me. "Have a seat in my office. Can I get you some coffee? Water?"

I shook my head. I'd hit three Starbucks along I-20. Any more caffeine right now and I'd see noises. "Thank you for offering. And thanks for seeing me."

"We're funny about our security here," she said. "You said something about a missing person?"

"Yes, ma'am. She volunteered here at one time. I'm looking for people she might have known or stayed in touch with, anything you can think of no matter how trivial you think it may seem. Lindsey Decker?"

A look I couldn't quite place flickered across her face so quickly I couldn't swear I didn't imagine it. Not shock or worry, exactly, but not anger or sympathy, either. She sucked in a sharp breath, a worried crease popping up between her brows as she leaned forward. "What on earth happened to her? Is her baby okay?"

"Her baby is fine." I pulled out a notepad and pen. "When was the last time you saw her?"

Emberly hunched forward, long strawberry-blonde hair falling around her face in a curtain, her hands rising to support her head.

"It's been probably three months since last time she was here." She directed the words at the heavy leather desk blotter.

"And how long did she volunteer here?"

"Oh, she came in every week for more than three years. She was our most faithful volunteer for a long time. I was quite sorry to have to ask her to stop coming."

"You asked her to stop?" I tipped my head to one side. "How exactly does one get fired from a volunteer position?"

She sat up straight, brushing her hair out of her face. "I liked Lindsey, Officer...?"

"McClellan," I said.

"Pleasure to meet you. Lindsey's a sweet girl. Maybe not the brightest I've ever met, but sweet. She likes to help other people. It's why she was so faithful about being here every week in the first place. But sometimes that urge to help can go in a misguided direction." Her chest heaved with a deep sigh. "Lindsey brought one of our residents an old cell phone. They swore it was only for games, but we have a strict rule that no phones come into the building. I don't even have mine, and I spend most of my time here, so I almost never have mine."

Damn. Spyware, the kind pimps and traffickers and asshole husbands can buy on the dark web, gets more sophisticated and impossible to trace every month. For a place like this, a cell phone is a little light-up target for the very people the residents are trying to hide from. A total ban is the easiest way to make sure the location isn't compromised. After three years, Lindsey should've known that.

"The internet is a wonderful terrible thing," I said.

She snorted. "Isn't that the gospel truth? Sometimes I find myself thinking longingly of the days when my car phone weighed twenty pounds and the internet was a military device, and I wouldn't have to worry about our address getting into the wrong hands and ending up blasted all over some creeper forum where a trafficker could find it. Trying to give these kids some security when they've known so little for however long is a twenty-four-hour-a-day job."

I leaned forward, resting my elbows on my knees. "So, you let Lindsey go for bringing the phone into the building?"

Emberly nodded. "I had no choice. I got proof that Lindsey was where the phone came from and I just can't allow that. Our rules are rules because they keep us alive and able to help people. Not because I like being a killjoy."

I tapped the pen on my notebook. "So you didn't actually see Lindsey bring the phone into the building?"

Emberly's almond-shaped green eyes narrowed. "AT&T said it belonged to her. And it was discovered in a pillowcase in our dormitory during bed check."

Pretty damning. Certainly not worth arguing about right now.

"I understand why you have to take a hard line on things like that," I said. "Mrs. Marland, were there residents here Lindsey was particularly close to? Important to?"

"I suppose she got attached to several of our residents. It's difficult to separate the personal from the professional, even for me, and I've been in social work twenty-three years."

I knew that struggle. "Was there anyone on that list who left recently? Anyone who might have tried to find Lindsey in the real world? Maybe could have led someone to her unwittingly? Especially since she'd given the police information on some traffickers a couple of years ago?"

The question had been nagging at the back of my brain since I left Amarillo, but I didn't fully understand it until it popped out of my mouth. Lindsey wasn't snatched out of that parking lot because she happened to be there. Whoever took her was in the lot because they knew she'd be there. They were waiting for her. Which meant they'd been watching her. And I was sitting in a place the sort of people who kidnap young women literally for a living might have targeted her.

Emberly drummed her fingers on the desktop, shaking her head slowly. She spun the chair. Stood. And strode to a tall oak and chrome filing cabinet in the corner. Pulling a drawer out, she plucked a file from a tight mass of manila folders and returned to the desk, spreading it open in front of her.

"Jeremy," she said, pulling a photo out and handing it across the desk to me. "He came to us from a police sting operation last summer. He was here for ten months. Computer technology training. He was forwarded to a work program where he could attend classes at the community college in exchange for a reduced salary in the IT department there."

My eyes still on the angular planes of the young man's face, I nodded. "Where is the college?" I asked.

"Austin," she said. "We don't place anyone back in the community they came from because their former traffickers might spot them. I've sent people as far away as Oregon and Massachusetts, but Jeremy wasn't in that world for long, and the program in Austin was too perfect for him to pass up. He was sweet on Lindsey, though."

I tapped the edge of the photo on the desk. A history of victimization can sometimes make a person the aggressor. "Would he have taken her?"

I wasn't sure what I wanted her to say. Kidnapping because she was the object of an obsession gave me an excellent chance Lindsey was still alive. But damn, I hate picking up kids who have been abused and seeing them go to prison because that fucked up their heads.

Emberly's full lips disappeared into a thin white line. She threw up her hands. "I don't want to think so, but honestly? I don't know. He never talked much in therapy group about anything. He left with us not knowing much more than we did when he came in. We give them all their space for the first thirty days, but I have some of the best therapists in the area working with our residents, and nobody could pry anything out of him. He's a master of deflection. And he's only nineteen."

Different, but not unheard of. Everyone deals with trauma in his or her own way, and depending on what happened in this kid's life, shutting it out or burying it might be his best coping mechanism. Psychologically, men are better at this than women—but I knew the process inside out.

So the trick would be to avoid projecting onto this kid, to see him for what he was and not what I wanted to see. It's a tough wire to walk, and one I've taken a few tumbles from in my career.

Not this time.

"Can you tell me where I can find him?"

"The program we placed him in is at St. Francis Community College. If he's still there."

"How long ago was this?"

"Six weeks."

Shit. Long enough to stalk Lindsey and grab her two weeks ago.

I started to ask for more information, but didn't get the words out before the door swung open behind me. "I thought you said we was going to church this morning, woman," a deep voice boomed with more than a hint of West Texas drawl.

I turned.

"Who the hell are you and why haven't I seen you before?" His face stretched into a wide grin, his shoulders going back under his expensive sport coat when he stood up straight.

I flicked a glance at Emberly, who didn't seem to notice or care.

"Darlin', I told you I would try," she said. "As it happens, I have work to do."

"This is a hobby, not a job." He grinned at me again, leaning in like he was sharing a secret. "She never does get that work is supposed to make you money. This doesn't do a thing but cost me, and still, she sleeps here, eats here, and calls it work."

"Let's save round 347 of this discussion for later, Miles," Emberly said. "I'm sure Ranger McClellan here has no interest in your opinion."

His eyes popped at the name and I stood, smiling at Emberly. "Do you mind showing me around a bit more before I go?"

"Sure," she said, walking to the door and opening it with a *stay here* glare cut over my shoulder at her husband. "We house anywhere from twenty to forty survivors at a time, though sadly we seem to be full more often than not these days. In five years and two months here, we've worked with various agencies to help two thousand one hundred and forty-two survivors find a new life. Our residents remain with us until we can feel reasonably sure we're placing them somewhere that they will thrive. Some go to school, others to halfway houses and jobs until they get on their feet. Everyone is provided access to community counseling services with each placement."

We walked back to the great room, where *Friends* was playing on a flatscreen bigger than the pool table, three young women in pajamas curled on sofa cushions eating Captain Crunch.

"Sundays are lazy morning days. No groups, no classes, just downtime." Emberly tipped her head toward me, keeping her voice low. "They have to find a way to be comfortable and unguarded when they're not busy, and we've found it's the most difficult accomplishment for some of them."

The smallest girl, with dark hair in short pigtails and honest-to-God footie pajamas covering her from neck to toes, laughed at the TV.

"What's your average age of a resident here?" I asked.

"Currently? Nineteen. With a range from fifteen to twenty-three."

"Fifteen?" I kept my eyes on the tiny girl. She couldn't have been more than five feet tall, which I could see even with her legs folded under her.

Emberly followed my gaze. "She's our youngest right now, fifteen and two months, been here nearly a year. She was brought to Texas by a step-uncle and sold to traffickers when she was nine."

Nine? My head snapped around. Emberly said quietly, "One thing this will teach you quickly, as I'm sure you know yourself, Officer—there's a whole lot of evil in this world."

True statement. But it's still hard to stomach the spoils of that evil, especially when they're in freaking footie pajamas, laughing at Monica Gellar on a Sunday morning. "What happens to her when she leaves here?"

"She's so empathetic. A fantastic listener. I'd like to see her go into counseling victims of what she's been through, personally. But that's going to require school and college. We're catching her up in her studies, but she's still only reading at a sixth grade level."

"So can she just stay here for however long it takes?"

Emberly laid her index finger across her lips. "Not according to the state." She winked.

Ah. They had the money to break rules, like Roundtree said. And Emberly Marland exuded privilege from every perfectly tightened pore. As Ruth McClellan's daughter, even though I didn't usually like to admit it, I could spot new money a football field away. Emberly was way too classy for that. The kind of attitude that let her enforce what had to seem to Lindsey like an arbitrary rule with a no-tolerance policy, yet break the actual law governing her center without batting a tucked and lifted eyelid—that was old money strained logic.

But I just nodded, because I would let the girl stay, too, in her shoes.

"Hey—is the person Lindsey got the phone for still here?"

Emberly shook her head. "I'm afraid I can't talk about that," she said. "Confidential client records."

There it was again. Pigtail girl, I could have her whole history without even asking. But the phone recipient, she used privacy to stonewall me on. How come?

Before I could ponder it, she turned and waved an arm toward a large, industrial kitchen. "The dorm is back there."

"Can I take a peek?"

"I'm happy to—" she began just as Miles bellowed, "I'm getting tired of waiting, Emberly Jane!" from her office. Her head whipped back and forth three times before she waved me on with a hasty "I'll catch up."

I didn't take the opportunity lightly, hurrying my stride to the wide door on the left of the kitchen.

I flung it open so fast I narrowly missed a thin young woman with purple hair and guarded gray eyes. "Sorry!"

She stepped backward, her expression flat. "No worries."

I stood to the side and held the door for her. She took half a step before her eyes fixed on my badge. They popped wider. "Are you here about Jeremy, too?"

Jeremy, the kid who was crushing on Lindsey? I could be.

"Did you know him when he was here?"

She shook her head. "I'm not sure how many people actually knew him, at all. I can't believe he's dead."

Um. "What?" I couldn't stop it from popping out.

Her eyes widened again as her fingers flew to her mouth. "Was I not supposed to say that?"

I shook my head hard enough to wreck my ponytail. "You're fine. I'm sorry. I'm actually looking for Lindsey Decker. I was hoping to find the friend she gave her old phone to."

Her forehead wrinkled. Mouth opened. Closed.

I tipped my head and flashed the *talk to me* half-smile.

She stared straight through it and sighed. Folded her arms across her chest. "Well, I'm probably not supposed to say this, either, but what the hell? Lindsey brought the phone in to Jeremy. So they could compete on some word game she liked to play. He was real smart."

And he left a few weeks after Lindsey and now he was dead and Lindsey was missing. That was a hell of a coincidence.

"Do you know Jeremy's last name?" I asked.

Her lips disappeared into a tight line. "I don't even know if Jeremy is his real name. That's just what we do here, you know?"

"And the police were here asking about him?"

Fear flared in her eyes. "I didn't say that," she said.

I was pretty sure she had, but she was moving again, and I couldn't exactly stop her.

"I appreciate your time," I said as she stepped through the door and toward the kitchen.

"Don't mention it," the girl muttered, her eyes on Emberly, who was hurrying across the long room smoothing the skirt of her Donna Karan suit.

Ten-four.

"Are you already done?" Emberly asked, slightly breathless. "I'm so sorry. It never stops here. I hope I was able to help. Lindsey has a good heart, and her son is precious."

So why hadn't she told me that Jeremy kid was dead?

My eyes skipped between Emberly and purple hair, wondering if this was a case of "consider your source." I didn't exactly have a good way to ask, but I could do my homework and follow up.

Emberly led me to the door, pausing after she threw the first lock and turning back to me. "Why haven't I seen anything about Lindsey in the news?" she asked. "If you're looking for a missing person, isn't it helpful to have as many pairs of eyes as possible helping?"

"I'm not sure what happened before I was sent here Friday, but I talked to Chip Johnson at Channel Seven, so hopefully word will spread from there."

She flashed a bright white grin. "Excellent. Please let me know if there's anything else I can do for you."

I shook her hand again and thanked her, not pausing outside to listen to the locks clicking back into place.

By the time I got back to my office in Waco it was after lunch, and I knew way more than I had twenty-four hours before, but somehow didn't feel like I'd made any progress. A text from Sheriff Benson said the trunk was clean and the car samples were at the lab, no luck on remains yet.

So maybe Lindsey was still breathing.

15

Darkness erased the world outside the windows of the empty office building. I stood back to survey the case wall I'd spent hours creating, rolling and rubbing a right shoulder sore from the effort. The whiteboard closest to my desk was crammed with neat, color-coded lists of facts, acquaintances, suspects, criminal histories, and evidence. The map had pins for every location I'd visited that had anything to do with Lindsey, including a green one in the far right corner for the car, since the Amarillo area wasn't pictured.

The photo of Lindsey and Jake was a reminder to keep writing when my arm started to get tired. To keep going when I got weary and discouraged.

I clicked the cap onto the marker. There were some decent leads on that board. Sheriff Benson had called again at 8:30 to tell me they hadn't found anything and were calling it for the night, but he'd keep me in the loop.

"They didn't find her because she's not dead." I laid the marker in the metal tray under the board, my words echoing faintly in the empty office. "I'm going to find her and get her home."

The answer was right there in front of me, somewhere. All I had to do was run the board.

* * *

I spent Memorial Day chasing down the vehicles registered to everyone on my list and adding them to the board before I searched traffic feeds for their plates. Emmett Worthington's white BMW 530i was the only one a traffic camera put near Southpoint Mall on the twelfth of May. Add in the sketch in Lindsey's book, Darla's shitty attitude, and the look on Lindsey's face when Emmett spoke to her the night before she disappeared, and I had a prime suspect. I headed back to Dallas before dawn Tuesday, fairly confident I was on my way to find out what happened to Lindsey and praying it wasn't what I feared.

I parked my truck across from the Worthingtons' red brick McMansion as the sun peeked over the eastern horizon. I had almost given up the surveillance when Emmett's white BMW backed out of the three-car garage at 9:30. I gave him half a block and fell in behind, figuring I might get more out of him if I caught him before he went into the office rather than ringing his doorbell. Except he didn't go to the office.

He went to Lone Star Joe at Southpoint Mall.

I watched Emmett and tattoo sleeves take a table in the corner. Emmett's left foot bounced so fast it was almost a blur, his eyes on the table as he spoke. Tattoo sleeves sat back, shaking his head, before he leaned forward and reached for Emmett's hand. Emmett shook him off. They sat in silence for ninety seconds or so until Emmett said one last thing before he stood and strode away. He shoved the door so hard it clattered into the concrete behind it. Temper, temper.

Damn. That part didn't look so good for Lindsey.

But maybe I was wrong. Maybe he wanted to talk to Lindsey. Maybe he wanted to sleep with her. Maybe he thought keeping her from her kid would get her to do something for him. He probably didn't get told "no" often—even Lindsey's talent didn't do him justice. He was, objectively, hotter than an August afternoon in El Paso.

I caught up with him as he pushed open the door leading outside.

"Mr. Worthington?"

He paused, the door half-open. "Can I help you, Officer?"

"I sure hope so." I waved for him to go on outside and followed before I stuck out a hand to shake. "Faith McClellan, Texas Rangers. I'm investigating the disappearance of Lindsey Decker, a young woman who worked in the coffee shop you were just in. Do you know her?"

He took a small step back, folding muscular arms across his broad, defined chest. "I go into the coffeehouse on a regular basis."

That wasn't an answer to my question.

I kept my voice even. "I hear they have the best lattes in town. Lindsey is about this tall." I held a flat palm up next to my shoulder. "Blonde, with a pretty smile."

He waited a beat. Four. Ten.

"I know who she is. She used to know my wife. Darla said the police were asking about her the other day, but I'm afraid I can't help you."

He turned, pulling his keys out of his pocket.

"Why did you break up with him?" I didn't shout, not that there was anyone around to hear me anyway. I had enough to take him in for questioning, but a guy like him would call a lawyer and shut right up if I tried. Getting him chatting was the fastest way I'd learn anything about him and his relationship with Lindsey, but he needed a reason to come back and talk to me.

His shiny brown wingtip paused in mid-air. Looked like maybe I'd lifted the right rock there.

He turned. "What did you ask me?"

I stepped forward. "I think you heard me. I'm sure your wife told you Lindsey has a son who misses her. I just want to get her home to him. Is there somewhere we can go to talk?"

He shoved his hands into the pockets of his pressed Armani suit pants. "I don't have her."

"Do you know who does?"

He sucked in a deep breath. Blew it out slowly. "Jason said she'd been getting flowers at work. They're all worried about her." His teeth closed over his lower lip. "I think maybe I said something I shouldn't have."

"What do you mean?"

"My wife, Darla. She's not ever been terribly...forgiving. I told her something about Lindsey that wasn't even true. I had no idea Darla knew her, you know—coffee shop baristas aren't exactly her usual crowd."

"Sure." I waited.

He ran his left hand through his hair, the sun throwing tiny rainbows over his chestnut curls from the diamonds on his wedding band. "Jason and I, we've been on-again off-again since college. Before I ever met Darla, even."

Stay quiet. Let him talk.

He huffed out a short breath and cleared his throat. "Everything was rocking along fine until I got too comfortable. Too brave. She saw me in the coffeehouse with him last year. So when she confronted me, I told her it was the blonde girl I was there to see, that I'd been seeing her for a while."

The police report had clued me in to what came next, but he kept talking. "She grabbed a knife out of the butcher block and came at me." He shook his head like he still couldn't believe it. "I had to call the cops. I tried to warn Lindsey and she told me she thought she'd recognized me before but didn't want to believe it because she knew Darla from the playgroup." He shook his head, words spilling out faster. "I felt awful about what I did to her; I stayed away from the coffeehouse and from Jason for months. But it never works with us, the staying away thing.

"Darla went to a spa for Mother's Day weekend and I got a sitter and came by on Saturday night. I tried to tell Lindsey I was sorry, but I don't think she wanted me to tell her much of anything. A few days later, Jason mentioned that he was short staffed because she wasn't showing up for work. Then Darla said the police were asking about her. I don't think Darla could...you know..." His head fell back. "Right? I couldn't be married to someone who could hurt another human being?"

So much for prime suspect number one. His story made perfect sense, right down to explaining the look I'd seen on Lindsey's face in the surveillance film. I believed him.

I also didn't believe Darla was incapable of violence any more than he did.

"I think maybe I need to talk to your wife. Was she still at the spa the evening of May twelfth? Is there anyone who can corroborate that?"

"May twelfth?" He pulled out his phone and tapped the screen. "Lindsey went missing on Mother's Day?"

"She did. From this parking lot."

"Darla was with me. There was a benefit thing, a Mother's Day dinner to raise money for breast cancer." He tapped the phone screen again and flipped it around to show me photos. Emmett and Darla Worthington, smiling for the camera at a chic rooftop bar downtown. Timestamped 6:38 p.m. on May 12.

There went prime suspect number two.

I flipped through three more photos and handed his phone back. "Thank you for your time, sir."

"Does that mean Darla didn't do anything wrong?"

"Sounds to me like she's done plenty, but it doesn't look like she took Lindsey Decker. Please do give me a call if you remember or hear anything that might help get her home." I handed him a card and started for my truck, my thoughts a dozen steps ahead of my feet.

* * *

On cursory investigation—which was as deep as anyone else would go into his life—it seemed Jeremy had left Harbor House and vanished into thin air. Nobody by that name was enrolled in a computer program at any university in Austin, no instructor claimed to have had a student placed by the shelter—not that I knew if anyone would tell them that—and Mrs. Marland was chronically away from her phone.

I spent Thursday haunting alleys and motels in seedy sections of Austin that crawled with traffickers. I asked around at businesses in those areas. No leads.

Friday, I was on my last hope, repeating my steps through Dallas' sketchier neighborhoods, when I hit pay dirt. Kind of.

"He don't work down here." The waifish brunette in the too-short skirt didn't look at me, her eyes on the Whataburger bag in my hand. "He works the airport."

Hot damn. I passed her the bag and was out of the alley and in my truck before she got the paper off the burger.

Dead or alive, this guy might be valuable to my investigation, though I was hoping for alive.

It took me two phone calls and a fifteen-minute hold to get an appointment with the head of the DFW Airport Police Department. Another hour and I was seated across from him watching his head bob as I described what I roughly knew of Jeremy.

"Sad story. He's been back and forth through our international terminals for years, bought and sold maybe a dozen times." He steepled his fingers under his chin. "I thought he'd gotten away from them, heard he was in a shelter a while back. And then he turned up in a hotel room a month or so ago, filleted like a prize heifer, wrists and ankles tied to the bedposts."

Jesus.

He spun his chair and opened a drawer. "The hotel was here on airport property, but we passed it along to the city because we don't have a homicide division." He pulled a folder free and passed it across the desk. "They made a pretty quick ID, a Russian national here less than three hours at the kid's time of death. Cameras had the guy going in and out of the room."

I opened the folder and skipped right past the photos of the scene, scanning the report the detective in charge sent over. I needed to sit down with this killer, to make sure Jeremy's murder wasn't a mask for Lindsey's disappearance.

"They let him leave? Are they kidding?" I thumped a fist on my knee.

"Nobody let him, he just did. Strolled right out of the murder scene and got on a plane home. I'm sure you know we don't have an extradition treaty with Russia. Our justice department could press for their authorities to prosecute, but it's a complicated issue. We can't exactly start a war over a dead teenage prostitute."

I stood and turned to leave before my mouth got away from me. Four days gone and all I had to show for it was a cold-hearted colleague and a dead end. I couldn't interview the prime suspect in the murder because he'd gone home, and I couldn't interview the kid who knew Lindsey because he was dead.

Back in front of my board, I crossed through Jeremy's name in red. Lieutenant Boone stuck his head out his office door. "Nothing yet, huh?" Sympathy cloaked the words. "The switchboard is about tired of the calls coming in from your TV turn in Dallas—but maybe they'll be helpful. On your desk."

I turned and snatched up the little blue message slips, letting them fall to the blotter as I counted. Twelve leads. Maybe one of these was the right one.

* * *

Another Friday rolled up on my calendar without a single credible lead from Chip Johnson's viewers to show for a week of chasing a whole flock of wild geese all the hell over half the state.

I stepped into a south Dallas pawn shop for the next-to-last interview on the list. The owner swore Lindsey had dropped off a necklace the day after she disappeared.

The brass bell over the door tinkled a second time as it slipped shut behind me. A round man with a gleaming hairless head looked up from a newspaper, his scowl vanishing when he saw me. "Miss McClellan?" The fluorescent light gleamed off sweat beading across his forehead and his upper lip.

"Thank you for calling in, Mr. Peters," I said. "Do you have that surveillance footage we discussed of Lindsey Decker?"

I glanced up, finding four cameras pointed at the counter.

"Huh? Oh, sure, sure." He rounded the end of the counter and tried to smile at me. I think. It was more of a leer, and I had to stop myself from stepping backward.

I didn't like this. Or him. Something felt off.

"Right back here." He motioned for me to follow him.

What if he had seen Lindsey? I swallowed my reservation and obliged, squelching the little voice in my head that whispered about trusting my gut. He was half a foot shorter than me and not in fantastic shape. I could handle myself.

He punched a code into a door at the far end of the shop, and I watched his fingers work the keypad. 55468. I repeated it to myself until I was sure I wouldn't forget, swallowing hard as I stepped past him into an office.

Where a pasty pale white man twice Graham's size waited, not an ounce of fat visible over all the muscles he was flexing, his blue eyes hard as they raked over me.

Shit.

I spun back for the door.

My sweaty little friend who saw me on the news pulled it shut, his girth blocking the entire frame.

I jumped back into the opposite corner and reached for my Sig.

The big guy leveled an old school sawed-off double-barrel shotgun. "I wouldn't." He spoke with an accent I couldn't identify other than to point in the general direction of Eastern Europe.

I let my hand fall back to my side.

He'd blow me clean in two if he fired that at this range. Which meant I needed to get them talking, buy some time and figure out what they wanted.

I turned to Sweaty. "You didn't see Lindsey Decker, did you?" I asked.

He shook his head. "But I did see Chuck McClellan's daughter giving out her phone number on TV. And my buddy here has a bone to pick with your old man."

Oh, you've got to be fucking kidding me. I didn't say that out loud.

"I knew there was a good reason I hated talking to reporters." My voice was icy and calm, my breathing even, thanks to intensive and regular crisis management training. There would be time to panic after I got out of this room.

"Not as many bones to pick as I do, I promise." I turned to focus on the one holding the gun on me. "I hate to burst a bubble this big, but my father is not going to give a shit that you have me."

"I know. If he cared about anything, someone would have caught the men who killed your sister. But the Bible says an eye for an eye, and McClellan refused to sign the clemency form that would have saved my daddy's skin." He raised the gun. "Can't much argue with the Bible. I figure he'll probably miss you at least a little. We got it all planned out, Willie and me. We'll be to Mexico before they ever find you here, and your daddy will get our regards from south of the border."

I had never wished harder in my life that Archie was my actual blood father. My fingers closed around the cool metal handle of a desk drawer.

"My father understands loss. You said yourself, my sister was already murdered."

"Not by me." His finger landed on the trigger.

He'd counted on the close range, because he only had one shot with that thing. My play was to make him miss.

I ripped the drawer free, swinging for the business end of the gun with everything I had. Papers and pens and rows of unused staples flew. Sweaty screamed.

Muscles' trigger finger twitched.

A roar absorbed all other sound, and Willie hit the floor as I wrenched my Sig from its holster and trained it on the big guy. His mouth was open for a wail I couldn't hear over the ringing in my ears as he fumbled for more shells for the shotgun.

My foot whipped up, connecting just below the trigger guard and sending his weapon end over end into the wall behind him.

His face twisted into a red mask of fleshy fury as he threw a punch my way. I dodged, my foot catching on Willie's calf. Keeping my balance—barely—I watched Muscles recover and draw back his left fist. Locking my elbows, I fired at his right shoulder.

That scream I heard, and a gurgle from Willie, too, which meant he wasn't dead. Muscles slumped back onto the counter.

"You shot me."

"I wasn't aiming to kill you."

"Your father..." He didn't get the next word out before he noticed the blood pooling under his friend's middle, and his own running down his arm. His eyes rolled back to solid white. I jumped into the blood puddle to keep him from landing on me when he fell.

Stepping over them both, I pressed the right numbers to open the door. Pulling it shut behind me, I dialed emergency services from my cell and gave them the rundown before I went to my truck and locked the doors, my hands shaking as I listened to the sirens draw closer.

If I made it to midnight without a cigarette, I'd consider myself well and truly reformed.

I tapped my phone to life and used my finger to draw a line through Chip Johnson's name on a photo of my whiteboard.

No more TV pleas. There had to be a better way to get leads.

* * *

"You almost got yourself killed, kiddo." I held my phone away from my ear, Archie's bellow plenty loud enough, anyway. "How many times have I told you to trust your gut? Do not try to tell me you didn't know something was wrong as soon as you walked in there."

"Who the hell was Ernie Galbacci, anyway?" I didn't want to think about or admit that I had indeed known I shouldn't have followed Sweaty Willie into the back. Much easier to be mad at myself for talking to Chip in the first place and go on with my life.

"Head of the Houston Aryan Nation. He led a lynching in Sweetwater in 1991. I don't believe Jesus himself would've signed a stay of execution for that man."

I shivered in the warm, waning sunlight on my porch. "Apple didn't fall half an inch from that tree."

"The Dallas PD is booking this guy on everything they can throw, including the illegal parking of his pickup in the alley behind the store. He won't see a free day again until he's an older man than I am." I heard his fingers drumming the desk, punctuated by a long breath out. "You scared me, Faith."

"I'm fine, Arch. Not a scratch. Just a deeper resentment of TV cameras than I already had, and about a million hours of reports to fill out in addition to the searches I'm doing for Lindsey Decker's car. Going to be a fun weekend. What are you up to?"

"I will join you in your current resentment of the news business, for now. Still chasing a weird one," he said. "Assistant DA found outside Sea World on Easter Sunday."

"I saw something about that—did they really find her naked?"

"Indeed. And every damned reporter in five counties has been up my ass all day every day since I caught the case. Channel Nine called me out on the air twice this week for not returning calls. I'm not sure how they think I'm supposed to catch a killer if I'm spending all my time giving interviews."

"Preach any more and I'll start singing a hymn," I said. "Thanks for checking on me."

"Listen to your instincts. And take a friend along every once in a while."

"Yes, sir."

"Still nothing on your MP?"

"I'm afraid I'm going to lose this one, Arch. I've run background on everyone she ever so much as smiled at, practically, I've checked her credit cards and bank accounts every day. Hell, I even called the lab last week and asked them to run her son's pacifier against every rape kit processed in forty miles of Southpoint Mall, thinking maybe that's why she won't say who his father is."

"Smart."

"The lab tech wasn't pleased."

"Work your case, McClellan. It's not time to give up yet," Archie said. "Just don't follow any more shady characters into back rooms."

I promised I wouldn't and clicked the *End* circle, watching the last sliver of the sun disappear. Another Friday gone. And I wasn't any closer to finding Lindsey than I'd been the day I first heard her name.

* * *

Two more weeks passed in a blur of research, interviews, and police reports interspersed with more phone calls than I'd had from my parents in the past decade. Not that they cared about me almost getting shot. They wanted me to tell the story to every member of their security detail, which I did, just in case.

On a blistering Friday afternoon when even the air conditioner was wilting in the heat, I had whittled my case wall to the final ER doctor on the vet's spreadsheet, looking for who might have previously owned the finger in the coyote's intestines.

Hold muzak played soft and low in my ear as I surveyed my scribbled-over, marked-up whiteboard.

One by one, I'd crossed off every item on every list. And I'd come up short. I swallowed a hard, icy lump of resentment.

I didn't lose.

Detail. Persistence. Organization.

I always found the magic rock. I always got the answer.

I'd never worked a case where the victim wasn't dead. And I was beginning to think Lindsey Decker was no different than the rest. Would changing gears, looking for a murderer, help me see something I hadn't?

A voice finally came on the line.

"Hi, Dr. Kemp, this is Faith McClellan with the Texas Rangers. I'm calling to ask about a patient from several weeks back, a man who came in missing the middle finger of his right hand?"

"Oh sure," he said. "Missing digits are always fun. Surgery saved that one—he was a mechanic, got it caught in the timing belt in an engine he was fine tuning. His buddies threw it in a cooler full of Lone Star and brought it in, and we managed to reattach it."

So it wasn't in an animal's gut causing gangrene, then. "Glad it worked out. Thanks so much for your time."

"Sure thing. Sounds like I'm not helping you, but I hope you find what you're looking for."

I put the phone back in its cradle and stood, crossing off the last open lead on my board.

Me too, doc. I just wish I knew where to look.

"McClellan?" Boone's voice came from behind me. "Can I see you for a moment?"

* * *

I knew what he was going to say before he opened his mouth, but I couldn't argue before I let him speak.

"I have an assignment for you." He measured the words.

"I'm still working the Decker case, sir." I tried to keep my irritation from creeping into the words, but he heard it anyway.

He raised both hands. "I come in peace, McClellan. I hear you've been working pretty much around the clock, even after your scare with the skinhead a couple of weeks back. Take it from an old man—that's not good for you."

"I could take up smoking again in my off hours, or move into the office," I said. "But you'd have to deal with Archie on the first one and there's probably a rule against the second."

"There probably is. You honestly think this girl is still alive?"

"We'd have found her by now if she wasn't." I said it maybe a dozen times a day, and couldn't have sworn I was trying harder to convince him than myself.

"Maybe. There are some we never—"

He stopped talking when I put my hand up. I knew that. But those cases weren't common.

"You asked me to do this, remember? You showed me a picture of Lindsey and her son, who is now staying with a kind neighbor because CPS has a shortage of foster parents and the kid has no family except a meth addict uncle, and you asked me to find her. I don't walk away until I have an answer. It's not how I'm built. This is my case, until it's done. I don't know another way to do my job. Sir."

He didn't speak until he was sure I was finished.

"I understand that." His already thick Texas twang was heavy with some emotion I couldn't put a sure finger on. "I even respect the hell out of it. Look, McClellan, I gave you a lot of shit your first few months on my team, and I don't know that there are many things in my career I regret more. You are a damned fine cop and I'm proud to have you, no matter who your father is. But there are things you do still need to learn, and when to cut your losses seems to be a big one."

"This isn't a spreadsheet. It's not a number. She's a person. Her kid is a person. I don't relate cutting losses to people." I didn't bother with the 'sir' that time, my temper flaming right past the compliment and lending edge to the words I might regret myself, at some point. "I get to the bottom of things."

"And what have you gotten to the bottom of, in four weeks? Almost six since she disappeared?" He wasn't angry, his voice gentler than I was used to. "I have never seen anyone work a case harder in my life, and that's saying something. I appreciate your drive, but you told me yourself just two days ago that you don't feel like you're closer to finding her, and you don't know where to look next."

I opened my mouth to protest—with what, I didn't know, because he was right. I had said that, and I'd meant every word. My board was clear, and I still didn't have an answer. Boone continued before I could decide how to argue.

"This isn't my choice anyway, just so you know. Your splashy record with murder collars caught the attention of Governor Holdswaithe. He called the commander into his office this morning to ask personally that you be assigned to a serial Baxter is working in Austin and San Antonio. Skye Morrow has apparently spotted a connection between these murders and the governor doesn't want the whole damned hill country in a panic heading into the holiday. He called you 'the big gun,' as I understand it."

I snapped my mouth shut. Opened it again. Closed it.

What the fuck was I supposed to do with that? You don't tell the governor no. I probably knew that better than anyone drawing breath, and I hadn't ever even met Holdswaithe.

"Archie needs my help?" I finally asked. Focus on the good. I loved working with Arch, and opportunities for it didn't come that often.

Boone's brow furrowed. "Actually, that's the odd part of this—he called me ten minutes after the commander did to tell me I needed to buck them on this. He sounded dead set on not having you in this case, but he wouldn't tell me why. Told me to tell the commander to fuck off—those were his exact words. Like I wouldn't tell that jackass where to get off every day of my life if I could get away with it."

"He worries. The thing at the pawn shop in Dallas shook him, that's all." Ever since I was running away from pageant makeup chairs to ride horses and climb trees, Archie had been the single constant in my crazy world. We knew each other so well we practically finished each other's sentences. He was family. I knew without asking that it wasn't that he didn't want my help—it was that he was scared of sucking me into something that might get me hurt. That's why he'd been so quiet about his case. I couldn't fault him for that. And while I had to admit I was curious, I also wasn't thrilled about being reassigned without an answer on Lindsey, no matter who thought I was needed elsewhere.

"I'm not letting go of Lindsey Decker." I folded my arms across my chest.

"Look, I can't force you to drop it completely, but experience tells me you're chasing your tail there. What I can do is tell you that you must give your full attention to Baxter's psycho for the time being. When the governor calls you into a case, you don't half ass it."

I knew that. "Did he seriously call me the big gun?"

Boone's lined, fleshy face widened into a grin. "So I hear."

I wasn't sure what I thought of Holdswaithe. He was the kind of politician Chuck McClellan loathed, skilled at bobbing and weaving through the modern political minefield, charming voters and hitting his talking points without actually committing to a stance on much of anything. The only thing I knew for sure about the man was that I agreed with his use of his veto pen most of the time. But in the Rangers, being on the governor's radar—in a positive way, anyway—is a good thing.

"Last I heard Archie was working that prosecutor in San Antonio they found in the woods Easter Sunday. But he hasn't said a word about a serial. You have a file for me to look over?"

He shook his head. "They're keeping it tight. Tighter than tight. I was told rather unceremoniously that it was none of my fucking business."

"What on earth?" I stood, holding up a finger, and ran for my laptop, shutting the door behind me when I walked back in.

"McClellan, if you know how to hack into HQ's case files, I don't need to be privy to that," Boone said.

I did, but like he said, he didn't need to witness it. "Anybody can find a news report. If they have cases Skye is sticking her nose in, they're not the only people who know about them." And if Skye Morrow could spot the link, I damn well better not miss it.

Murder, Austin and surrounding areas, search.

I got eighty pages of results. News—most recent.

Eleven since April. "What the hell is the matter with people?" I muttered.

Boone snorted. "You figure that one out and we'll put you up for the Nobel Prize."

I let my eyes wander, waiting for them to light on something. Most major cities have a murder about every other week, and Austin is no exception. Blood still gets coverage, but murder is overwhelmingly a crime of passion—the killer is nearly always someone the victim knew. If Archie had a serial who was on the governor's radar, I wasn't looking for typical.

There. A pastor, found Memorial Day weekend. The story was way too cursory for Skye, with almost no detail given. Except that Graham Hardin was heading the investigation for the TCSO.

Huh. I'd been too buried to pay any mind to the fact that I hadn't heard much from him lately. Seemed he was, too.

Looked like I was about to find out why. "Do I have to go right now?"

"You're due at HQ first thing tomorrow. Serial cases don't stop for weekends. Finish up any loose ends on your missing woman so you don't have distractions." Boone stood, grabbing his blue coffee mug with the Boy Scout motto stamped on the side in white letters. "McClellan, if Baxter has a nut job on his hands and he's scared enough to not want you there..." He crossed the room to lay a hand on my shoulder. "You watch your ass."

"And the rest of me too; yes, sir." I returned to my desk, nodding as he went on to the break room. "I'll check in."

"Good luck."

I'd only ever seen Archie scared once in my life: the morning after my sister was taken. If this case—or cases, maybe—had him freaked out, we needed all the good luck we could get.

I scoured notes and files for the next hour, looking for any little lead I might have missed. Short of finding Adam Decker or getting those DNA runs back, there wasn't one. Lindsey's brother was still nowhere, and the lab was estimating another two weeks thanks to short staffing and backlogs. I tapped my computer back to life and searched for recent drug busts, like I had every other day for the past month.

Except today I got a hit in Lake Whitney.

Still processing, perpetrator list pending. Hot damn. I grabbed my keys and phone. If there was any chance Adam Decker was in a city jail cell outside Dallas, I wasn't missing him waiting on Bill Roundtree to return a call.

* * *

It wasn't him. A younger, luckier version of him, maybe—their opiate epidemic at the high school was sourcing from a science teacher who'd discovered Oxy as a college football star and sold his students cheap, dangerous shit to feed his own high-dollar habit. I left the station at seven-thirty glad Roundtree finally had his man, but frustrated as all hell that my chance at finding Lindsey Decker was probably officially dead.

The right thing to do was to go tell Mrs. Poway I'd failed to deliver on my promise. I drove that way, feeling sicker with every mile closer to Lindsey's house. When I spotted Jake and the dog in the yard as I turned the corner, I had to stop and catch my breath.

I couldn't do it.

Keeping my eyes on the road, I rolled right by.

I'd have to come back eventually. But maybe chasing Archie's killer could buy me the time or perspective—or both—to at least leave them with better than "I don't know."

16

"I heard you didn't want me around, but I have orders that come from pretty high up."

Archie didn't answer me Saturday morning, grabbing my wrist and leading me to his Crown Vic. In the car with the AC blasting, he shook his head as he backed out. "Holdswaithe wants good press more than he values good sense. I know exactly how good a cop you are, but this...this is one of the most sadistic pieces of shit I've ever seen. Since you're here, you might as well see what we're up against. New Braunfels PD has a third victim this morning."

Nothing like being chucked straight into the deep end. "You're sure?" I'd never worked a true serial.

"Our guy is pretty specific." Archie sped up the onramp to 35. "And we've managed to keep details to ourselves, no small feat in the age of online news and drones with cameras. I'm sure."

He flicked the knob on the radio and I listened to Willie Nelson and Merle Haggard sing about Pancho and Lefty as I watched the parched, brown summer landscape roll by the windows. Archie didn't want to talk about the case. Just exactly what was Holdswaithe throwing me into here?

Three switchback turns after Archie pulled off the freeway, I figured out where we were headed. "The river?"

Archie stayed quiet, rolling the car to a stop at the edge of a low stand of trees along the banks of the Guadalupe. A football field away, emergency lights flashed as a few straggling tourists with shell-shocked expressions talked to Comal County deputies.

What a lousy vacation memory. Bodies that have been submerged before discovery are hard on the eyes—and the nightmares—even when you look at dead folks for a living. We ducked under tape and walked past a six-foot stack of inner tubes outside a rental shack to the edge of the water.

A petite deputy with freckles lining her green eyes waved to Archie as she picked her way through the tall grass. "Mr. Baxter, it's an honor," she enthused. "Claire Leavy, CCSO. The captain asked me to show you around."

"I appreciate the hospitality." Archie rested his fingers on my elbow. "This is Ranger Faith McClellan, she'll be working with me on this case."

Deputy Leavy tossed me a "nice to meet you" before she pointed to the medical examiner's van downriver. "They're finishing loading up the body there. I'm supposed to ask if you have a preference on the ME."

"If y'all could send her to Jim Prescott at Travis County, I'd sure appreciate it," Archie instructed.

I surveyed the scene, used to people fawning over Archie. He'd earned it, and I was more interested in what I could see out here than what she could tell me, anyway.

Three officers in wetsuits and scuba gear, arms linked, bobbed above and below the surface of the water. They'd made it about halfway to the far bank, walking a staggered, expanding grid up and back against the current. Standard procedure, but more difficult in moving water than it would be in a lake or pond. They had to keep their lines moving out in the direction of the current to make sure any evidence they were hunting didn't wash downstream.

A team of four combed the bank on our side, while two more worked the far bank upstream. I counted a dozen deputies just in my line of sight.

"How long was she under?" I asked.

"She wasn't." Leavy glanced at Archie. "Did someone misinform you, sir?"

"She was in a tube, Faith," he said. "Floated right up into a group of college kids."

I opened my mouth to ask why he was so sure she was murdered, and closed it when I remembered his short words and long silence on the ride up. I pointed to the divers instead. "Then what are they looking for?"

"Her finger. She's missing one, maybe the perpetrator, maybe local wildlife. She came out of the water up there." Leavy pointed to the deputies working the bank just up from us. "So since it would have traveled faster on its own, we're looking down that way."

I watched Archie's face as she spoke, and even I couldn't tell if that was an important clue. But I couldn't help thinking of the coyote by Lindsey Decker's dumpster, either.

Leavy returned her attention to Archie and I wandered downstream, my eyes on the grass, looking as much for missed evidence as watching for snakes.

I stopped behind the open rear doors of the ME's van and leaned to peer inside when the usual sickly-sweet smell of death didn't smack me in the face.

That was definitely a body bag. A full one.

A tall, spindly man in a navy county-issue Polo rounded the back of the van and put a hand out. "They said the Rangers were coming. I'm Ben Winters. What can I do for you?"

"Faith McClellan. From the lack of stench, I'm wondering if you have a ballpark on TOD."

"Not more than five hours," he said. "Less, maybe, but someone will know more when they get an autopsy. I'm waiting for marching orders on that."

"Travis County. Ask for Jim Prescott." He was due back at work Monday. Nice welcome we were sending him.

"They said she was in an inner tube? ID?"

He pointed to a black and white forensics truck. "The SO took the float into evidence. I got prints for them to run. She didn't have anything on her."

"And her missing finger? How long had it been gone?"

"Eyeballing it, I'll say since just before she died. Blood at the site, but no clotting I could see."

Nice. "Thank you. If anyone at Travis gives you any trouble with the intake, tell them I sent you."

He closed up the doors and turned for the front of the van. "Miss McClellan, I've been doing this job a while now, and I've never seen anything like this. I hope y'all catch whoever's responsible for it right quick. I have a feeling it won't stop here."

Me too. I just didn't say why. "Do me a favor and don't tell the press that?" I said.

"No need to worry about me there, ma'am. I'd rather wade through a whole stream of water moccasins than talk to Skye Morrow."

Her reputation preceded her even way out here. Nice. I thanked him and spun a slow circle, looking for the thing everyone else had ignored.

Behind the tube rental shack, a stocky, bearded young man stomped out one cigarette and lit another.

"Faith McClellan, Texas Rangers." I put my hands in my pockets so I wouldn't try to bum one as I walked up. "Are you okay?"

He puffed twice before he answered me.

"This job is supposed to be fun, you know? Easy. Summer on the river. Nothing stressful. Nobody fucking said anything about cut up naked women."

"I heard she was upstream a piece from here," I said.

"Sure. But they all came screaming out of the water needing a phone, and I was dumb enough to walk down there. Plenty of people overdo beer and sun out here and pass out. But I never saw anything like that. The words...I thought she had a tattoo at first, but they were carved. Like into her skin."

Words? Someone cut words into her flesh? Hard to keep my flat expression behind that, but I managed.

I glanced at the big stacks of black inner tubes behind him. "Did anyone rent a tube this morning? Really early maybe, or late last night?"

He took another drag, shaking his head. "We're always busy right around the fourth, but it's still dead after eight and before about ten."

"Anything else odd the last several days?"

He raised the butt back to his lips, stopping just short. "You know—the chain on the big stack was cut." He fanned fingers out. "Friday morning, I guess? Clean break. I figure it was kids being assholes, bored with school out a month already."

Maybe. "Was anything missing?"

"I'm supposed to count them all when I close up, but I don't always. This is my fourth summer here and nobody's ever messed with anything after hours. But it didn't look like there was." Two more puffs. "You don't think it was, like, one of my tubes she was in down there?"

"Are they all marked?"

"Most of them are stamped, but maybe not every single one." He scuffed one orange Croc in the dirt.

Which probably meant he was supposed to mark them.

I pulled out a notebook and pen and jotted that all down. "You have a security camera here?"

He shook his head. "Like I said, we don't ever get trouble around."

I thanked him and turned to look for Archie. Not difficult, he was two steps behind my left shoulder talking to a couple who'd been out here for a few days, at least, from their sunburns. I waited until he'd dismissed them and fell into step beside him as he walked the bank. "Body's on its way to Jim. Guy in the rental shack didn't see anything and has no security video, but I'd bet the tube she was found in is the one stolen from his hut last week. The ME said she'd only been dead a few hours, though."

He didn't look surprised by the advance prep. "They're processing everything they've got for prints and fibers. They won't find any, but we'll let them do their jobs. Not much else we can do here—let's get back to the air conditioning and sort out what we've got. I'm guessing it's not as much as we want to think, when we get right down to it."

I followed him back to the car in silence. I'd never seen Archie so morose. He was the go-to guy for the hard stuff. My nerves thrummed as I watched the grass for signs of disturbance. I didn't see so much as a bent blade.

* * *

We rounded the corner into the main conference room at HQ and found Graham leaning on the edge of the big mahogany table, files and photos he was studying obscuring most of the surface in front of him.

"I can't find anything that links them before they died," he said, his eyes still on the fat file folder under his nose. "But the burns, skull fractures, and dehydration are consistent across both."

"The one from this morning, too, according to the Comal County SO." Archie shut the door. "Governor Holdswaithe sent us a new set of eyes."

Graham stared at me, not saying a word before he turned to Archie. "This morning? There are three now?"

Archie waved at the folders. "Faith, come on in and meet Daphne and Stephanie. We'll have a third name and another file soon enough, but for now, tell me if you see anything that might help us avoid a fourth."

I walked to the table like Graham hadn't been dodging me for weeks. I'd been so wrapped up in Lindsey's disappearance, the truth was I hadn't pushed it. A few voicemails and a couple of texts to Graham that got one-word replies, and I figured I'd have time to figure out what was up his ass once Lindsey was safe at home with her kid.

But he wasn't talking to me because he was here with Archie. The last time I saw them both together was the day Graham showed up with Skye. If Skye was asking the governor's office for comment on a serial, she had details on this case nobody else did. Details she hadn't aired yet.

I had missed something big.

I grabbed the nearest folder and flipped it open.

"Archie said y'all had managed to keep this quiet, but Skye Morrow is nosing around about a serial and has Governor Holdswaithe running scared. Why are you two talking to—" The "her" died on my lips when I turned the page.

A sterile pad on a steel counter. With a human finger lying on it.

Evidence marked as received by Skye Morrow via US Mail.

17

"Never mind." I put the open folder back down on the table.

"She's holding back on the biggest part of the story for now because the governor called in a personal favor," Archie said. "But even he can't hold that woman at bay forever."

I went to the whiteboard and picked up a marker. "How many victims?"

"Three. That we know about," Archie said.

I made three columns.

"In how long?"

"April 23, May 25, and today, apparently," Graham said.

I put the dates at the top. "Right about a month apart."

Graham snorted. "We hadn't noticed."

"I wasn't trying to be condescending," I said. "Who are these people? All women? Ages?"

"All women," Archie said. "Our first two were both missing for several weeks before they were found."

I stopped with the marker in midair and spun slowly. "I'm sorry?" Ding ding ding. I'd found the bigger reason they wanted me to stay away. They knew how invested I was in Lindsey's case. They didn't think I'd be reckless in general; they thought I might let my desire to find her override my sense of personal safety.

In all fairness, they had Sweaty Willie and his pal from the pawn shop to back them up.

Graham sighed. "I know. But people disappear every day, and we don't know enough to know whether your case might be related. Both of these women were missing for a while before anyone knew they were gone. But there's no evidence either of them were violently abducted. They just disappeared. Cars gone, doors locked. In both of these cases, it took until they ran out of leave at work for someone to start looking. The only thing they have in common, other than how they died, is that they lived alone."

Which Lindsey definitely did not. But her car was gone.

"And there was no trace of them until they turned up dead?"

Archie shrugged. "We have varying degrees of effort put into the cases, none as much as you've given Lindsey Decker. When adults who aren't an Alzheimer's risk vanish, especially when their affairs are in order and there's no sign of foul play...I mean, what would you think if you got that call?"

Now, I would think I needed to look deeper. But I wasn't like everyone else.

I turned back to the board so I wouldn't yell at them.

"Credit card usage?"

Graham shook his head. "Nothing."

"Shouldn't that have been a sign to someone that they didn't go on vacation?"

"It was, after someone reported them missing and people started looking," Archie said.

"But by then it had been weeks, and they could have been literally anywhere," Graham said.

I tapped the marker against my leg. Tell me about it.

"And the living alone thing was all they had in common?"

"We have to wait for details on the new vic, but from the surface on these first two, that's correct," Archie said.

"So this is like a bona fide serial. Random victims with no connections, presumably torture." I raised my eyebrows and they both nodded. "Rape?"

Archie shook his head. "Nope."

That was different enough to note.

"The ME at the river said someone carved words into the woman this morning," I said. "The others, too? Is the message the same?"

Graham brandished a folder. "The other two had the messages, not the same, about redemption and selflessness."

"This new one is contrition," Archie said.

"Religious?" I turned to write those three words on the board.

"Not from any part of the Bible I've read," Archie said. Archie's late father was a Baptist preacher. There wasn't a single verse he didn't know backwards and sideways.

I scribbled *Source?* under the words describing the messages. "Ages of the victims?"

"Forty-six and thirty," Graham said.

I noted that. "Cause of death?"

"Severe head trauma. All three."

Ugh. I made a face and shook my head. "Jesus."

"It will consume you if you let it." Graham's voice was quiet, his eyes on his fingers, twisted together in his lap. He was all in on this one.

"I got a call this morning from the church where Stephanie Allen worked," he said. "The associate pastor using her office found a threatening letter tucked away in a drawer. I came by to see if you wanted to ride out there with me."

"Shall we all go to church?" Archie stood. "I'll drive."

Graham insisted I take the front seat even though his legs had six inches on mine. Archie turned left out of the parking lot and nudged me with his elbow. "I know it's a lot to take in, but you catch on fast. So what does your psychobabble say?" He liked to give me good-natured shit about my degree choice because he'd wanted me to study criminal justice.

I'd never worked a serial before. Sometimes an extra body turns up in the course of investigating a murder, but even most people who can kill another human don't do it more than once. And something like this, where someone had taken pleasure in torturing other people before bashing their heads in—that was way scarier than a gambler with a bad debt or an abusive boyfriend off on a bender.

"It takes a special kind of crazy to completely devalue human life." I blew out a slow breath. "And unless we can figure out how to see the world that way, the killer has the upper hand. Hopefully the pastor's hate mail will give us a clue."

The church was big—Graham said it used to be a Costco—with inspirational messages in bright colors dotting the walls. I followed Graham to the office.

"Isn't it weird that anyone here would think she'd just not show up out of the blue? It's not like she worked at the daycare—she was the pastor," I whispered to Archie as he pulled the door open for me.

"Apparently the staff thought she'd been struggling with something, needed to be alone," he whispered back. "But that's a good question."

A month after her death, Stephanie Allen's name still gleamed in silver letters on her office door. Behind the desk outside it, a young man in a lime green T-shirt stood to greet us. "Nice to see you again, Officers." He turned to me. "Nice to meet you, Miss—?"

"Ranger. McClellan."

"My apologies. Y'all take a seat if you'd like." He picked up an envelope. "This is what Quent found in Stephanie's desk last night. I'm not sure where it came from, and neither is anyone else here, but we thought you ought to take a look."

Graham opened the envelope and Archie leaned in from his left, sending me circling his elbow to the right.

"An eye for an eye is the way of the Lord. The laws of man might disregard you, but you are not above punishment." Graham read it aloud.

"Sounds like my skinhead from the pawn shop," I murmured. "Had Pastor Allen done anything that you know of to provoke this?"

Surely Archie and Graham would know that by now.

All three men shook their heads. "That's part of why it's so weird," the one without a badge said. "Ask anyone here—she was unfailing in her generosity and tireless in her work."

That her employees knew, anyway.

"Do you mind if we have a look in her office?" Archie asked.

"Please. I'll be around if you need me for anything."

The space was big, bright, and inviting, with an oversized blue jacquard sofa on the near wall and a spindle-footed wood desk painted in soft gray dominating the center of the floor. A credenza and two oak file cabinets sat against the wall to my left, with books and photos displayed on the shelves lining the back of the room. I crossed to the pictures, examining each, my eyes going wide when I spotted my father in one.

It was a standard grip-and-grin, no context other than they were outside in front of a wide oak tree with graceful, sweeping branches.

The books were mostly of the spiritual and self-help variety, with a notable absence of the televangelists who write most of the books in Lifeway window displays. I picked up five at random and rifled the pages. Nothing fell out, no highlights or comments in the margins.

"That note was definitely on the religious side." I ran one hand along the back of each shelf, feeling for anything the pastor might have hidden. "What did the messages on the victims say? Was the lawyer big on church?"

"A free society must provide the weak, the afraid, the plagued, a place to claim safety," Archie recited. "That was the lawyer."

"So not religious, but to do with her job." I flipped photo frames forward to look behind them. "Which kind of mimics this note. What was the message the killer left on Stephanie?"

"True effort requires attention to detail," Graham said. "Which is not religious even a little bit."

"I keep telling you, I don't think the messages are for us." Archie didn't look up from the desk drawer he was rifling through.

"Who exactly is the killer talking to, carving stuff into dead women, if it's not the cops?" Graham's tone said he was tiring of a discussion he'd had before.

Time out. I turned and stepped between them, pointing to Archie. "Yours sounds like a line from a political speech," I said. "Did y'all Google it?"

"I do know something about how to use the computers." Archie's voice was dry.

"It seems to point to some sort of miscarriage of justice, but we can't find one in her files," Graham said. "By all accounts, Daphne Livingston was good at her job."

"How far back did you go?" I asked.

"Two years."

That ought to get it. "The eye for an eye thing—it's weird that the guy who tried to shoot me a few weeks back said the same thing someone sent in a note to your victim." I moved to the credenza and opened it. Nothing but a couple of dust bunnies, a blanket, and a stack of CDs.

"But that asshole is still sitting in Dallas County lockup. He didn't kill anyone this morning," Archie said. "It's a common phrase."

True. "Let's assume for a second this note Pastor Allen got was from our killer," I said. "Like the message inscribed on Ms. Livingston, it alludes to her line of work and some sort of wrongdoing. But nobody knows of the pastor or the lawyer doing anything wrong. So then we look at the other side of it."

"What other side?" Graham put down the file he'd just pulled from the cabinet to my left. "These are church financials for like the last ten years. She's doing a good job, I guess—they're in the black and earning more every year."

"The killer's side. What if our guy isn't acting out based on what they did, but based on what he's done?" I pulled the stack of CDs from the cabinet and flipped through. Not so much as a scratch or a missing liner note in any of them. "If you guys checked the cases the attorney worked and didn't find any dropped balls, what if she's a warning? Like the killer picked a lawyer with a good record and this isn't intended as a rebuke for her, but as a warning for her colleagues? Or even someone she knew? Our killer is still walking free, and therefore the weak and afraid aren't safe, right? And the lawyers should fix that? And for our pastor, maybe our killer is saying people like her should pay more attention to detail to stop him from killing? So maybe he goes to church?"

Archie held up a piece of white office paper. "Maybe this church."

I returned the CDs and crossed to him, looking over Graham's shoulder again. "Repentance is painful for the wicked in the face of the Lord," I read. Like the other note, the line was typed in place on a sheet of plain white office paper. With a guy this clever, dusting it for prints was likely useless, but it didn't mean we shouldn't do it anyway. "It's not folded," I said.

"And the other one wasn't mailed." Graham went back to his file cabinet and I took the second one while Archie finished up with the desk.

"So the killer walked it in here?" I flipped a dozen folders about a building campaign.

"Or to her house, or left it on her car," Graham said. "Hard to say when we can't ask her."

Archie's phone buzzed. "Got an ID. Ramona Mathers, 51, empty nest widowed mom of four." He sighed. "No prints or fibers found on the tube or the body. Prescott has her in his queue, but he's not officially back until Monday."

I stuck my head out the door. Lime t-shirt wasn't at his post, but a blonde in a pink sundress sat in his chair. I stepped around the doorframe so she could see my badge. "Did anyone in the congregation dislike or disapprove of Pastor Allen?" I asked. Sometimes the element of surprise gets people talking.

"The usual nut jobs. Mostly men who think women have no business in church leadership. But she always handled it with grace," she said.

I thanked her and went back into the office, shutting the door again.

"What about a misogynist?" I asked. "Women in high-profile positions, messages about their performances. Maybe it's not anything they did so much as that they were doing it."

"I don't hate it." Archie stood as Graham closed the last file drawer. "Anything else?"

"If these letters are from our killer, they suggest that these weren't random." I pulled the door open again. "They were targeted. Which at least gives us a square to start from."

Archie picked up the other letter on the way out, and we took photos of both and dropped them at our print lab on the way back to the war room.

* * *

I added Ramona Mathers's name and age to the board, pausing with the marker in midair. "She was a stay-at-home mom." My voice deflated around the words.

"So?" Archie asked.

"So, she didn't have a leadership position a guy like this wouldn't want her in," Graham said. "That, or the quasi-Biblical language is a decoy."

"I'm not sure we know enough about her to know that yet," Archie said, looking up from his phone. "According to the Bexar County DA, Daphne's office was cleaned out and they donated all personal effects to a women's shelter, and sent all the non-professional papers to the incinerator."

Damn. "Should we head to Ramona's home to see if she got letters?" I asked.

Archie shook his head, raising the phone to his ear. "Our job is to see the big picture. But I'll advise Comal County to search. Even if she did, there's no guarantee she'd have kept them—most people throw that kind of shit away because it scares them. I say we assume they were being watched until something proves us wrong."

True. They shouldn't. But they do. Like the note in Lindsey Decker's laundry basket.

But I wasn't supposed to be thinking about Lindsey. Focus, Faith.

Archie reeled off instructions about any kind of written correspondence to Deputy Leavy and hung up, and I started pacing. Three victims. Perfectly planned. Perfectly spaced. Perfectly executed.

"Psychopaths often see the world upside down," I said. "But three murders so close together, all of them this immaculately carried out, isn't a novice. I'm willing to bet the lawyer isn't our guy's first kill. Just the first one he wanted us to know about."

"If a killer is focused on killing, why would he want us to know about any of the murders?" Graham asked. "Why wouldn't he want to just fly under the radar and keep killing more and more people? The guy wants attention."

I shook my head when Archie opened his mouth to argue. "I don't think he does, Graham. It's easy to get there on the surface of what we see here, because it fits the narrative we've all been fed. Like the Zodiac sending letters to the newspapers, our guy sent a finger to Skye. But Zodiac didn't write on his victims."

"Zodiac was also never caught," Archie said. "Let's keep the focus on someone who was. Take Bundy or Manson. How did the detectives handle the case?"

"Old fashioned police work," I said. "I'm not saying don't do that. I'm saying let's do both. I'm good at this stuff, Archie, and I've never had much of a chance to use it. But whatever this is"—I swept an arm at the stacks of folders in the room—"I don't think it's the screenplay stereotypical serial wanting to play cat-and-mouse with the cops. My gut says his game isn't *Catch Me if You Can*, it's more like *Codebreaker*. He's trying to tell us something. Whether or not it leads to him...who knows? What did he write on Ramona, Archie?"

"'Evil lies not in the shouts of the guilty, but the silence of those watching.' Deputy says she was still the bake sale coordinator even though her last child had long since left the public school system."

"Watching what? A high school soccer tournament?" I asked. "And that's not a non-traditional role for a woman."

Archie and Graham didn't answer because they knew I wasn't talking to them.

I shook my head. "Do these read like social media memes to anyone else?" I flipped open my computer. "Take them off charred flesh and onto a black and white photo of a hazy mountain, and they're inspirational."

I typed the words into Google, even though Archie had already done that.

He was right, there wasn't a match or source available.

"Traffic cameras?" I asked.

"Avoided. Carefully," Archie said. "The body discoveries were all made in places accessible via backroad."

"So someone who knows the area." It was obvious, but saying everything out loud is the best way to make sure nothing gets missed.

"Or knows the computer well enough to look up camera locations and use GPS to avoid them," Graham said.

Always a hundred possibilities.

Three victims in, we had to think there was one on deck. Crime scene photos spread in front of me, I wanted with everything I had for it to not be Lindsey Decker. "Y'all have pulled all the recent missing persons files from the area?" I asked.

"It's alarming how many of them there are with such a broad window, but we've got a team of guys at the sheriff's office running backgrounds and feeding us information. Local police departments are handling video footage and credit card monitoring." Archie tapped his phone screen. "Ramona Mathers last used her debit card at a gas station at 11:34 p.m. on June second."

I stood and added that to the board. Twenty-two days before we found her.

"So he's holding them a while. What else makes this guy different?"

"He sent Skye a finger," Archie said.

"So gross it almost makes me feel bad for her. Which victim did it belong to?"

"Daphne, the lawyer," Archie said. "That's why Graham brought Skye here the day you were here last month. He knew I was working that case, and he'd just found Stephanie."

And they'd told us this morning Ramona was missing a finger. So was the killer taking them?

What the hell for?

18

Three floors deep into the bowels of the building, the cold case unit provided a purgatory for thousands of people we hadn't been able to help. Lives cut short, condensed into plastic containers, and stored on a shelf until a fresh lead or a gut feeling made someone open a box.

At some point near midnight Saturday, we'd decided if our serial had attempted practice kills before this murder spree, the case details might be right there in our basement. Then we'd decided to start the search after sunup.

Already on our third Sunday morning coffees before 8 a.m., Graham and I followed Archie into the long, silent room.

"We're assuming a lot," Archie muttered. He heaved a weary breath. "Shit, it's worth a shot. I don't know where else to look."

"Wouldn't they have to be, you know, pretty old? To be down here?" Graham stammered over the words, his eyes not meeting mine as he talked.

"It depends," Archie said. "Every department does their own thing. Sometimes we catch cases that are barely a few months old, because it counts in their stats as cleared when it comes to us. Other times, locals hold onto stuff for whatever reason and we only get it if the detective assigned moves or dies. It's a hell of a haystack, but Faith has a good point about this not being our guy's first rodeo, and we just might find an important needle down here. I'm kind of annoyed that I didn't think of it myself."

Shelves and boxes as far as I could see, the rows blurring together when you looked down them long enough.

"So is there a classification system, or do we just start looking?" Graham asked.

Archie's head swiveled slowly toward him. "I know our badges are old fashioned and sometimes people are surprised we still exist, but we have managed to transition successfully to two new centuries, now." He pointed to the computer on the tall counter. "Faith?"

I ripped my eyes from row seven, moving to the keyboard and powering up the unit. "Looking for women, but nonspecific age. Race?" I glanced at Archie.

"Our three were all white."

"What about wounds? The finger thing is weird. Right?"

Of course it was. It was also worrying around my head way more than it should be, given the layers of crazy we were trying to see through, here. Focus, Faith. The finger that vet in Dallas cut out of the coyote Lindsey was feeding was odd by itself and extraordinary stacked next to this, but over-reading coincidences where you desperately want to find connections is a pitfall in this job, and until Jim had examined the vet's find, I couldn't let myself get on that train. Lindsey was young. She didn't live alone. Serials stick to their pattern, it's part of the fixation.

"If there's a way to search that, absolutely," Archie said.

The records search screen loaded. I clicked the box next to "Identifying marks," and typed burns, head trauma, finger missing. Go.

A black and silver wheel spun in the center of the screen. Five seconds. Fifteen. Forty.

No results found.

I shook my head at Archie. "Strike one."

"I know we can search by age," he said, stepping closer.

I clicked the box for that. "Eighteen to what? Seventy-five?"

"Might as well go wide," Archie said.

"Locals, or no?" I asked.

"Not for now," Archie said. "But if we need to narrow it we can try that first."

I typed the range, hit the box next to "female," and clicked the *Go* button.

"Six hundred forty-seven hits."

"Damn," Graham breathed, but I only half heard him.

My eyes stayed on the screen, my sister's name screaming from it in all caps.

First match. MCCLELLAN, CHARITY LYNNE.

Archie saw it. Moved behind me and put his big, warm hand over mine on the mouse, scrolling down. "Sorry, honey. I did that."

"What?"

"I asked the IT guy to make it so that whenever Charity is a result in a search down here, she's the first one that comes up. I didn't think about it until I saw your face. I just wanted to..."

I spun on one heel and threw my arms around him, burying my face in his shoulder so nobody would see the tears escaping my lashes. "Thank you," I sniffled, my face still planted in the woodsy-aftershave-scented cotton of his shirt. I'm not much on the hugging thing, but sometimes people just don't give you a choice.

Archie stiffened momentarily, then wrapped his thick arms around me and patted my back.

I tipped my face back to look at him. "Thank you for keeping her relevant. Making sure people would see her name as much as possible so the guys who work down here think about her."

His mouth turned up into a sad half-smile. "Yeah. Something like that."

"And you say you don't believe in my psychobabble crap." I stepped back.

"I loved her too, kiddo."

I turned back to the computer. "My sister was buried with her fingers all intact," I said. "So that's one down. Now what?"

Archie folded his arms across his broad chest, stretching up to his full six-four. "Knock out everything older than five years."

Graham raised his hand.

I stared at him. Waited. Pointed. "Are we in class now, Commander Hardin?"

He rolled his eyes. "Sorry. Something about this room. Requires solemnity. Respect."

Archie nodded. "What, Hardin?"

"Are we sure five years is a big enough window? I mean, there have been serials who ran for decades before anyone caught up to them."

I shook my head. "But there have been three in three months, now. Let's see what's here. We can always go back further if we find a reason to."

I clicked two more boxes and typed a date. Tried "burns" for identifying marks.

"Twenty-six," I said when the results came up.

Archie tapped Graham on the shoulder. "Your back in decent shape, son?"

Graham laughed. "I think I'll come in handy."

I rolled my eyes. "So will the elevator and that dolly." I pointed.

"You people give everyone this much shit, or am I special?" Graham asked.

"Try getting a job here." I winked.

I sent the list on the screen to the printer and ran a finger down the first page when it came off. Nothing on aisle seven. I took it, and divided the other two pages between Archie and Graham. "Last one done buys drinks," I said.

They took their pages and disappeared, Graham muttering that the new guy always gets stuck buying drinks.

"If it makes you feel any better, I've never been down here on a case, either," I said. Someday—this room was the whole reason I'd spent a decade busting my ass for that star. But for the time being, my work was in the here and now.

At least, usually. If my gut was right and we could close one or two of these when we caught this guy—and we would catch him—I'd call that a job well done.

* * *

Sometime long after the last streaks of lavender-lapis sunlight had faded from the inky sky outside the windows, I flopped into a chair, the conference room strewn with folders and photos and reports, along with the white boxes that used to contain those things.

"Two maybes and a strong possibility," I said. "How about you guys?"

"I have one possibly and a bunch of nothing," Graham said.

Archie shook his head. "I'm 0 for 7."

"How many boxes left?" I asked.

"Four," Graham said.

"How did you find so many when I didn't get a single one?" Archie asked. "It's not like you to be overly optimistic."

"But I am thorough," I said. "Just making sure I don't miss anything. One of my maybes had a pinkie finger and two toes missing. One is a Jane Doe. So is my probable."

Archie stretched his arms their full eight feet over his head, his shoulders cracking like old, brittle plastic, before he limped over to my chair. I frowned. "Your knee bothering you?"

"Lifting plus sitting equals stiff. I'm fine."

He was not. But he knew I worried. He'd busted that knee tackling my father. I was twelve, and an anti-death penalty protest turned deadly (the irony not lost on any reporter in America) when one deranged dude in the crowd pulled a .357 Magnum, screaming "Let's see how you like it, McClellan!" and charged the rope line as my parents walked out of a speech to the Wardens' Association.

I saw the whole thing on video, twelve times in three days. Skye Morrow always gets her story. And the shooter still got cameos in my nightmares now and again—every time, I woke up drenched, heart racing, after dreaming he'd hit Archie.

I pointed to the two folders spread on the table nearest me. "Jane Doe, forensics puts her between eighteen and twenty-five. Found in a shallow grave near an oil rig two years ago in April. Head bashed in, but no dental, no prints to match…so no luck."

Graham stood, picking up a Dr Pepper can and downing the last of it before he crushed the aluminum and tossed it at the wastebasket in the corner. Even half-trying, he made it. "That sounds familiar," he said.

"Original jurisdiction?" Archie asked.

I flipped a page in the file. "Loving County," I said. "That's at least a dozen exits past the middle of nowhere, isn't it?"

"They have like three cops and a part-time janitor," Archie said, reaching for the file. "Her fingers?"

"Two missing." I flipped a page. "Doesn't say which ones. This report chalks it up to animal activity. She'd been there a while."

Graham moved to stand behind my chair, resting his fingers on my shoulder while he peered at the file. "But she was buried, this says. Our victims were almost on display. The guy had to have wanted them found."

"Sure he did, and before decomp set in. It's the only way his notes get read," Archie said.

I stood. Back to the board.

Smart.

"What if he was learning?" I asked. "A first kill? The burial versus the display scene means something, too. If a serial changes his pattern, it's for a reason."

"And you think this is confidence?" Archie put the folder on the table.

"I'm shooting in the dark, but maybe. If it was two years ago, it's not illogical that he was getting his toes wet."

"Could be." Graham picked up the file and flipped pages. "Wait. Their coroner estimated she had been out there for more than a year when they found her," he said. "That's three years. We've had three killings here all about thirty days apart."

"Because he found his footing," I said. "If he's gotten by with this one for three years, even after she was found, that would lend itself to that kind of confidence."

"This file is thin, y'all," Graham said. "The coroner's report is cursory, no DNA evidence noted. No mention of her fingers other than there were eight accounted for."

I sighed. "And that's not a certain indicator of anything, if she was buried in an oil field for a year. Could be for any reason from animal scavenging, to decomp, to a careless recovery team."

"So then how are we supposed to decide if this is worth pursuing?"

Archie laughed. "Old fashioned gut work, kid," he said. "I know the two of you think DNA is the be all and end all of crime solving, but I remember the days when there was no such thing. We worked on tips and clues and hunches, and every man in this building had an eye and a mind like Faith's." He tossed an affectionate wink my way. "That's why I always knew you'd get here if you wanted it. Because you have the technology of your generation, and the skill and instincts of mine. So, McClellan, what does your gut say about this victim? Should we add her to our board?"

I looked at the board. Turned to look at the file folder on the table. "Something about it raised the hair on my arms. I think she stays. At least until evidence removes her."

"I agree," Archie said. "So what have they got, Hardin?"

Graham shook his head. "Not mu—"

Archie and I both stepped toward him, hands out for the case file, when he paused.

Graham folded his arms around the thin collection of paper and frowned. "Hold up. Maybe someone did take her fingers. The coroner noted striations on the bone inconsistent with known area wildlife."

I made a grab for the file and came up with a scrap of a green page corner. "What? Where? I didn't see that."

"Because it's not in the ME's report. It's in the bottom of the sheriff's notes. Homicide, victim's identity unknown."

Archie shook his head. "That doesn't make any sense. If the sheriff was in over his head he would've just called us."

I crossed the room and reached for my laptop, logging in with my credentials and opening a records search. "Date?" I asked.

"April 27 of '17," Graham said.

I punched it in. Clicked *Homicide*. Go.

No results found. "Doesn't look like he did." I wiggled my fingers at Graham. "Give me that, please."

He handed the file over and perched on the edge of the table. "So why is his file in your cold case room?"

Archie sighed. "It's a shitty thing to say out loud, but young women go missing or turn up dead in this country every day. A lot of them, nobody gives a shit about." He pointed to the folder. "Given the choice between this file and a Jessa DuGray or a Tenley Andre, where the parents are on TV every twelve seconds and the whole damned city is up in arms, which are you going to pursue with limited resources, especially when nobody explicitly asked for your help?"

Graham's face twisted into a pained expression that told me he didn't want to answer that.

"Yeah," he said finally, half under his breath.

Archie patted his shoulder. "Welcome to the fun decisions of police command staff, Commander."

Graham shook his head. "I don't have to like it."

"Yeah, but what are the odds they've had more than one murder in a place that tiny in the last like, twenty years?" I asked. "This wasn't about a choice. Lack of resources, or ability, or...something has to be closer to the truth."

Archie turned back to me. "Maybe. So my first question is, who was the sheriff out there at the time and why the hell didn't he call in help? And my second is, is there a way past this dead end if this was our guy's handiwork?"

I put my fingers back on the keyboard. "Graham, how did they find her?"

"Says here a worker called it in when he went out to check on the rig after a storm. Rain churned up the mud."

"Witness statement?" I asked, looking up.

Archie shook his head. "Gone when the sheriff got there. Figured he was a junkie who didn't want to talk to the cops. A lot of the roughnecks out there get hooked on opiates that progress to meth—that's not work for the intolerant of pain or faint of heart."

I typed in the dates and "Loving County Sheriff" and clicked *Search*.

My eyes rolled up before I could stop them when the results came up. "Of course. Bud Colvin, sheriff from November of '95 to August of '17. When he died."

"So the investigation got dropped when they lost their department head," Archie said.

I slumped back in the chair. "I'd bet the new guy sent the file to us when he couldn't make any headway, if he even tried."

"What's his name and number?" Archie asked. "I'll call him and see what I can get."

I copied the information from the top of the county website and sent it to his cell. "You'd think I'd have long since stopped expecting things to be easy by now. Magnifier?"

Archie rummaged through a drawer in the credenza along the back wall until he came up with one.

I laid it over a photo of the half-decayed young woman in the muddy field, the stark, rusty arms of an oil rig rising to the sky behind her. When there was no way for me to index a scene in person, I combed photos for what other folks might have missed. And out in the middle of nowhere with no budget and no help and a one-page report on a murder vic dump, I was betting they'd missed plenty.

"No end is ever truly shuttered until every inch of it has been explored," I said, moving the glass slowly, my careful eyes not missing a blade of grass or droplet of water.

"Huh?" Graham and Archie asked in unison.

"It's Nietzsche. It means if you look hard enough, there's always an answer. The first thing we need to do is take stock of what information we already have. What someone who didn't have all three victims and their messages might not have known to look for."

I was irritated that the lieutenant had pulled me off Lindsey Decker, no lie. I felt like a failure for the first time in my entire career, but down in darker places I didn't like to acknowledge, I had been beginning to think I'd lost Lindsey for a couple of weeks now. The chances that we'd find her alive and relatively undamaged, able to return to her normal life, grew slimmer every day. I wasn't ready to give up, but it was a twisted sort of nice to have something else to focus on.

This was my wheelhouse. Devil in the homicide details. Little things that led to big arrests.

It felt good to be home.

I moved the glass up the rig. Back to the mud.

To the water droplets shining iridescent in the sun all around Jane Doe's right eye socket. Water, not mud. The drops reflected the red-orange of thick layers of rust on the pump piston of the rig.

"Gentlemen, there's still something to be said for good old-fashioned gut instinct and observational skills," I said. "Because whoever found this body found it because they knew it was there. It seems likely from this that the witness called it in and took off because they wanted it found." I flipped a page in the file. "Caller was male, gruff, hesitant voice. Maybe because he was trying to disguise his voice?"

"If you got away with murder, why would you want the body found?" Archie asked.

"Because you wanted people to know the victim was dead?" I was assuming a bit, applying logic from our three connected cases to a great big maybe over this one. But if we were going to follow this trail, following it all the way was the only useful option. "But then the Jane Doe thing must have infuriated him." I tapped my fingers on the edge of the table. Stood and began pacing.

"What now?" Graham asked.

"I'm just...there has to be a reason he went back and dug her up." I stopped and re-read my board. "Wait. What if—and I know we don't have anything definite connecting her—but what if she was a test?" I started moving again, walking faster this time. "Like, what if the killer left her in the middle of nowhere, buried, to see if he could get away with it? Then called attention to himself and helped them find her to see what would happen?"

"Why?" Graham asked.

"Well, we've said it a dozen times, these bodies need to be found, right? For the messages. If the killer didn't want to get caught, he needed to know if he would still get away with it if the police got involved."

Archie pulled a notepad to him, scribbling. "I don't hate that. Worth keeping in the hopper, for sure."

"And if she is the first victim, we're closer to the killer than we think we are," Graham said.

"Maybe if we knew who the hell she was or how she might have possibly known the killer, sure," Archie said.

"That's what we have to find out, but we know one thing," I said. "Our guy was in Loving County three years ago." I spun and made a note on the board in bright red ink. "Whether he knew this victim or not, the first kill is nearly always someone in the killer's own backyard. They start off hunting close to home. And the population of Loving County in the last census was 82. So who moved from there to here in the past three years?"

"That's going to take some research," Graham said.

"You got anything better to do?"

He smiled. "Faith McClellan always gets her man."

I let the possibility of a double entendre go. "Maybe not always, but damned close," I said. "I'm not losing two in a row." I gestured to the file open on the table. "He was careful with her. But then they didn't find her, so he waited as long as he could, for whatever reason, and then he handed her to them on a platter. There's something bigger at work here than the thrill of the kill."

19

Murder cases are complicated equations, each one made up of a thousand variables that must be in an exact order if we're going to have a shot at getting the right answer. Not a letter or clue out of place. Not any old solution, but the right one. The only one that gets evil off the streets and away from innocent people.

Somewhere in the folders in front of us, there were variables in the wrong places.

I dropped the file on Graham's dead pastor for the sixth time and went to the break room in search of another Dr Pepper.

"You're getting annoyed," Graham said when I turned to lean against the cracked Formica countertop. I opened the can with a hiss. He added, "And you're pissed at me."

I shook my head before I tipped it back to down half the can in one swallow. "I'm not." I swallowed a burp between the words.

"A lady is only as genteel as the persona she presents to the world." She'd said it a thousand times. Ten thousand. Standing behind a salon chair with her hands on my shoulders, staring into the reflection of my blue eyes in the wide, brightly lit makeup mirror. *"Remember, Faith, that every judge on that panel will see you through his or her own eyes. With his or her own biases. You*

must be lively enough to impress the ladies, but demure enough to avoid upsetting the gentlemen if you want that crown."

I didn't give one sliver of a damn about any of the crowns. She did. She still had every single one, and I'd won more than anyone's share before I stopped caring about pissing her off.

Graham crossed the room and leaned next to me. I stiffened. He bumped my shoulder with his. "I'm sorry."

"For what?" It came out an octave too high and way too tight. I cleared my throat, my eyes on the pointy black toe-tips of my favorite worn-in snakeskin and leather boots.

"I've been too wrapped up in this case to be a good friend. You were starting to panic over your MP in a way I've not seen you freak out since you were so wet behind the ears my grandmomma wouldn't have let you outside in January for fear you'd catch your death. And I was too far into my own shit to call you back."

I blew out a long breath. So he wasn't mad at me? I stayed quiet, though. Let him talk.

"It's this fucking promotion," he continued. "This is my first high-profile case, a pastor murdered in cold blood, and I knew Archie was right when he said even the governor couldn't keep the link off the TV forever. I think listening to you talk about that Morrow woman all these years has worn on me. I was too worried about getting crucified on live TV to call you back." He ducked his head and turned puppy-dog widened eyes up at me. "I suck. But I didn't mean to."

I tried to swallow a laugh and forced Dr Pepper up my nose instead, whirling for the sink and reaching for a paper towel. "Dammit, Graham," I muttered, blowing soda out my nose and laughing anyway. "I get it."

"So, how's it coming with the missing mom? I bet you were pissed when they reassigned you."

"It's almost like you know me or something. Boone actually gave me a speech on Friday about cutting losses." I shook my head. "I need to focus, though, because the sooner we find this bastard the sooner I get to go see if I can still save Lindsey."

Except. I paused, sliding my eyes sideways. "Do you still have that friend at the lab?" It came out way more casual than I felt, thankfully. The idea of Graham dating someone rankled in a way that few things unrelated to dead people did for me.

He twisted his mouth to one side. "I don't think I do. The last time I saw her she threw a beaker at my head. I'm rusty, but I think that means she doesn't want to talk to me anymore. Why?"

"Remember the blood samples I found on the dumpster?"

"You mean the flakes of something you hope was blood? I do recall that happening."

I didn't even roll my eyes, years of dealing with Graham's that-grass-is-not-green-until-we've-ruled-out-every-other-color-and-sent-samples-to-three-labs attitude letting the words float by with no offense taken.

"I took them to the lab myself, but my one good contact there moved to Colorado last year, and I'm stuck in DNA limbo. I know I'm right. Someone took her. I'd just like the lab-certified proof so Boone will stop looking at me like a pity case. Grasping for any way I might get the report in a more timely fashion than the usual too late to never." I blew out a long, frustrated sigh. "This whole damned thing has been one roadblock after another, and it's making me more than a little nuts."

"Amen to that. I'll keep my ears open for another connection we might be able to exploit. Which lab? Here or Waco?"

"Any lab you can find. Thanks."

He pulled out his phone and tapped the screen a few times, thumb-typed a short message, and looked up. "That make up for my workaholic tunnel vision of late?"

I leaned into his shoulder. "I just don't understand why you didn't call me before now. Since when do you need the governor to send me to look at your files?"

His chin dropped to his chest, low voice directed at the floor. "I wanted to do this one on my own. And I could tell from your messages you were eyeballs-deep in your own bog of misdirection and missing information. I didn't want to bother you."

"You should know better than that by now, Hardin. We'll find this guy." I drained the can and tapped the empty aluminum on the countertop. "I'm missing something. Hours of staring at every pixel of every photo and reading every word of every report, and I have a decent grasp of how, if not why, but I'm not any closer to who."

"You're working off other people's notes." He pulled a bottle of water from the fridge and twisted the top off. "It's more difficult to study a homicide long-range."

"Through his or her own eyes. With his or her own biases."

I went still from the ends of my hair to my summer-polished toenails. My mother. Helpful. Who knew?

I could worry about the long range psychological ramifications of that later.

I grabbed Graham's arm, squeezing so hard I made him wriggle. "That's it. That's what I didn't notice," I said.

"What is?"

"Like my mother used to tell me about the pageant judges—it's the same with the other cops who did the ground work on these cases—they saw it with their own biases. So we have to read these reports and study these photos not only looking for what they missed, but for what they might have seen differently than it actually was because of their personal life experience."

"But I was one of them. So was Archie," he said.

"I know. Lucky me." I spun and ran back for the conference room, not pausing to see if he was on my heels.

It was the dead sheriff from the cold case that was the problem. Which meant I needed some time with Google and a little bit of luck to see what he might have let pass.

* * *

"If I wasn't convinced we're looking for a white male based on data, I am based on this," I said two hours later, sitting back in my chair.

Sheriff Bud was pretty much the last word in the law in a tiny border community for two decades. That told me he knew everyone, and probably thought he had a good bead on his people.

His jurisdiction was twenty miles, at the center, from Ciudad Juarez, across the Mexican border, with little in the way of INS presence that far northwest. The local paper, back in the 90s when there was one, had photos of him leading a volunteer local militia of sorts with dogs and rifles along the border after the only other murder I could find during his tenure. A local farmer had been found beaten to death and robbed in an old barn on the outskirts of the only town in the county. Never an arrest made in the case, but when you read between the lines of the newspaper reports, Sheriff Bud did a lot more decrying outsiders as a source of violence and calling his community to arms than actual police work in the wake of the tragedy.

"Good stuff on the late Sheriff Colvin?" Archie asked, not looking up from his laptop. He was poring over background information on all the identified victims, looking for something that might have been missed.

"Looks like he was big on the school of thought that outsiders made trouble in his quiet town," I said.

Graham tapped on the doorframe, pocketing his phone as he walked back into the room. "The lead detectives on the river victim will be here first thing in the morning. The sheriff in Comal County said his guys have some good stuff." He turned to Archie. "He also said to tell you hello and thank you for your help. Is there anyone in law enforcement in the whole damned state that you don't know?"

Archie kept his eyes on his screen. "Sheriff Bud Colvin of Loving County. He's the one I wish I knew best right this second, and I had never heard of him, Lord rest him, until a couple of hours ago."

"Outsiders is polite code for Mexicans, I'm guessing." Graham turned to me.

I touched one index finger to the tip of my nose and pointed the other at Graham. "Never caught the killer in the only other murder I can find there, but was convinced it was an interloper. I'd bet my last cigarette he didn't even look at people from around his town when this body turned up. He wanted it to be someone from anywhere else."

"You were supposed to quit." That got Archie to look up.

I rolled my eyes. "Seven weeks and counting. It's a figure of speech."

He pushed his computer away. "But if we're on the right trail, the sheriff was wrong."

I touched one index finger to the tip of my nose and pointed at him with the other. "Bingo. Which means we have to comb through his report for anything that might hint at something he let pass because of his personal bias."

Graham leaned against the doorjamb and folded his thick arms across his chest. "I'll be damned." He smiled, shaking his head at me. "Every case I work with you, I learn something."

I tapped my fingers on the edge of the spacebar. "A theory—even one with a direction—is just a theory until we find something solid. I'll feel better when we have an actual suspect to go with this one."

Archie leaned back in his chair and checked his watch. "We're headed for midnight oil territory again. Are you two still lucid and ready to keep digging, or do we call it a night and reconvene here tomorrow after we talk to the detectives Graham pestered into coming down here?"

The corners of Graham's lips tipped up. "I didn't tell you that."

"I've been in this game a lot of years. The sheriff is a good man and damned fine cop, but he's pissed that the governor sent me out there yesterday, and he's going to be more pissed when he gets wind that Faith is here." He nodded when I looked up with raised eyebrows. "Not Governor McClellan's biggest fan."

"Oh, then we have something in common." I stood and waved him to the door. "Let's go home, boys."

Monday meant command staff at small departments would be back at work, the Comal County detectives would catch us up, Jim would be back at work, and if we were lucky, the inches we'd gained this weekend would turn into miles pretty quickly.

20

Beat cops react to Rangers HQ one of two ways: abject awe, or pissed off resistance. Our visiting detectives were a walking illustration of the extremes Monday morning.

Officer Ballard looked fresh out of the academy, raising Graham's eyebrows when he said he did two tours in Afghanistan with the Marine Corps before coming home to settle down with his wife and new baby. He didn't look at anyone as he spoke, too busy twisting his long neck every which way, gawking silently at his surroundings.

His partner, as long in the tooth as he was in the jowls, leaned against the doorjamb with his arms folded across his wide chest, glaring daggers at Archie and Graham in the periphery, and at me in particular.

I ignored it until he started talking. "So the Rangers think throwing their token female at this one is going to get them good press or some horseshit? I remember when this organization was more about putting slime bags where they belong than looking pretty for the TV cameras."

I turned my head slowly. "Then you'll appreciate that I've closed a hundred and twenty-one murder cases in my fairly decorated career in law enforcement, Officer Stoneway. And I'm not looking to chalk up my first loss anytime soon." I clapped my hands hard, the sound cracking back off the acoustic tile ceiling, and looked at the four men around me in turn.

"Gentlemen, what do you say we stop worrying about who wears what badge and focus our efforts on saving some lives this morning?"

Ballard nodded a little too quickly, stepping to the table. "Anything you need, ma'am," he said. I kept my eyes on his partner. I wasn't blinking first.

Twenty beats later, Stoneway shoved off the wall with one shoulder, closing the heavy door behind him. "Whatever sick fuck could do that to another human being needs to go straight to death row, no passing go, no collecting prison girlfriends or internet fame. If we're all in agreement there, then I'm in." He gave me a once-over and inclined his head my direction. "Ma'am."

"Call me Faith, please." I pulled a chair out from the table and leaned on the back of it. "What have y'all found about how or where the victim entered the water?"

"We've identified three likely points, all within a half-mile of the discovery site," Ballard said.

I exchanged a glance with Graham.

"Let me guess—no traffic cameras on the access roads."

"There's not even a road to the one place," Stoneway said.

Ballard pulled out his phone and poked at the screen. "We're reviewing traffic cam video from the perimeter area of each, for thirty minutes around the ETA. Parks and wildlife was able to give us a fairly narrow window thanks to Friday's storm and a strong current."

Without a make or model of car, they were fumbling in the dark, hoping something on the feed stood out enough to catch their attention, or a violent offender had a record bad enough to get them a warrant. But I'd be doing the same thing in their shoes. Leads can come from the damndest places.

"How far out is the nearest camera?" I asked.

"From one site, we have one just over two miles away. Six turns, but it's not a busy road." Ballard poked the screen again. "A dozen vehicles turned toward the river from there in our window. We have a team of three running backgrounds on the owners, and we're running down plates today on the two that weren't visible."

The nearby camera made me think the odds that our guy picked that route were low. But I wasn't bursting Ballard's bubble.

"You know what does have cameras?" Archie asked. Every head in the room turned his way. "The post office. Hardin, do we have that box back from the lab yet?"

Graham stood up straighter, the look on his face telling me he was annoyed that he hadn't thought of that. "I have images of the postmarks," he said. "As far as I know it's still in line for analysis. That's more specialized testing and the packaging wasn't decomposing."

Archie tipped his head toward Stoneway. "You have men you can put on running down when and where something was mailed? See if we can hit a match on one of your plates, or spot someone with this box?"

"That's a long shot, and I only got a team of three for a murder case. What are you interested in postal activity for, exactly?"

Archie's eyes shot between me and Graham. The governor wanted this kept close, and the more people we told, the more we risked pissing him off. But if these guys were working one of the murders, they deserved to know what they were up against.

"There are two more victims," Archie said. "The governor wants that quiet for reasons I'm sure y'all can guess, but the thing here is, Skye Morrow over at Channel Two got a severed finger from one of the other victims in the mail a few weeks back."

"A serial killer?" Ballard's voice rose at least two octaves. "So like, there will be more?"

"Not if we can help it," I replied. "Archie is the only person in the room with experience in this particular arena." I glanced at Stoneway and he nodded agreement. "But we will find this person."

Stoneway removed his hat, lowering it to his side. "Travis County...the lady preacher from Memorial Day weekend? I never saw an arrest made in that one. So do you have suspect vehicles we should be looking to match?"

Graham shook his head. "The dump site in my case was a side road that can be accessed by seven different county roads without passing a red light or a camera for twenty-seven miles. That's why she sat there in the heat for almost a day." His voice oozed distaste at the memory. Graham hated the less delicate parts of working homicide.

"So this guy knows the traffic cam network." Stoneway surveyed the room. "Are we looking for a badge, then?"

I didn't love the thought, but it had crossed my mind. "We don't know enough to say," I admitted. "So we rule nothing out until we do." I bit my lip. "It seems your partner and I have a shared abhorrence of the local news media. How would you like to be in charge of keeping Skye Morrow busy, Detective Ballard?" He was cute. Boyish. He'd come across on camera as long as it didn't make him nervous. Skye would love him. I pulled out my phone and read him her cell number.

"That woman is meaner than a rattler, and she gives you less warning when she's going to strike," Stoneway said. "You've got your work cut out for you, kid."

Ballard puffed his chest out. "I can handle her. I watch her station. She likes to have things first."

"Exactly," I said. "So you keep her busy chasing after little things for a while. You can give her the bit about parks and wildlife helping look for the entry point, but nothing else, and then get her off onto other reports for the next few days. Anything you can find in the calls that's interesting, you tell her that's what you're working on. She'll go chase it down thinking you're still working this case. Just be kind of tight-lipped, don't say much, make her think you're telling her something you're not supposed to. And whatever you do, do not say the words 'serial murders.' I think she's onto it already, but we don't need to fan those flames. Think you can handle that?"

"Yes, ma'am," Ballard said. "Um. Faith."

I smiled. "Thank you so much."

"And what are you doing while he's entertaining Miss Austin TV?" Stoneway's tone was wary.

"We will continue to follow leads in these cases, looking for links and insight." Archie's voice boomed more than usual, and he cut his eyes my way with a nod so slight half a blink would have missed it. "What do you hear about the status of your autopsy?"

I watched, an admiring smile playing around my lips. He said 'your' autopsy on purpose—Stoneway was about to get pissy again about us being involved in this, and Archie knew that as the ranking officer in the room, deferring would smooth those ruffled feathers. He was a master at handling people, for all his gruff cowboy facade. I just didn't like it when he turned that particular talent on me.

"They transferred the body up to the high tech ME's office here. We're in the queue. But the state furloughed another three people on Friday." Stoneway's ire found a new—and solid—target in the budget fiasco, and Archie shook his head in proper exasperation.

"I might be able to help there," I said. "I have a friend at the morgue who should be back at work today after an extended leave. I'll see what I can do."

Stoneway grunted a thank you.

"I'd sure appreciate a copy of that report when you get it, and anything else you pick up that might help us tie all this up." Archie stepped toward the door. "We're not here to take your case from you, gentlemen. Our job is to offer our expertise and help resolve this as quickly and quietly as possible. If everyone keeps that in mind, we have a better shot at accomplishing it."

I nodded along, staying quiet. I knew that speech well, could have said it just as convincingly myself, but I've learned in fifteen years behind a badge that if another officer is going to respond better to words coming from a man... well, hunting killers is a more rewarding pursuit than banging my head against the thick, rough bricks of the misogyny wall.

Ballard shook everyone's hand again on his way out, his palm a touch clammy, and Stoneway tipped his hat when he turned back from the door. "I look forward to talking again soon," he said.

I shut the door behind him and turned to Graham. "Nice, the post office thing. I can't believe we didn't think of that sooner."

"I'm a little annoyed with myself, to tell you the truth. But we've thought of it now. And if they're spread thin, I have a rookie who's itching to do something besides bailiff duty."

"He's intimidating at first glance, too," I said. "Good choice."

Graham pulled out his phone to call Bolton and I turned to the map on the wall, my eyes on the river. It would be jammed full of folks celebrating their independence by drinking themselves silly in a couple of days.

A couple of days.

I spun back to the board.

"Shit."

Graham asked Bolton to hold. "What?"

I pointed. "The dates aren't just the end of the month. Easter. Memorial Day. Holidays are slow news days, Graham."

"We thought so too, but unless everyone is celebrating national guacamole day now, there was no holiday Saturday."

"But it was also the most public dump. How many people were in the river who saw her before someone realized what they were seeing?"

"So?"

"So the biggest holiday of the summer is day after tomorrow. If I were a killer looking for news coverage, I'd have a plan to take advantage of that. The fourth victim on the Fourth of July. The clickbait headlines will write themselves."

"From one body a month to two in a week?" His skeptical eyebrow, the right one, shot up. "You're reaching."

I wasn't. I could feel it. Cameras are great, but if they were the be-all and end all of police work, nobody would have ended up in limbo downstairs in the past decade. Archie opened the door and slid back into the room.

"Check your phones," he said.

I pulled mine out and touched the screen. Saw the Channel Two alert.

'Lock your doors, the Hill Country Phantom wants in,' a Skye Morrow exclusive. I flipped the screen around to show Graham.

"Why would she risk the governor's wrath?" I asked. "Skye likes being in the inner circle."

Archie held his phone up. "She called me. She got another present this morning. She's been around almost as long as I have, and she knows just enough about what's going on here to get herself good and worked up. She's afraid she's a target."

"How—" I stopped. She lived alone. She was pretty much the top of her chosen profession. And that would damned sure get attention. "But people would notice her missing," I said.

"But maybe if he's looking to make a splash on the Fourth like you said, then that wouldn't matter so much," Graham said.

I stared at the Channel Two logo on my screen. "So now I'm supposed to save Skye Morrow? The universe is twisted sometimes, y'all know that?"

"What I know is that Skye is freaking out, and you're grabbing any thread that might hold this quilt together," Archie said. "We don't know that she's a target. And what's all this about the Fourth?"

I explained. "Skye would be a way to get the message across," I said. I hated to even look like I might be thinking of siding with her, but she had a point.

I checked my watch. "It's after nine. Archie, are you going to call Skye back?"

"Oh, I suppose."

"Ask her what she's not telling us," I said. "That day she was here, after the first package came, she was weird. Subdued. Like, she gave me a little hell, but she backed off way faster than she should have. Maybe she was scared, but there could be more there." I turned. "Graham, you got Bolton on the post offices, just in case?"

"He's already on his way."

I moved to the door. "I'm going to go talk to an old friend and see if I can get us anything else that might help."

21

Jim Prescott leaned elbow-deep into a middle-aged man's chest cavity, reeling off commentary on human organs like most folks recite a grocery list. I let the door to the autopsy room click shut behind me to announce my arrival, my face breaking into a grin when he stopped talking and turned his head.

"It's working, huh?" I asked.

While I didn't love being another name on former Texas Governor Chuck McClellan's endless list of people who owed him large favors, the look on Jim's face was worth every minute I'd spent listening to all the ways I had ruined the life the governor had envisioned for me. I was so happy to see my friend looking better, I didn't even immediately notice the sting of the formalin creeping into my nose and throat.

Jim extracted his hands from the open chest on his table and pulled off his gloves and gown, wadding them up and tossing them into a large beige garbage can on his way across the room, where he yanked me into a hug so tight my feet left the floor. Jim squeezed for long enough to make my lungs burn before he put me back on the floor and laid both hands on my shoulders.

"Thank you."

The two simple words carried more weight—and more emotion—than any I'd ever heard. I nodded, swallowing hard. "You are so welcome." I directed my gaze to the table. "Who's that?"

"I don't much care, and you won't, either. He had a heart attack in the middle of sex with a fifteen-year-old girl. That warning on the Viagra bottle is there for a reason."

I wrinkled my nose. "Karma at work."

"True. But he had marks on his throat, so the DA wanted to be sure he wasn't strangled."

I stepped closer to the table. There were indeed deep blue-purple ligature marks peeking out of the fleshy folds of the dead man's neck. "I wouldn't blame her if she had," I murmured.

Jim barked a short laugh. "Me either. But she didn't. She swears he got off on the orgasm strangulation thing, and she said he told her to pull the tie that he put around his own neck. Regardless, he died of a massive heart attack. His left coronary artery is stopped up like Bigfoot's shower drain. His hyoid and lungs are fine."

"Since when do you look into the stories behind the bodies you get?"

He shook his head. "Since never. But the guys who brought this one in told Florence the whole tale and she wouldn't shut up about him when she welcomed me back this morning and saw I had him on the table. I still did my job fairly, but it gives me a new appreciation for what you do every day. Keeping objective when you know shit about people is hard."

Florence was Jim's assistant, the only one in the building who hadn't seen her job eliminated in the past year. Grouchy and particular, nobody liked her—except maybe Jim, but I couldn't even swear to that. Archie and I figured Florence knew where too many secrets were kept for anyone to risk pissing her off by firing her. But here, I agreed with her.

"Fifteen, huh?" I shook my head. "Makes you wonder what the hell kind of road a kid walks to end up in a situation like that."

"I'm just glad this road isn't headed to prison," he said. "Yet, anyway. But Rick Dershire over at the DA's office can probably fill you in if you're interested."

I stepped back as he donned another dandelion-yellow paper gown and snapped blue latex gloves onto both hands, returning to the table. "I wish I had time to save everyone, Jim."

"I know you do, McClellan," he said. "And I also know you're here today after information on the woman from the river, which is the third drawer in my lineup today, unless you need her to be the next. I hear the governor himself put you on this. Moving up in the world, and deservedly so." He glanced up from his work and smiled.

"Thanks. This case is bigger than anyone knows. And I'd appreciate her moving up—but I'm actually here to ask another favor, too."

He pulled silk thread, a needle, and a wicked-looking stapler from a drawer in the cart next to him and started putting Mr. Pedophile back together, arching an unruly gray eyebrow at me. "Is there some reason you think I'm going to decline?"

I shook my head. "It's for another case, and this one does need my full attention right now, but I can't just abandon this…" I shook my head. "Well, anyway. I brought in a human finger right after you left for Houston, and I haven't heard a word about it. The computer system just says it's processing. I need to know if there's a way to find out who it belonged to. Three women dead, one missing, and more than one disembodied finger floating around has me drowning in questions. I need to start finding a few answers if I'm going to save anyone."

"Save anyone? Since when did you defect to the land of live victims?"

"Since Boone assigned me to this one. So far I'm striking out. I'm scared shitless that I'm too late already, and I have to know I tried every possible road, no matter how weird. The victim was working at a coffeehouse, and feeding a coyote near the mall parking lot where she was taken. The vet who cut the finger out of the animal's insides said it was possible the coyote bit the offender trying to protect her food source."

"A coyote bit someone's finger off, and you think it's evidence? There's so much fucking weird about that I don't even know where to start asking. Who did you leave it with?"

"Florence," I replied. "Who else would I trust?"

Jim put the last staple in the guy's breastbone and pulled his sagging skin back over it, going to work with the needle, the stitches even and small.

"Huh. She didn't mention it, but I'll ask her. We'll find it. You said it went through an animal's digestive system?"

"Disgusting, I know, but the vet said there was still some flesh."

He shook his head, but didn't speak until the cadaver's chest was closed, a white sheet settled back over the man's face. He waved for me to follow him out the side door to a narrow hallway that led to his office. "Florence, did Faith bring by—" he began as we walked into the cluttered room that housed Jim's current files and Florence's desk.

She held up the small plastic container.

"I saw her name in the log book just now and remembered that you would want to see this guy." She shook the box and a low, wet thump emanated from it.

My reaction must have shown on my face because Jim snorted. "What exactly do you want me to do with this? I can tell you that a month later the chances I'm getting a print are pretty damned low."

"The vet said the print wouldn't be recognizable with it processed that far down her gut," I said. "I was hoping maybe for DNA we could run?"

I wasn't letting myself hope for anything else. Yet, anyway.

"I'll give it my best shot." Jim took the box and moved toward the door. "I assume you want this now, with your ticking clock?"

A grin broke over my face. "You're the best, Jim."

"Anything. For the rest of my days." He stopped when the last word choked off and turned back for the sterile environment of the autopsy room.

I moved to follow and Florence grabbed my hand. "Your father is a cold-hearted bastard," she said when I looked back, "but you…you're good people, Ranger Mac. Thank you."

The soft tone was so unlike her usual Janis Joplin growl that my lips moved, but couldn't find words for a few seconds. Kindness wasn't Florence's forte, even where Jim was concerned. But she had worked for him for coming up on three decades. "Anything for a friend," I said, returning the pressure she was putting on my fingers.

* * *

"Jesus, Jim." I clapped a hand over my mouth and coughed. Even the formalin didn't cover the sickly-sweet, acid-tinged stench of decay that had my eyes watering and my stomach twisting.

"There's VapoRub on the table there." Jim pointed with one gloved index finger, the words muffled by the mask obscuring the lower half of his face. "Masks in the drawer."

I hurried to the steel cart, dropping the jar's lid in my haste to smear a large glob of Vicks across my upper lip. I stuck my coated finger partway into both nostrils for good measure. Not much makes me queasy anymore, but that particular rancid smell was one I hadn't come across before.

Looping a mask over both ears to keep the more pleasant scent closer, I joined Jim hunched over a shiny stainless steel counter.

The bright light surrounding the magnifier between him and the counter glinted off the tools lined up neatly next to the blue-plastic-backed pad under the...oh, my.

The contents of Dr. Avery's box lay on the pad, lumpy and brown and not as decomposed as I would have expected, a fat gold ring strangling the flesh on one end.

"It's the ring that stopped it from going all the way through her intestines," Jim said, picking at the flesh with tweezers and scissors. He put the scissors back on the counter and picked up a scalpel, his eyes narrowing as he removed a slice of the outer layers and used the tweezers to lift it to the center of the powerful magnifier. He turned it six different ways, his breath coming faster.

"What?" I asked.

"I don't..." Jim shook his head, sidestepping to the microscope and pulling a clean slide from a drawer.

He placed the sample on it and put it under the scope, clicking on a light and turning a few knobs as he peered through the lens. Standing up straight, he turned to me. "I hate to burst your bubble, Faith, but this isn't human. It's not even flesh."

22

"I'm sorry?"

Jim shook his head. "I...yeah. That's some sort of polymer, maybe, but it's not flesh."

"But I—" I waved one arm in a broad sweep over my head. "The smell. It has to be."

Jim walked toward me, using the scissors to slice through the outer layers and pulling the ring free. He returned the mangled brown lump to the box, taking the ring to the sink and spraying it with hot water before he dunked it into a beaker he filled with water and industrial cleanser. I used the scalpel to pull the box closer, squinting at the half-digested object in it.

Ridged striations in the core Jim's scissors had exposed showed vertical variations in color, with slight scoring from the point of the scissors visible. I poked with the scalpel, leaving the barest indentation.

"Is this wood?" It was like I heard the words without saying them, bitterness crawling up the back of my throat. I let my head fall back, angry tears pooling so quickly a couple escaped before I could will them back. Deep breath.

His fingers closed over my arm, their warmth permeating the cloth of my sleeve. He stayed quiet, though. Because he didn't know what to say.

"I spent the last four weeks chasing my tail in circles on this. How does a hundred-and-twenty-pound fully grown adult vanish in broad daylight and just...that's it? I've had dreams about this finger cracking this open. Convinced myself that it was the key. And it's not even real. Now what?" I sniffled, my nostrils burning, raising my head to meet his eyes. "The kid won't get his mother back and it's my fault. I missed something."

"You're not Wonder Woman, Faith. No matter how much you want to be."

I dragged the back of one hand across my face, wiping a slick mixture of snot and VapoRub off of my lip. "It sucks to lose, Jim. You are sure, right? I mean, how did something that wasn't dead produce that god awful stench?"

He laughed. "McClellan, if I can't tell rubber from human flesh by now, the state of Texas has a serious problem. The smell isn't the thing in the box, it's where it came from."

"Huh?"

"Dead bodies float because of the gasses that get trapped in the intestines, right?"

"Right. Body Recovery Scenes For Dummies."

"The same thing happens to animal innards as they decay. Your vet wasn't super diligent about cleaning that up before she put it in the box, and she didn't put formaldehyde in there with it or anything."

"She said she didn't want to damage anything the lab might be able to find."

Jim rolled his eyes. "If this ever happens to you again, tell them I beg of them to preserve whatever they're sending me. When your eyes started watering? That was the gasses from the coyote's intestines. They'd been building up in that box for weeks while it sat in a drawer in Florence's overheated office. Damned near knocked me over when I opened it. I'm glad you lagged behind—that was enough stomach stink without mopping up puke, too."

I winced. "Sorry."

He shook his head. "Not like you could have known."

"But what about the ring?"

"You're welcome to look at it when it's clean—it's your evidence, after all. Didn't you tell me this girl disappeared from a mall parking lot?"

"She did."

"So, I have a theory." He grinned entirely too wide to be appropriate for the situation. "I think the coyote ate the ring, maybe even some time ago from the tissue that was grown into the outside of it, and then she managed to turn up a discarded mannequin, bit off a chunk, and it got stuck inside the ring and stopped up her gut." He paused. "How did you come across this animal, anyway?"

"Long story short, she tried to attack me, and a mall cop who isn't old enough to buy beer shot her with his dad's Saturday night special. I made the kid come with me when I took her to the vet. The vet busted her ass to save the animal, but she lost that fight and decided to play Kay Scarpetta, wildlife edition. And here we are."

"That's a hell of a story. The kind I'm sorry didn't get us the bad guy for more than one reason. I could get a journal article out of that one, for sure."

I snorted. "Truth is stranger than fiction, huh?"

"Thirty years in this place and I'm convinced of it."

"So. Back to Archie's vic."

"She's next in line. Between the furloughs and the holiday weekend coming up, I've got the place almost to myself today."

"If you could have a look at her and give me a call, I'd appreciate it. Send the report to the process officer at Comal County first, though."

"Pissing war?"

"Just a tiny battle, but I'll give him this one to keep him happy," I said. "Let me know if there's anything weird I need to jump on, though?"

Jim turned back for the door. "Sure thing. You want this ring?"

"I'll look at it when I can think about it without getting pissed off."

"I get it. But sometimes the best way to solve one problem is to focus on another. I've examined thousands of brains, and they truly are miraculous things. Yours has always been better than average at this kind of shit. Think about the murder vic and let the missing woman marinate on her own. If you missed something, your subconscious might just turn it up for you."

I squeezed his arm and thanked him before I turned for the lobby, hoping he was right about more than just coyote guts and pedophiles this morning.

23

Even in the dark, she could always see the ring.

As big as a quarter glinting off the back of His hand, she could've sworn He moved it in and out of the sickly, filtered gray-green half-light from the bulb at the top of the steps on purpose. Normal weapons and normal fears weren't His thing.

The ring had a sharp edge and a blunt surface, could cut skin like a knife through summer-picnic-warm butter and made her cheek feel like it had exploded—once even all in the same swift strike. He'd had to sew her face up that time. Said it might get infected and He couldn't stand the thought of losing her. But He never minded losing the others.

She wondered about them. Did He hurt them, maybe even kill them? Or did He just throw them back, because He couldn't find anyone to replace her? He said once, that's what He wanted. To replace her.

She didn't bother to wonder what would happen to her if He did.

The others always came, screamed, and disappeared. While she slept, usually on days when she didn't manage to avoid the drugs. He thought she took the pills, but she didn't. Not unless she couldn't hide the fact that she wasn't. He tried telling her once that they were vitamins. To keep her strong because He loved her. But no vitamin made a person fall helplessly into a sleep too deep for dreams. When she could still remember the sun, she'd started with locking her jaw. Then spitting them out. The next time He came He brought the needles, and when she could sit up and talk again she asked for the pills back.

The ring was cold and hard and flat against her jaw as He stroked her face, His voice going high-pitched and soft. "Such a good girl you are. I knew you were a good girl the first time I laid eyes on you. I need a good girl." He cackled. "It balances the bad in me. I told you, you're my other half. This was written in an old place. And we'll be together forever now. Nobody can take you away. Good girls get love and privileges."

It was the only time in her whole life anyone had ever thought she was special. Worthy. And damned if she didn't wish she could melt into the floor and go back to being trash.

Fate has a dark, mean sense of humor.

24

I dialed Archie on my way back to my truck. Got him on the first ring.

"How's our favorite death whisperer?" He didn't bother with hello.

"About to start on your victim," I said. "He had just finished sewing up a pedophile who died of a heart attack when I left."

"Karma. Any luck with your missing girl?"

He knew me too well.

"I hung a whole lot of hope on one piece of evidence that turned out not to be real. So no. But I'm not giving up. Governor's orders first, though—how's Skye?"

"Jumpy as a long-tailed cat in a room full of rocking chairs. And hell-bent on catching this guy herself. She got an ear this time."

"From the soccer mom in the river?" I asked.

"Nope. I double checked with the on-site coroner. She had both of hers. Skye also never got a piece of Hardin's lady pastor, but he swears she wasn't missing an ear, either."

"Maybe it's his? He thinks he's Van Gogh?"

"At this point, I'm accepting any and all theories. I have to tell you, I've known Skye a lot of years, and I've never seen her like this. I tried reminding her that the governor doesn't want this on the air, and she did not give one single damn."

I shook my head. "That's not like her, Arch. There's something she's not telling you. Is she getting threats? I mean aside from the normal ones." Skye was no stranger to hate mail. The body bits were gross, and being addressed directly by a murderer was scary as all hell, but there was a deeper motive here for her than wanting to land the headline first.

"I asked if there were directions for her to put it on the air, or a message of any kind, and she insisted there wasn't." Archie didn't sound convinced.

Neither was I. "You need me for anything right now?"

"Nah. I've got feelers out on dentals and DNA for the cold case Jane Doe. I found seven women who went missing around that time, and I'm waiting to hear back from some folks. That close to the border, she could have been getting dental work done in Mexico for all I know. But maybe it's just a tiny town and a tiny office and nobody responded in a timely fashion last time around. The new sheriff in Loving County said he knows nothing about the case, other than that it was never solved and he didn't want to put a toe in it."

"Any other homicides with similar MOs in the surrounding area there in the past few years?" I asked.

"He said no, but I'm checking records as we speak." I heard his keyboard clicking away in the background. "So far everybody was buried with all their fingers. I was thinking—the left ring finger is the wedding ring one, you know. Should that matter?"

"Maybe? Could the messages be some sort of commentary on the modern American marriage?"

"There are so many possible trails to chase here I have no fucking idea which one is the right one," Archie said. "That could be important. Or it could just be the easiest one to cut off. Maybe it's the right length or weighs just enough to mail cheaper. Who knows? Like when a high school English teacher goes on about the symbolism of the roses blooming outside the prison door in *The Scarlet Letter*. I always wondered if Hawthorne actually meant anything by that or if maybe he just liked roses."

I laughed. "You think we're over-reading?"

"Maybe. Or maybe we're not seeing enough connections. I can't say anything without flat ass guessing."

"I'm going to see if I can get to the bottom of at least one thing," I said. "If you need me, call me."

"Go get 'em, kiddo," he said. "For real."

I touched the *End* button and dropped the phone in the cupholder as I turned out of the morgue parking lot.

Channel Two was right up the road. It was almost noon, and Skye frequented the coffee shop across the street.

She owed me. Archie might have let her dismiss him, but she wasn't getting rid of me so easily.

* * *

Skye's perfect curtain of platinum hair hid her face as she hunched over her phone at the back corner table. I got closer, noting her furious thumb-typing, her face twisted into a scowl that would give her plastic surgeon fits.

The upshot of whatever was bugging her was that she didn't see me until I sat down in the chair opposite her.

"Boy, this day just keeps getting better." She plunked her phone face down on the table.

"Something bothering you, Skye? Maybe more than one thing?"

She leaned back in the chair and crossed her arms over her chest. Everything about her body language screamed "go away."

"Getting body parts in the mail has to be unsettling even to you," I prompted.

"I've had better care packages. But we both know you're not here because you're concerned for my health, mental or otherwise. So why don't you just tell me what you want so I can get back to arguing with the governor's secretary."

"They saw the teaser? Hill Country Phantom has a decent ring to it."

"Three people are dead, and from what I can't get out of Hardin and Baxter I can infer that you're no closer to catching this guy than you were when he killed Daph—" She paused. Let her eyes shut. Her sigh said it all; she was frazzled and frustrated and she'd let that slip when she didn't mean to.

Bingo.

"You knew her?" I leaned forward. "And you didn't tell Archie? Skye, that's not only dangerously close to obstruction, it's stupid on your part. Why would you keep that to yourself?"

She tapped three scarlet talons on the polished wood tabletop. "We used to be friends. We weren't anymore. I didn't want that clouding Baxter's investigation."

"Bullshit. You know good and well that's the kind of connection he needs to know about. It has potential to speak to how well the murderer knew the victim." I paused. "Why weren't you friends anymore?"

Skye shook her head, pinching her lips together like the answer might escape against her will. "She was a good person. A good lawyer. She skipped out of journalism and went to law school because she wanted to help people, and she did. Every day. If this is what she got for it—" Her voice faded to a horrified whisper. "Maybe I deserve to be next."

Damn. I had no love for Skye Morrow, but even I found it difficult to sit there and watch her talk that way.

"Listen, nobody I've ever met has done anything that would qualify them as 'deserving' of this," I said. "And you know exactly what sort of people I grew up around. Whatever you are, Skye, it's not that."

"I think that's the most backhanded kindness anyone's ever uttered," she said. "And I'm still going with my story. You need help, McClellan, and deep down, you know it. Besides, the people have a right to know they could be in danger."

"I thought you were convinced he was coming for you," I said.

"I didn't say convinced. I said I thought he might. What I know is that somebody has seen something, and you don't have the reach to turn them up. So I'm doing it myself, since it might be my ass on the line."

I sighed. "I tried that a few weeks back. Didn't get a single credible lead. All it did was waste my time. Are you sure you want to waste our time right now, Skye?"

"I have to use my platform." The words had a steel edge, and the slightest tremor. She was downright terrified.

"Why did he kill your friend?"

"I would tell you if I knew." She stood. "Daphne was a good kid. Smart. Kind. Her only problem was that she always tried to be too fair. That played better in court than it did in the newsroom. The guy who tortured and mutilated her before he bashed her fucking brains in shouldn't walk away because y'all can't get your shit together and the governor wanted your face attached to this case so he could play hero when an arrest is made."

She grabbed her phone and shoved it into her bag, the scowl back. "He can kiss my entire ass. And shove his inner circle right up his own. The story is going. And I'm not leaving this alone until the person responsible for Daphne's death is locked up or in the ground with her."

My jaw loosened as she strode to the door. I'd never seen her so pissed. I'd also never seen her care about anything so much.

Archie was right—the clock was ticking faster. At least now I knew why.

And she had given me an idea.

* * *

We had a killer on our hands who was smart. Maybe the scariest smart bastard I'd ever personally dealt with. He'd gotten away with three, maybe more, brutal murders without leaving us so much as a flake of dandruff. I knew Archie had worked a couple of high-profile serials decades back, and I remembered him getting called away somewhere to assist with a serial investigation when he was on my father's detail. Men like Archie Baxter are a special breed, able to take in the very worst humanity has to offer without letting the evil seep into who they are and how they see the rest of the world. I struggled with that myself, sometimes, and I wondered, when I was Archie's age, would I still be able to say that? And would I have the guts to walk away from the job if I started to feel like I couldn't? For now, having his experience on board made me feel better.

Driving to the sheriff's office to find Graham, I replayed my talk with Skye. She was right about more than I wanted to admit. I knew I was here for more than just my brains and my record. The governor needed some good press, with the budget stalemate starting to put more of a squeeze on voters as they saw unemployment rise and CHiP health insurance slow thanks to lack of funding. If the teachers refused to return next month with the state unable to guarantee their pay, Holdswaithe was screwed come November. Except. A high-profile serial killer, caught before anyone even knew he was working, by a team Holdswaithe could claim rights to assembling—a team that included poor Faith McClellan, who'd lost her sister and never stopped chasing demons...that was redemption enough for a lot of folks. The trick was keeping the serial part of that out of the news until after we'd caught him, and we all knew it.

It was pulling it off in the age of smartphone cameras and constant vigilance that was the tricky part.

Which was where talking to Skye had come in handy. "Somebody had to have seen something," she'd said.

Smartphone cameras.

Constant vigilance.

And a new trick we could pull from our sleeves.

I kicked the door open and hotfooted it into the sheriff's department, talking before I got all the way around the corner into Graham's new office. "Somebody saw what happened," I said. "In every single case except maybe the one where snakes outnumber people three to one, and Archie's still trying to figure out if that one's even related. We need a warrant for whatchamacallit at Google. The surveil—"

I stumbled to a stop in the middle of the word when I stepped through the doorway. Captain Jameson and Deputy Bolton stood on the side of Graham's desk closest to the door.

"McClellan." Jameson's smooth tenor was spiked with a shot of the smarmy that mid-grade salesmen and small-time politicians exude. "Welcome back. Good of you to remember where you started."

"Captain." I put out a hand to shake his. I wouldn't apologize for my outburst—not to him. But I telegraphed a *what the hell* to Graham when Jameson turned back to him.

Graham curled his full lips between his teeth and bit them into a thin line, our old signal for "help." And me with no clue how.

"Good, I'm glad it's settled." Jameson got to his feet, patting Bolton's shoulder and moving to the door, prompting me to slide out of his way. "Bolton here is the most promising recruit we've had since..." Jameson's eyes flicked to me almost involuntarily from the speed with which he redirected his gaze. "In a long time." He clapped his hands. "Appreciate it, Hardin. Good luck."

He disappeared. Bolton stayed seated. And suddenly I could read Graham's face clearer than a New York Broadway marquee. We were stuck with the rookie. On the biggest, most dangerous case either of us had ever seen.

* * *

"Is the post office closed?" I asked, drawing confusion from Bolton and a smirk from Graham.

"Skye's package was mailed from a contract postal location in Gruene," Graham said.

"Let me guess—no cameras." Damn, this guy didn't miss a trick. Tiny tourist town, cute little main street where people mail gifts and trinkets home every day, nobody watching.

"No cameras. And, nobody remembers anything now because it was a month ago and tourist season started. But the captain thinks it's an excellent idea for Bolton to remain involved with the case."

Shit. I stared at the rookie. We needed a way to get rid of him.

Skye.

What else had she said? That the lawyer lady was always trying to help people. And Graham's victim was a pastor, that was sort of their thing.

I plucked a Post-it from the pad on Graham's desk and wrote Ramona Mathers's name on it.

"Officer Bolton, the first thing we need right now is to know if this woman did any volunteer or career counseling. I understand she used to work in IT. Anything resembling charity, or anything else you find, you bring it to us," I said.

Bolton lumbered to his feet, taking the paper and nodding to Graham. "I'll get right on it, sir. Thank you."

Graham nodded and watched me shut the door after Bolton ducked to get out it.

"Thank you." Graham kept his voice low, even with the door shut.

"Happy to help. And by the time he's done, we'll be gone."

"Is he going to find anything useful?"

I shrugged. "He might, if my hunch is right. But while he's chasing that, we're going to go chase down a warrant, because I'm smart. And of all people, Skye Morrow gave me an idea."

My phone started buzzing in my pocket. I raised it to my ear with a grin at Graham. "Hey, Jim," I said by way of hello.

"Skye Morrow is teasing a segment about a serial. This is his handiwork, right?" Jim's voice was tight.

"It is," I said. "I wasn't on the scene, but Archie was. Why do you sound so weird?"

"This is maybe the weirdest thing I've ever had on my table, and I've been here too long for that not to carry the weight of an anvil."

I stood up straight, clearing panic out of my throat. "What's wrong?"

"The cause of death here was definitely the head trauma, though I can't imagine this combination of razor marks and burns didn't make her want to die before she did. But this woman has been completely drained of blood, Faith. Like, not a drop. Nowhere in her hair, on her head. It's gone."

"I." I stopped. "What? How would that work?"

"The most efficient way to do something like this is to blow an artery, then keep up chest compressions until there's no more blood. Her carotid has been severed, but there are marks on her ankles that suggest she was hung upside down. But someone still would have had to keep her heart beating after her skull was cracked open. And it took a while."

I closed my eyes, the imagery playing on the backs of the lids anyway. "Wow."

"Yeah," Jim said. "What the hell are you getting yourself into, McClellan?"

"The governor got me into it," I said. "And honestly, I'm not too sure. You got ideas on a weapon?"

"Not the first clue. The bone shows evidence of a sharp edge in places and a blunt one in others. Maybe there were two?"

"Maybe he made his own?"

"Not much would surprise me here. I'm not through yet, but I had to tell you about this. I see people who've bled out this way or that all the time, but I've never examined a corpse that was devoid of blood."

"Thanks, Jim. Let me know what else you find."

"Watch your ass out there, Faith. Most humans aren't capable of seeing another person lose large quantities of blood. Whoever you're hunting for helped."

"Noted." I clicked the end circle and tucked the phone back into my pocket.

"Ramona from the river was drained of blood," I told Graham. "Jim is shaken. Said someone had to keep her heart pumping after she was dead to do that."

Graham sat up in his chair. "Why? And why her and not the other two?"

"What if it had to do with the location of the discovery? We talked to the guys leading the combing of the bank this morning. If there's no blood, there's no trail."

Graham pointed. "And now we're back to what you were saying when you walked in. Google. You're talking about the cell phone net, where we give them times and locations and they provide a list of all the phones within a certain radius. I read that article too."

"If Parks and Wildlife has an estimated time of entry for the body into the water, we have someplace to start, because we have two other locations we know our guy was at." I turned the doorknob. "Let's go."

25

I didn't have time to get on anyone's schedule, which can take weeks with the backed-up dockets plaguing almost every courthouse in the country, and I learned long ago to take my advantages where I can get them if it means bringing a killer to justice.

Which meant Graham and I spent the next hour zig-zagging the stifling July courthouse halls, popping in on three judges I'd grown up calling "Uncle Bob," "Uncle Jeff," and "Uncle Dan" before we found one who was both in his chambers and available to see us.

Daniel J. Brinkman wasn't a big man, but his supersized intellect and deep, booming voice could fill a room—and knock the wind out of an opponent—more completely than a dozen professional football teams. Of every jurist the governor ever played golf with, Uncle Dan was my favorite. And he'd always had a soft spot for me, too, in his quiet, unassuming way.

"Well now, Ranger Faith McClellan, all grown up and hauling in murderers." He stood behind his massive, chocolate-brown oak desk, pushing his wire-rimmed glasses up his nose. "To what do I owe the pleasure of having my Monday brightened this way?"

"I need a warrant, Your Honor," I said, striding to the front side of the desk and putting my hands out to grip both of his. Uncle Dan got me. He wasn't a big hugger, either.

"Please, with that 'Your Honor' nonsense. You've been calling me Uncle Dan since you were being paraded around in tiaras and I won't answer to anything else." Graham's breath went in sharply behind me. He didn't grow up in my world—first and pet name familiarity with sitting members of the state's most coveted bench was a stretch for him.

"A warrant, huh?" Uncle Dan continued, sinking into his chair and assuming a stern expression. "State your case, Officer. Grounds?"

I didn't flinch. He took his job seriously, and he didn't believe in favors. My name and some good memories got us in the door, but I would have to work for what I wanted.

"We need witness and possible suspect identification on three murders we believe are related." The switch to legalese was so automatic I didn't even notice it until I caught Graham side-eyeing me in my peripheral. "Using the local media for such requests has proven to have limited, often time-consuming results, and they're on the decline with the societal change in viewing and news consumption habits." I sounded like a cross between a lawyer and psych professor, but Uncle Dan was a smart man who knew just how smart he was, and having my facts in order and well-presented was the shortest route to getting him on my side.

Dan sat back in his chair and steepled his fingers under his chin as my phone buzzed in my pocket. I ignored it, watching the judge's face.

"But a cornerstone of the role of the free press in our society has always been to inform and, when applicable, protect the American public," he said. "If you're not talking to the press about a possible serial killer, you're leaving people with their guard down. And while I remember well how much you enjoy talking to the press, your motivation must always be to protect those you serve despite personal bias."

I knew that was coming, and I was ready for it. "I do whatever is necessary to perform my sworn duty to the best of my ability." The words tumbled out so fast I wasn't sure they were in the right order. "If you check the website for Channel Seven in Dallas you'll see that I'm not averse to TV news pleas for leads—but that case also illustrates my point perfectly. I spent three weeks chasing wild geese without a true lead to show for the time and effort, and almost got myself killed because a viewer had an old grievance with my father as a bonus. Not only do we need this data in the most timely manner, but the taxpayers shouldn't have to pay for us to run down nonsense if there's a more efficient route to the information we need." I paused for a breath. Cleared my throat. "Sir."

Dan pursed his lips, nodding slowly. "Well played. Good stewardship of taxpayer funds should be every public servant's concern." He leaned forward and plucked a pen from the marble stand at the head of his Aggie maroon leather desk blotter.

"Exactly where and when are you planning to search for this data you seek?"

"That's part of the beauty of it: we don't have to search. We can focus on analyzing other clues while the search people search. Have you ever heard of Google Sensorvault?"

He pushed his glasses up again and tipped his head back, looking down the bridge of his nose at us. "I read something not long ago about a technology dragnet and a serial rapist in North Carolina. Is that what you're referring to?"

Graham, who I couldn't swear had drawn a breath saving the one I heard when we first walked in, nodded. "Yes, Your Honor. It's been used with success in several cases around the country, and while it's not a magic answer machine, it will help us see patterns and find information we'd spend months tracking down the old school way, if we ever found it at all."

Dan swiveled his head. "I don't believe I've had the pleasure, Officer," he said, extending a hand.

Graham stood to shake it. "Lieutenant Commander Graham Hardin, sir. Travis County."

"Forgive my lack of manners, gentlemen," I said. Oops. Introductions first. I had known that since practically before I could walk.

"You're trying to catch a murderer, you said." Dan smiled. "I think we can overlook a slip in etiquette in favor of the big picture."

"Big picture," I echoed, the phrase pinging around my head for a reason I couldn't pin down.

He opened a thick leather folio and poised his pen above a skinny-lined yellow legal pad. "Why do you believe these murders are connected? And do you have reason to believe there will be more?"

"Yes, sir. Three women, all burned and mutilated in the same fashion, all left in public places with messages on their skin, all with their heads bashed in. If we can find out who was in these places near the times the bodies were dumped and either identify a pattern or find a witness, all of a sudden our rapidly cooling trail is red hot."

"And this service will help you do that? What exactly am I compelling these people to release?"

"Cell phone data," I said. "It's not perfect, because not everyone uses their programs, but people who do are tracked. Constantly. So if we have a warrant for the phones that were in the vicinity of these coordinates along the Guadalupe's banks between 11 p.m. Friday and 6 a.m. Saturday, we might get a bead on the killer. At the very least, we could turn up a witness who doesn't even know they saw something. If we get lucky, we find somebody who took video with their phone."

Dan's pen faltered. "That's skating the edges of invasion of privacy," he said. "People have talked other judges into issuing these sorts of warrants? Really?"

"Only in cases of public danger, which this is," Graham said hastily. "And the initial report we get will be coded with numbers that reveal nothing about the owners of the devices—we'll just be able to see if the same device was in the vicinity of more than one dump scene, for instance. And who might have been close enough to see anything at either. Once we narrow it to a few people we need to speak with, we have to request contact information separately."

"Will you need another warrant for that?"

Graham shook his head. "No sir, just the one will cover both things."

Dan tapped the pen point on his paper, raining tiny black dots on the margin. "Technology is wonderful in a lot of ways, but I worry about the future of mankind some days," he said. "What are the odds that when you do find this person, he got his ideas from the very information web we're using to track him down?"

"We're? So we can have the warrant?"

"Give me the timeframes and locations and I will get it ready for you before the end of the day." Uncle Dan winked. "Nice arguments, young lady. I hope it does everything you think it will. It sounds like someone's life may depend on it."

The scene with the finger at the lab this morning had taught me to avoid putting all my hopes on one idea, but this was a good one, and we'd cleared the first hurdle. Sensorvault wasn't widely known even inside law enforcement yet. Which meant chances were decent our killer didn't know to leave his phone at home. And everyone always has their phone.

Graham pulled his out and poked at the screen, calling off the latitude and longitude of parameters for each scene. Was there an app for that? I stood and moved to look over his shoulder. I'll be damned. There was indeed.

"As Faith said, between 11 p.m. Friday and 6 a.m. Saturday for the first location, and then anytime from 5 p.m. May 24 to 9 a.m. May 25 on the second. The oldest one, we need from 4 p.m. April 20 to noon on April 21." Graham fidgeted with the corners of the phone before he returned it to his pocket. Mine buzzed, long and insistent, for the fourth time since we'd walked into Uncle Dan's chambers.

"What?" I muttered, digging it from my pocket and making an apologetic face to Dan when I saw Lieutenant Boone's name flash up. "I'm so sorry; it's my boss." I noted that the three missed calls were, too. "Can you excuse me?"

"I should get back to work, but this has been a lovely—and enlightening—surprise. I learn something new every day, just about, even after all these years. Thank you for being my teachers today. Stay safe out there," Dan dismissed us.

I put the phone to my ear before we were even out of the judge's chambers.

"Answer your damned phone much?" Boone huffed. "I know you're on a fancy special assignment for the governor, but I am still your superior."

"I was in a judge's chambers seeking a warrant, sir," I said. "I picked up the second I could. What can I do for you?"

"It's what I can do for you, though I'm aware I might be complicating your day more than making it," Boone said. I paused in the too-warm hallway, backing into an alcove to get out of the bustle of rushing lawyers and bailiffs.

"Sir?"

"Waco PD just picked up a young woman walking, third degree

sunburn, dehydrated and emaciated. She won't say much, but she's repeated Lindsey Decker's name a half-dozen times."

Shoving off the wall, I took off at a dead sprint, Graham on my heels and manners forgotten, as murmurs rippled through the crowd parting for us.

* * *

I vaulted into the driver's seat of my truck, Graham jumping in on his side. I put the phone on speaker and dropped it into the cupholder before I jammed the key into the ignition and cranked the engine.

"Where'd you say they found her?" I asked.

"I didn't." Boone's voice was tinny and far away on the little speaker, Graham's breath hissing in again as his eyes widened. "That's the other weird thing." Boone cleared his throat. "She was walking straight down the yellow line in the middle of 35 about ten miles north of the city limits. They stopped her because they thought she was on something."

My breath went in sharp enough to make me cough before I thanked him and hung up, turning the car onto the northbound freeway and laying a hand on Graham's knee to let him know I'd explain as soon as I was done weaving through traffic like I was driving for NASCAR.

Walking far enough to get burned that badly aside, tractor trailers fly up and down that flat corridor at more than a hundred miles an hour all day every day.

What the hell would somebody have to be running from to make that look like a good option?

26

Every single bone was visible, though I had to look past the angry indigo-crimson blisters to see them.

I'd spent so many hours staring at photos of Lindsey Decker, I'd recognize her in a crowd before I picked out my own mother. The girl in the hospital bed wasn't Lindsey. I wasn't sure I'd really expected her to be, but the back of my throat burned with disappointment anyway.

"Jesus." Graham walked right into me when I stopped short, the scratchy ER bay curtain curled tight in my fist.

He cleared his throat, nodding to the lanky WPD uniform sprawled in the chair next to the cot. "Eddie."

"Hardin? What the hell are you doing this far outside Travis County?" The guy's long, oval face broke into a grin that exposed big, shiny white teeth when his eyes flicked to me. "I don't believe I've had the pleasure, ma'am." He rose, towering over me and even dwarfing Graham, one hand outstretched. "Eddie Hennings, Waco's finest."

Graham snorted, stepping around me before I could greet his friend. "This is Faith McClellan, Texas Rangers." The words were clipped.

"*The* Faith McClellan?" Eddie returned to his chair without comment on Graham's sudden lack of manners. "I can see why—"

"What are the doctors saying, Eddie?" Graham stepped to the side of the narrow cot in the center of the space.

"Nothing much yet," Eddie said. "They had to put her IV in her chest because they kept blowing her veins. She came to for about twelve seconds, long enough to scream when that happened." He pointed to a gauze dressing on her right forearm. "The nurse went to pick up her arm to try to start an IV to hydrate her and her skin just came right the fuck off." His head shook as he spoke. "She's breathing. They were going to call someone from the burn unit down in Austin, but nobody has come yet."

I swallowed hard, watching her chest rise and fall, my eyes lighting on tiny pinprick purple dots on her left arm, almost lost in the burns. I walked to the other side of the bed and leaned down. Needle tracks. I counted nine.

"Did they run a narcotics panel?" I asked.

"I told Bill she was flying on something when we found her, walking naked down the middle of the road like that," Eddie said. "I just don't know what, and nobody here is getting a blood draw out of her for a while yet."

I rocked back on my heels, forcing myself to take a hard look at the still form in front of me, the soft *whir-click* of the IV pump and low beep of the heart monitor the only sounds in the tiny space.

All of our victims had been naked when they were found.

But that in itself wasn't a link. She didn't have any other wounds that we could see, and we didn't know enough about the situation for me to make assumptions.

Objectivity is a real bitch sometimes.

Impossible to guess her age, with her skin stretched so tight over her bones. Somewhere between fifteen and thirty, which wouldn't even narrow the missing persons database to a zip code, let alone a ballpark.

I shook my head, going back to the arm with the tracks peeking out of the dressing.

"She's not a random junkie."

Eddie returned to his chair, tipping his head to one side. "What makes you say that? It sure seems like she's got all the trappings of one."

I lifted the blanket off the end of the cot to check her feet for tracks and wished I hadn't. Her feet were downright charred, blackened skin curling back in thick layers to reveal muscle and tendon and even bone in a couple of places. My breath hitched in on a sharp hiss.

"Why the hell aren't these dressed?" My fist tightened around the covers.

Eddie grimaced. "I know. The doc who came in when we got here said burns like that are sterile for several hours and he wanted to wait for the specialist. The initial treatment is important, he said, and he ain't ever seen anything like that, not even from accidents at the fertilizer plant or the factory. He didn't want to mess anything up."

Jesus. I got it, but my feet hurt inside my boots just looking at hers. Resolve settled in my gut. Whatever happened to this woman, it wasn't because she was hunting a fix. "You ever seen anything that would mask the kind of pain burns like these would cause, Eddie? She walked on blacktop in the July sun for—what? Hours? Days, maybe?" I settled the cover back in place gingerly. "Any high would've worn off and sent her inside the nearest building." I pointed to her cracked lips. "Absent the burns, she's dehydrated. Stick-skinny. Probably weak as hell. But she was still on her feet when you found her. Right?"

"Yeah, she was."

"She wasn't running after anything," I said. "She was so determined to get away from something she was able to push through pain no human should ever have to endure."

"She puked in the back of my car three times, and she was dry heaving before the doc put her out," Eddie said. "She's dehydrated from that."

"This much sun will do that to a person. But one round of vomiting didn't do this to her."

I stepped to the head of the bed, wanting to brush the fine hair off her forehead but scared to touch her. "What are you afraid of?" I asked her, my voice soft.

Eddie snorted. "We tried every question we could think of. She didn't say a word except the Decker girl's name. And she sure as shit ain't talking to you through all the Demerol they put in her a while ago."

I ignored him. I wasn't expecting an answer. I always talked to my victims, though this was the first time I'd ever seen one who might talk back at some point. And she was a victim, this girl. Her outward injuries might be self-inflicted, but there was no way in blue bloody hell I'd buy that she got them over a fix.

"Did you get prints off her?" Graham asked. I felt him move closer behind me. "We can try to figure out who she is and where she belongs while we wait for her to wake up."

"They're not great, but we're running them," Eddie said. "No hits the last I heard, but that was a half hour ago."

I opened my mouth to ask him to check again when the IV pump next to the bed bleated an alarm. Forgetting Eddie, I turned to the little beige box. Error code 756.

"I'll get someone," Graham said, the words barely hitting the air when the curtain scratched back in its metal track. I pulled my eyes from the girl's face—even her eyelids were burned and swollen, like she'd been walking with her eyes closed—and scooted to the side so the nurse standing behind Graham could get to the pump. She pulled a bag of fluid out of the pocket of her Hello Kitty scrubs and hung it from the metal hook, looping the line through the pump before she straightened the blanket and looked up.

"Afternoon," I said, reaching out to shake her hand. "I'm Faith McClellan, Texas Rangers. Can you tell me when this young woman might be able to speak with us?"

Her clumped-together lashes flickered over soft brown eyes, pink-gloss-slathered lips popping into an "o".

"It's important," I said.

She turned the corners of her mouth down into a tight little frown as her gaze skipped from one badge to the next around the room. "I'm not sure what the doctor has in mind here." Her tone was professional, but short. "I don't have much experience with burn patients, and the expert we called isn't here yet."

She gathered up the empty fluid bag before she stepped past Graham to leave, closing the curtain behind her.

I tipped my head back to look at Graham, my eyes going to his left shoulder before I thought about it. He knew plenty about burn healing times. I'd only seen his scars twice in all the time I'd known him, and he never talked about it.

He didn't recoil, his gaze holding mine for three beats before he flicked his eyes to Eddie and tapped the back of my hand with one finger, our old partner signal for "I've got something I'll tell you later. Hush up for now."

"Did they give you an ETA on the doc?" I asked Eddie.

He shook his head, his eyes on his iPhone screen. "Depends on when she left and the traffic on 35, I suppose."

Graham cleared his throat. "Call me when she gets here? Or if anything changes?"

"Sure, man," Eddie waved the hand not holding the phone, his gaze locked on the screen. "Y'all don't seriously think she knows where that coffee girl is, do you?"

His tone said he was still dismissing this blistered young woman hanging over the threshold of death's door as a crazy junkie. If we hadn't changed his mind yet, we weren't going to.

"Have a good one, Eddie." I slipped through the crack in the curtain in front of Graham. I wasn't telling that dude it was nice to meet him, no matter how deeply my mother had beaten the reflexive phrase into my brain, because it wasn't, particularly.

Back outside the air conditioning, I watched sweat bead on Graham's head and tried to ignore it trickling down my sides under my starched button-down. "They're going to keep her asleep a while, aren't they?" I asked. "I wasn't wrong to leave?"

"If they let her out from under anesthesia before Wednesday I'll shine your boots," he said. "I'd bet my stripes this doctor will want her transferred to the burn unit at University, like yesterday. Looking at her feet, I can't believe they didn't send her already."

I didn't want to think about looking at her feet. My focus was better spent on finding what had pushed her—scared her—into doing that to herself. And what the hell it had to do with Lindsey Decker.

Graham swung one arm toward the truck. "What now?" he asked.

I walked that way, pulling my keys from my jeans pocket. "Starved. Naked. And a desperate desire to get away from something. What if she was running from our serial?"

Graham's boots clomped on the pavement as he chased after me.

"I can't say no, but we don't have enough to say yes, either. We haven't had a victim this far north. And none of the others had needle tracks. You sure you're not reaching because you want to find Lindsey Decker?"

"I'm not sure of that at all. But I've been trying not to see a connection here for three days and it keeps creeping around the edges anyway." I turned left out of the parking lot, away from Rangers HQ.

"Where are we going?"

"The lab. If I have to stage a sit-in, they're running those blood samples for me today."

27

Four weeks of roadblocks and frustration everywhere I'd turned left me utterly unprepared for the file folder a fresh-faced tech named Elena handed me when I asked for a status update on my samples.

"It was in my stack to process out to you today," she said. "It looks like it's been a while. I hope it helps."

I thanked her and flipped the file open. Please God. Something. Anything.

"That's pretty thick for DNA results," Graham said.

I held up one finger, turning pages. "That's because it's all here. Everything I dropped off, all in one place."

I ran my finger down the first page.

"It was blood. And it was hers. The DNA from the side of the dumpster is a match for the toothbrush I swiped from her bathroom."

I needed a chair.

Five weeks of my life poured into my gut telling me somebody took Lindsey that day, and here was proof I was right. I had worked the case like a kidnapping almost from the beginning, and I'd been sure of it since Amarillo PD found blood in Lindsey's car. But irrefutable proof she'd been accosted made it all feel more visceral and urgent.

So what else could the lab tell me?

I looked over Jake's DNA report. He was Lindsey's little boy all right. But none of the rape kits I'd asked to have run against his profile were a match. I was glad to be wrong about that, in a way, but frustrated that I didn't have anything else to go on.

I closed the file, drumming my fingers on the front and raising worried eyes to Graham. "I've been thinking for days now that maybe Lindsey was taken by our friend who's been taking women here. Now we have proof she was kidnapped, violently so. Now we have the naked burn victim who kept saying her name. I think it's worth considering."

"I've been considering it for three weeks, since Archie and I figured out there was such a long span between when our victims were last seen and when they were found," Graham said. "I just haven't found hard evidence that links the two, and in the back of my mind, I still wondered if she'd taken off." He pointed to the folder. "That says she didn't. But I don't think it's time for us to change our focus, either. If we just keep working the other case and she's connected to it, we'll find her."

I wanted to find her alive. But I just nodded, because whether the phantom's next victim was Lindsey or someone else, he was right—stopping anyone else from dying was priority one.

I stood, tucking the folder under my arm. "Let's get after it," I said.

Elena came running out of the double doors leading to the lab. "Officer McClellan? I thought we had everything in your file, but I just found this in the expedited tests." Her brow furrowed. "I didn't see you earl—" She stopped, looking at the top of the page. "Oh wait. This was dropped off by a courier to return to an Officer Baxter." She pointed to the folder under my arm. "May I see that for a moment?"

I obliged, meeting Graham's eyes over her head. He raised his brows. I shook my head. Archie hadn't said a word to me about sending anything to the lab.

Elena looked up. "But it is a match for this sample that you left with us," she said. "A toothbrush belonging to a Lindsey Decker?" She turned her head toward the lab. "Maybe there was a mix up. Can you wait here for a moment?"

"Of course," Graham and I said in sharp harmony.

She disappeared and I pulled out my phone and opened a text to Archie. *Did you send a sample to the lab today?* I typed.

I watched the screen. Delivered. Three seconds. Gray dot bubble.

Buzz. *I did. After you left this morning. Why?*

What was it? Send.

Five seconds. Seven.

My phone buzzed an incoming call, Archie's name and shield flashing on my screen.

"What's up?" I put the phone to my ear.

"I'm confused about how you heard about this."

"I came to the lab to ask about my DNA samples in person, and they had them ready. Then the girl brought me your thing too. She said it was supposed to be in my folder because it matched the toothbrush that belonged to Lindsey Decker. Then she took it all back. I can't figure out why."

Archie sucked in a sharp breath.

Elena reappeared in the doorway with the folders. "The machines were cleaned and calibrated, and these weren't run back to back," she said. "Should I send this along with you, or have the courier take it to Officer Baxter tomorrow?"

Graham put a hand out for the folders. Opened the thin one. "Tissue sample?" He rolled his eyes up to me.

"Want me to bring your labs by?" I asked Archie. "And then you can tell me where you got a tissue sample from Lindsey Decker?" My throat felt tight, strangling the words.

I was pretty sure I already knew.

"The package on Skye's desk this morning." Archie's words made me cringe. "I don't know what you said to her, but she turned up here an hour ago asking me to help hide her. She's still in the conference room. The governor ordered the speedy DNA run in exchange for the station killing her story. Their security video is on its way over, and APD is on standby to haul whoever dropped the package off in for questioning."

I murmured a thank you and touched the red *End* circle.

For weeks, my whole life had been about finding any sort of answer in Lindsey's case.

Having this particular one didn't make me feel better. Lindsey wasn't just taken from the mall. She was being held by a serial killer and missing an ear she might have still had this time yesterday. In trying to stay objective, to avoid assumptions, had I missed signs that would cost little Jake Decker his mother?

28

"*What are you afraid of?*"

The words leaked through the darkness, low whispers swirling all around, whoever said them invisible.

She was used to it. The darkness was familiar. Once terrifying, now almost comfortable.

And she never answered that one.

She wasn't afraid of anything. Not anymore.

Day two sixty-one was the last time He'd so much as laid a finger on her, and He'd never touched her in bad places. It was so much easier to just give herself the shots than to fight. He brought the vials and waited. Whispered about her nightmares. Her story.

She locked her jaw and listened as the whispers drifted away, her eyelids heavy. The screams were always the last thing she heard.

The dark was relentless. Never more than a bit of gray for a couple of hours that helped her mark the days, and sometimes not even that. She counted. Waited. Planned.

Twice, she stuck her arm with empty needles. It was dark, He couldn't see.

Eighteen days.

The new girl had lasted twice as long as any other before her. Too long.

The new girl wasn't special—just smart enough to copycat the silence. But she wasn't sticking around to see if she'd been replaced.

Wherever the others had gone when they vanished, it wasn't good, and she wasn't about to sit in the dark and wait to see it for herself.

He would chase her. Outside her box, where she could find a weapon, she'd be ready for Him.

If the new girl was really smart, she wouldn't stick around to see if He came back.

29

Longish, greasy hair tucked under a gray ball cap, black denim shorts, and a threadbare T-shirt for a band that recorded one album in 1997—that was all we could see of the person who brought the padded yellow envelope containing Lindsey's ear into Channel Two at 7:39 Monday morning.

Archie played the video for the fifth time, slowing it to half speed. "I can't see his face at all," he said. "Certainly not well enough to find him."

I leaned closer to the monitor like that was supposed to help. "Why the hell did the receptionist take this to her? Don't they have protocols for packages? Especially when someone got a finger in the mail last month?"

"Nobody knows that," Graham said. "She opened it long after it was just a skeleton crew in the newsroom for the holiday weekend, and she brought it to me because too many of her colleagues have good sources at the APD."

I shook my head. "I still can't believe she didn't run on a live shot with it, but okay. Still, shouldn't someone be vetting these things?"

"Should? Probably. Doing? Nope," Archie said.

"How do they not have exterior door cameras?" I leaned on the table, not expecting an answer. "If we could see which way he went, or have a longer angle on his face..." I stopped. "Wait. The coffee shop across the street has a camera on their patio."

"APD says no," Archie said, flipping a page on his notepad. "I asked about exterior camera permits for the whole block."

"They may not have a permit, but I know I saw a camera," I said. "I was just there this morning. The angle might be weird, but it's worth a shot."

"You going yourself?" Archie asked.

"I'll go with her," Graham said.

His face told me he was worried. Between the girl in the hospital and Lindsey's ear turning up on Skye's desk, a case that had consumed him for weeks in its theories was suddenly all too real.

"It's just a video request. And it's still light outside," I said.

"You don't want my company?" Graham pretended to look insulted. And my last trip to look at security footage hadn't gone so smoothly.

"You don't do pitiful well." I grabbed my keys. "Come on."

Graham was a good man. I knew that so deep in my bones, anyone who got a marrow transplant from me would know it, too. I wasn't offended by him wanting to keep me safe, even if I thought he was being a little over the top. Things were finally sliding back to easy between us, when our jobs weren't getting in the way. And the sparks I'd noticed back in April hadn't ever lit any sort of a fire, but they hadn't sputtered out, either.

That part was flat-ass maddening when I let myself think about it, which is why I chose not to most of the time. And with both of us up to our eyeballs in dead women, it could wait until we had time to figure it out. I hoped.

We climbed into the truck, my fingers brushing his knee when I went for the shifter and missed. He flinched.

"Sorry," I muttered.

"No need to apologize. I was just thinking. About that girl at the hospital."

I put my hand slowly on his knee, on purpose this time. "You've never told me about that night."

"Not a whole lot for me to tell, really. I don't remember most of it. I was a rookie, three months out of the academy and six off the diamond. Routine traffic stop. I was walking back to my car to run the guy's license and something knocked me to the ground."

Graham was six-four and a former professional baseball player—that in itself was a story. It took strength to take him down.

"I didn't get my wind back before I felt something cold and wet pouring over the back of my shoulder. I thought for a second the guy was pissing on me, but then that wouldn't be cold. I remember because it's the last thought I had before he dropped the match on me, and I don't remember anything after the flames caught but pain until almost a week later."

I reached for his hand without thinking about it, squeezing. After I was assigned as Graham's partner six months into my decade at the TCSO, I finally read the file. Austin PD arrested the driver twelve miles down the road after a doctor on his way to the lake for the weekend had stopped and put the fire out before he called 9-1-1 from his car. Dude had a trunk full of smack, which Graham would've known to look for when he ran the license and saw all the distribution priors. The offender hadn't had a gun, but he did have a full gas can in his trunk and a book of matches in his pocket. He tackled Graham, set him on fire, and left him for dead, and then hadn't even bothered to dump the evidence before the next patrol unit down the freeway spotted him. I hadn't ever asked Graham about it. He kept the scars covered and the memory to himself, and I'd never felt it was my place in all the years we'd spent ten hours a day two feet from one another. Something about watching his face in the ER today and just now left me unable to keep the questions in.

"How long did it take you to heal?" I asked.

"I was out of the burn unit in seventeen days, back at work in a month on restricted duty."

My nose wrinkled at the idea of Graham working at a desk.

"I remember wondering if I would ever be able to get in a patrol car again," he said. "Then you came along."

Huh? I hit the brakes at a red light and turned a loose jaw on him.

He smiled, tucking a wayward lock of hair behind my right ear. "I never told you that, either. But yeah. It was you. Walking in like you owned the place, ready to hunt down killers after what your family had been through. I was in awe of your bravery. I wanted to be like you. So I asked Jameson to pair us up, told him I'd go back to patrol if I could go with you."

I just stared, my lips forgetting how to work.

"That's why I was so pissed when you left. I knew it was better for you, but you...your drive got me back out of the station, working cases, helping people." He shook his head, sitting back in the seat and pulling both hands back into his lap. "I don't think you realize how special you are, Faith. I'm not sure why you don't see it, but I do."

Wow. My ribs expanded with the first breath I'd remembered to take in a while. "Back at you, Hardin."

He leaned forward ever so slightly, his gaze holding mine until there was nothing and nobody in the world but us. This was crazy. We didn't have time for personal entanglements in the middle of all these dead people. But I couldn't tear my eyes away, couldn't move other than to lean right back toward him.

A horn beeped behind us.

Green light.

Probably just as well.

I hit the gas pedal and cleared my throat. Graham let out a nervous laugh. "Didn't mean to go so serious on you, there."

I shook my head. "No apology necessary." I risked a sideways glance and found his cheeks burning peachy-pink under the soft cocoa brown. "Really."

Four minutes later I stopped outside the coffee shop and pointed to the little white camera aimed at their patio but covering the front of the news station in the background. "See?"

"I never doubted you."

He held the door open and waved me inside, following close on my heels and pausing for a half-second, like every good Texan, under the high-powered air conditioning vent over the door.

I asked for a manager and got a wide-eyed nod and an invitation to wait at a table. I chose the one Skye and I occupied that morning.

"Did she look nervous when she saw my badge, or was it just me?" I asked.

"Something was definitely off," he said. "Maybe coffee isn't the only thing they sell here?"

Hmmm. Could be the reason they had an un-permitted camera up outside. I didn't get a reply out before a skinny guy with a man bun appeared from the back room.

I stood.

"What can I do for you, Officers?" he asked.

"We'd like to review the security footage for the camera on the patio. From this morning, between 7:30 and 8."

He blinked. "Camera?" he asked.

"The one in the corner of the patio outside," I said. "Look, I know you don't have a permit and I don't care. Right now I also don't care why. I just need to see if your camera picks up the building across the street, and I need to find a specific person in the feed if it does."

He rocked up on the balls of his feet, balanced there for a three count, and shrugged. "Sure, whatever." He waved us to the back.

"We get sketchy folks around here sometimes," he said, tapping the keys. "The cameras are set up to run overnight, but sometimes that one is on during the day, too. Here you go."

A grainy color image filled the screen. He clicked play.

Graham and I crowded him away from the desk, leaning over the monitor. "The doors are there, but that's a lot of people and cars in between," I murmured, my eyes peeled for the black shorts and gray hat.

We watched in silence for six minutes, the coffee shop manager giving up on small talk when his first couple of questions fell unanswered.

At 7:39, I spotted him. Leaving the building, just a flash of gray hat and stringy hair. "There!" I whirled. "How do I pause this and back it up?"

The manager stepped forward and clicked a few keys. "Like this."

I took over the board, running it back three times. "It's the box truck," I said. "There at the light. We can't see him go in because of the truck. Which doesn't matter so much except that this blue car makes it so we can't see his face when he comes out."

I clicked play, watching the frame until he disappeared to the left.

"You don't happen to know a kid with stringy hair and a gray ball cap, do you?" I asked.

"Can't say that's a familiar one, but there are loads of homeless kids hustling down here every day," he said. "Most of them would do just about anything for a buck, especially one they didn't have to split with a pimp. Just saying."

I slid my eyes to Graham, his tight jaw saying what I was thinking. We could go look, but street people rarely talk to cops, so it probably wasn't worth our time.

I watched the screen until the timestamp got to 8:01, hoping he'd come back.

He didn't. But at 7:59, I saw a face that made me suck a breath in so fast I choked on my own spit. Coughing, I pressed keys. Watched again. A third time.

I stepped to the side and pointed to the screen. "Do you know this guy?" I asked.

The manager craned his neck. "Oh, Adam? Sure. He's been coming in a few mornings a week regular for the past..." He clicked his tongue against the roof of his mouth. "I don't know, couple of months?"

"Any idea where he lives?"

He shook his head. "Nah, I don't get that personal with customers," he said. "I could give him a message next time, though."

I shook my head, thanking him for his help and turning to stride quickly outside.

Graham stayed quiet until we were in the truck.

"That was Lindsey's brother." I started the car. "I'm almost sure of it. He's got a long history of addiction, he disappeared right around the same time Lindsey did, and the manager at the flea hole motel where he lived outside Dallas gave me the impression he was running from someone. He's done a great job of keeping himself hidden—I've run every search I know to run and haven't found so much as a whisper until just now. If Adam Decker is somewhere in Austin, I'm not going to bed until we talk to him."

"I'm in." Graham pulled out his phone. "I'll let Archie know we didn't have any luck with the video."

I pulled back into traffic. "Where's your seediest motel? We'll start there."

30

Adam Decker seemed to nomad between shitholes of the lowest order, unusual for a kid from the pruned-garden and white-picket-fence suburbs.

The woman behind the counter at the Stop n' Sleep off Highway 28 was way less interested in protecting Adam's privacy than getting Graham and me out of her line of sight. I probably could have gotten a key with the room number, but I didn't want to push my luck.

I drummed my fingers on the bottom of the worn leather steering wheel in my truck, staring at the door with the red-stenciled 236 on the yellow paint, everything I knew about Lindsey and the three dead women playing on a loop in my head.

"I feel like we're missing variables here," I said. "We've looked through everything for a connection between these women and can't find one. The guy at the other motel hinted that Adam Decker was at least in with a trafficker, and I know it's not uncommon for junkies desperate for a fix to lure girls into that cesspool. But nothing about the rest of it fits. Let's say Adam sold Lindsey to a trafficker. Then how did she end up with our killer?"

Graham shifted in his seat. "And, I mean…his own sister?" He winced. "When you deal in a world like that, you know what happens to the victims."

"It also doesn't explain the others. I've seen reports of teenage girls from the suburbs getting trapped in that cycle, but successful professional women? Nobody bought the other three victims." I reached for the door handle. "Let's go see what the hell is going on."

"He might not be here," Graham cautioned, pushing his door open and striding to the front of the truck.

True. I didn't see a car. "Damned shame if he's not, wouldn't it be?" I winked.

"You cannot search this guy's place without a warrant, Faith." The words were muttered low and tight, just enough to carry to my ears, but not a centimeter past. Graham was the master of low, private speech, even in a crowd.

I rolled my eyes. He was also the king of by-the-book. "Hotels aren't residences," I said. "I bet she'd even give us a key."

He shook his head. "She wasn't arguing with us over his room number, but if you can find someone who runs a joint like this and wants a reputation for letting the cops into the rooms, I'll buy drinks for a year."

I hated it when he was right, and even more when he was smug about it. If I found something in there that proved Decker was the mastermind behind the whole thing, he might not go to jail because I didn't have a warrant and I wasn't the owner. The thing was, right then, I cared more about finding Lindsey than anything else, and I didn't think Adam Decker was smart enough to be our killer. He might know our killer, but I wouldn't be shocked if he didn't realize it if he did.

"Whatever this guy is, he's not in charge of jack shit," I said. "He's no mastermind, and traffickers sell humans for the money. Adam is definitely not making the money if he's living here." I started for the door. "Let's just give it a knock and see what happens."

Graham walked beside me to the door. After half a lifetime studying what makes the evils of our little corner of the world tick, I knew a good man was in the little things: the way he listened even when he didn't want to, or shortened his stride to walk beside me when his legs are half a foot longer and it would be so easy for him to take the macho road.

I raised my fist and rapped hard three times, the hollow plywood amplifying the sound with an echo as the lightweight wood rocked loose in the frame.

Graham's hand went to his sidearm.

We didn't dare breathe too loud, watching the door and the curtains in the window to one side of it.

Not a twitch.

I knocked again. "Adam? Please open the door if you're able."

"No judge anywhere is going to buy that this was a welfare check," Graham muttered.

I knew that. I didn't care, though.

I waited thirty seconds and tried the handle. Unlocked.

"What do you know?" I asked, pushing the door open.

"Faith," Graham began in an I'm-losing-my-patience voice. I didn't wait to hear the rest of it.

Adam Decker was seizing, his body coming up off the bed with the convulsions, a rubber tube still slack around his bicep and a hypodermic that looked like it had seen cleaner days hanging from his arm.

I took the distance from the door to the bed in a long leap. Hurling the needle in the general direction of the bathroom, I straddled Adam's thin, sunken chest and put my hands on his shoulders. His eyes were rolled so far back I could only see bloodshot whites, yellowing foam collecting in the corners of his open mouth as his skin went from pale to bluish.

He was trying to swallow his tongue.

I heard Graham summoning paramedics behind me. "I need something to keep his airway clear," I said, barely hearing the words over the blood rushing in my ears.

Graham grabbed a spoon from the nightstand and thrust it at me, tucking his phone back into his pocket. "This is all I got."

Gross. I wiped it on my jeans and nodded to Adam's shoulders. "Hold him."

Graham put one big hand squarely in the center of Adam's chest and one over his forehead. "Go."

I wedged the spoon between the roof of Adam's mouth and his tongue, careful to keep my fingers clear of his teeth. Pushing hard, I managed to return his tongue to its proper place and hold it there, restoring his airway. His chest heaved under Graham's grip.

"That's it, kid. Breathe," I muttered, holding the spoon in place.

I heard sirens in the distance. Even if we could keep Lindsey's brother from dying, he wouldn't be able to tell us anything tonight. And I was running out of places to look for the lead that would tell me how to save her.

We had twenty-nine hours until the Fourth.

31

I leaned on Graham's shoulder, watching the medics load Adam into the back of a blue and white ambulance.

"Damn," I said as they shut the doors and took off.

Graham turned. "Shall we see what he took?"

"Too much of something, it looked like." I shook my head. "Not sure the spoon will help us, but we can try."

I surveyed the room, spotting a small plastic baggie peeking out from under the edge of the bed. "Here." I retrieved it.

There wasn't much powder left, but probably enough for a lab to analyze. Someday, anyway. "I wonder if Archie can call in any more favors from the governor?"

Graham took the bag and sealed the spoon inside it. "Only one way to find out."

I handed him the keys to my truck. "You feel like driving back?" I asked.

His eyebrows shot to his hairline. "How come? You okay?"

"I just want to think this through, and it's a ways back to headquarters," I said. "We're missing something, Graham. And if we don't figure out what, Lindsey Decker is going to die."

He laid a light touch on the small of my back to usher me out the door. "We'll find it," he said. "The Fourth isn't for two days, if your holiday theory is right. And those bodies were all pretty fresh when they were found. The writing wouldn't have been easy to read if they hadn't been."

His phone bleated and he held up one finger. "Hardin."

He stepped away. I tuned out his end of the conversation, surveying the parking lot of the motel, empty save for my truck and a small Mazda sedan outside the office, which I assumed belonged to the manager.

It had been almost seven weeks since Lindsey was taken. She could be anywhere. Before full-blown panic could set in, Graham was back. "Eddie got an ID on the girl with the feet," he said. "Britney Teague. Twenty-five, two possession priors, works for CPS in Austin."

My breath caught. "How long has she been missing?"

"Since Memorial Day. She's being transferred to University in Austin, they have the best burn unit in the state. Still out cold, according to Eddie, until at least tomorrow, and likely longer." He patted my shoulder. "Sorry. I figured as much."

I nodded, already walking to the truck. I still didn't buy that a fix had put her on that road. My gut said she had been where Lindsey was.

* * *

We were ten minutes from headquarters, running a list back and forth of everything we knew about the case, when Graham stopped at a red light.

"There has to be a link between these women," I said. "Lindsey didn't live around here. For all the hell I know she'd never even driven through here. Her car was found four hundred miles away, the other direction from where she disappeared. And now her ear turns up on Skye's desk. Not a damned thing about that makes any sense at all."

"A lawyer, a minister, a computer geek, a coffee waitress, and a journalist." Graham ticked them off on his fingers. "I can't figure it out."

I drummed my fingers on the door. "The geography just keeps getting wider. First San Antonio, then Travis County, then New Braunfels, and now the south Dallas suburbs?"

"It seems too big to be random, but aren't they almost always? Serials pick victims based on obscure stuff. It's part of the reason the term terrifies people the way it does."

I stopped drumming. "But a serial killer is driven by the kill itself above anything else. The drive is to avoid getting caught so they can stay out of prison so they can keep killing. That part doesn't fit with the body bits being delivered to Skye. What if it's not our attention the killer wants, but hers? Is he warning her? Did anyone check to see if the victims we have so far got packages in the weeks prior to their disappearance?"

Graham parked the truck in the lot at headquarters as the inky indigo twilight faded to dark. "Not that I know of."

"That DNA sample I got back this morning confirmed that Lindsey Decker was taken from a public place in broad fucking daylight, Graham. This guy is targeting these women for a reason, and he wanted Lindsey badly enough to risk getting caught, but he didn't want to take her from her home like he has all the others."

"Because of the kid?"

"I can't point to another reason. It's a weird code that murderers live by. Children are a bridge too far for a lot of folks who will cheerfully bash in the skull of a grown woman."

"So then we're still trying to figure out why he wanted her." Graham shook his head. "Why do I feel like we're kind of running in big circles?"

"Because we have been. We've resisted the idea of looking for patterns because serials don't often have them, but I think our guy is different. This is a mission. Which means he has a motive. I'm wondering if he's hiding under a rock I've been looking at for weeks without knowing it was special. I know Lindsey Decker better than we've gotten a chance to know any other victim in this case. And if the killer wanted her that badly, it almost has to be someone in her world. Someone I've looked at. I think."

Graham pulled the door open and waved me through. "So let's borrow your suspect list and see if something fits."

32

Lindsey had a handful of people in her life who might want to hurt her, but nowhere on my list could we find anyone with motive to harm any of the other victims.

Three hours closer to midnight, I looked up from a computer screen that was going blurry despite my best efforts. I knew why Darla Worthington hated Lindsey, and I could buy that she'd even paid someone to grab her so she'd have an alibi. But the computer couldn't link her—or her husband—to any of the other victims. Adam Decker was in a coma, but still breathing, but Daphne Livingston had never prosecuted a charge he was brought up on, and I wasn't sure he'd ever stepped foot in a church or watched a newscast. Sebastian the security guard wasn't strong enough to have carried Ramona Mathers to the river, and had no connection to her or either of the other victims. Plus, his boss had video confirming he was on the other side of the mall when Lindsey was taken.

"Strike three," I said.

Archie looked up from his screen. "It seems our Jane Doe from the oil field was a badge. Annmarie Hernandez, 28, Amarillo PD. There's no DNA to match to anyone here, but they found the profile from the victim in the lab files in El Paso and sent it to me this morning, and that's the match, double checked through the law enforcement database."

A cop. I met Graham's eyes over the top of my screen. I knew what he was thinking. "It has to be something to do with them being helpers," I said. "A pastor, a prosecutor, a cop." I looked at Skye, who was still lurking, claiming asylum, and forced more words out. "A journalist. Lindsey did volunteer work..." I trailed off.

I hadn't looked there because in my head, Lindsey and Ramona were the odd women out of the equation. But Adam had ties to shady people. I'd gone to the shelter looking for a path from Lindsey to the same kind of shady people, but I hadn't found a clear road. And then I'd gotten side-tracked by the apparent randomness of our serial killer.

Sometimes the best way to solve an equation is to isolate difficult variables.

"If we leave Ramona Mathers out of this until we know more, we have a link between the rest—they all worked to help others in some capacity. We know Daphne Livingston hadn't had anyone released from prison lately, but now we have a cop in the mix. Did Hernandez ever work anywhere besides Amarillo?"

Archie tapped keys. "San Antonio. Says she was terminated with cause, doesn't say why."

I reached for my phone. "I may know somebody who can tell us." I dialed Sheriff Carl Benson.

He picked up on the third ring. "Sheriff, I'm so sorry to call so late—it's Faith McClellan with the Rangers. I'm wondering if you can tell me anything about an Officer Annmarie Hernandez from Amarillo."

He cleared his throat. "Isn't she the one who got busted falsifying evidence in San Antonio to try to help out the DA? I remember it being a big dust-up when the chief over in Amarillo hired her. Even a year later the officers' association didn't want her there and they threatened a walkout. But he was determined that she wasn't a bad cop and wanted to give her another chance."

I scribbled every word as fast as my hand would move, my brain stuck on "DA."

He paused. Yawning, maybe. "I think she just picked up and disappeared one day, if I remember right," he said. "Seemed most of their department thought it was good riddance. There are some things people can be awfully damned unforgiving about. What makes you ask?"

I pulled in a deep breath. "I think maybe she didn't pick up and disappear." I kept my voice light, my pen tapping. "Did you happen to get the labs back from Lindsey Decker's car yet?" I had asked him to call, but he might have forgotten.

"Tomorrow, they said. I had it on my list to call you and find out where to send them in the morning."

I reeled off my email address and confirmed when he repeated it. "Thank you so much, sir."

I hung up and jumped to my feet, pacing. He didn't say which DA. But it had to be Daphne.

I turned to Archie. "See what you can find on a case in Bexar County"—I counted on my fingers—"four or five years ago, a mistrial due to falsified evidence from the PD."

I clapped my hands and turned. "Skye. May I borrow you for a moment?" I asked.

Archie and Graham fixed wide eyes on me. Even Skye's mouth popped. In three ticks it was replaced by a curious, confident smirk. "Of course, Ranger." She couldn't help the derisive little sneer on the last word. It was like a defensive reflex that came out every time she spoke to me. She wasn't getting a rise out of me today, though. I'd just realized something about Skye—right then, I needed her to get Lindsey back.

I shooed her into the conference room and shut the door, leaning against it. "You told me this morning that you and Daphne were friends once, but not anymore. Why?"

She looked at the table. "I did a story she didn't come off so well in," she said. "A few years ago, now, but she was angry, and she never talked to me again."

"Was it falsified evidence?" I couldn't sit still, standing to pace. Skye didn't watch.

"No. Daphne wouldn't have been party to something like that. My piece was on a RICO bust, a clearinghouse for every kind of illegal anything you can name that somebody would want to buy. Internet thing. There were multiple defendants, but the lead one had Corey Moats behind the defense table." Damn. That guy was my generation's answer to Racehorse Haynes, the legendary Texas defense attorney who could help folks get away with actual murder if they had enough cash. "Daphne wanted that win," Skye continued, "both because the guy was a scumbag and because she wanted to beat Corey. She screwed up and signed off on a plea bargain for a lesser defendant that violated the state sentencing statutes, and Corey called it abuse and had a mistrial declared."

Shit. "And double jeopardy still applies there," I said.

"Right. She wasn't actually mad at me. She was mad because he walked and they had to start over. They got him the next time, but it wasn't her case, and my story just rubbed salt in the wound." Skye shrugged, a sad half-smile playing around the corners of her lips. "So I lost a friend. Part of the job, sometimes."

That whole story sucked on a lot of levels. But it wasn't the one I was looking for.

I stuck my head out the door. "Archie. Anything Hernandez and Livingston both worked on?"

He shook his head. "I'm trying, but not so far."

I went back to Skye. "You knew Daphne Livingston," I said. "What about the others?"

Skye shook her head. "I would have told you if I knew any of the rest of them," she said. "I mean, I have heard of Stephanie Allen; we did a feature on her shelter program last spring."

"Homeless shelter?"

Skye shook her head. "No, it was a sort of halfway house for victims of human trafficking. Admirable work."

I grabbed a legal pad from the credenza, drawing a chart. "Does that mean something?" Skye asked.

"Maybe. The latest victim, she volunteered at a trafficking shelter in Dallas for a long time. Maybe they knew each other that way." I tapped a pen on the paper and spun for the door, returning a minute later with my laptop.

Google. Daphne Livingston and trafficking. Go.

I scrolled past three articles and two case file numbers to get to the images.

The fourth photo was of Daphne, posing and smiling in a long red evening gown next to a tuxedoed Miles Marland.

I sat back in the chair.

Surely not.

"Skye? What do you know about Miles Marland?"

"More money than God, fond of credit for the philanthropy he does to get tax write-offs, gets gropey when he's had one too many." She made a face. "He's kind of a creep. He's not a serial killer."

"But you know him? Have you seen him lately? Around the station, even?"

She shook her head. "They stay in their Dallas circle unless something to do with drilling is in front of the legislature. Why?"

I shook my head and typed in Stephanie Allen's name with Marland's after it.

Four photos, all from the *Statesman*'s society page, a fundraiser for the shelter.

I scrutinized each image. A smiling Stephanie Allen toasting Marland. The two of them sitting at a dinner table with Emberly Marland and Daphne Livingston and six other...oh, hell.

I zoomed in on the guy to Marland's right. Pretty sure he was Jim's strangulation victim. Variables shifted around Jim's voice echoing in my head. *A fifteen-year-old girl.*

Damn. I had talked to Miles Marland. Smiled at his borderline degrading jokes about his wife's work, even, because she laughed and it was the polite thing to do. My father knew way more than anyone's share of assholes, and I'd perfected the art of polite deflection and dismissal before I needed a training bra.

I typed the third victim, Ramona Mathers, and Marland.

No results.

"But she wasn't a public figure. Just because Google doesn't know he knew her, doesn't mean he didn't," I said, logging into the criminal records database and typing his name. "Google doesn't know he knew Lindsey, either."

The search wheel spun, and I yelped when the results came up.

He had a record.

"What?" Skye asked.

"Nothing." I shushed her. "Stay here."

I hopped out of the chair and half-ran back to Archie's desk. "Miles Marland."

"Like Marland Oil? You're kidding. Do you know how many armies of lawyers that guy has? No judge in Texas will give you a warrant to so much as breathe on him without video of him committing a murder, and even then, I think it depends on the judge."

"He knew them all. Well, I can prove three of our five, and just because the internet doesn't know he knew Ramona doesn't mean he didn't."

"How did all the victims know Dallas's real life JR Ewing?" Graham asked.

"Through his wife's charity work."

Archie scratched his head. "Huh?"

I closed my eyes, rubbing my temple with two fingers. "We've been driving ourselves crazy for days combing through these women's lives looking for a connection, and here it is. He has one violent prior for domestic assault on his first wife."

"Faith." I opened my eyes to sympathy rolling off Archie's face. "I know you can hear how thin that's going to sound to a judge. There's no way a guy with Marland's money and connections even comes in for questioning on a couple of pictures and an ancient charge. I'm not saying you're wrong, I'm saying if you believe you're on the right trail, build yourself a case."

I grabbed a marker and found a blank whiteboard. What did I know?

He knew at least three of the victims in some way.

Those same three were trying to help human trafficking victims. Lindsey's friend Maggie said Lindsey was working on a degree in social work to get paid for what she'd loved doing as a volunteer.

Marland had a whole lot of money and a whole lot of privilege, and wasn't shy about running his mouth.

Annmarie Hernandez worked in Amarillo, and she'd gone there to try to rebuild her reputation. Amarillo was the edge of oil country. Her body was found hundreds of miles away in an oil field.

"Do you see anything on trafficking in Officer Hernandez's background?" I asked, not taking my eyes from the board. I wasn't sure I trusted the idea forming in the back of my brain.

"Looking," Archie said. I heard paper turning. "I'll be damned. Yeah, she was lead investigator on a trafficking ring bust, the arrests were made about ten months before she went missing. How did you know that?"

I didn't answer right away. The photos were taken at a benefit. "Skye!" I hollered.

She appeared in the doorway to the conference room.

"Did Daphne Livingston ever successfully prosecute a human trafficker?"

"She was on a state special committee to study how to put a stop to it," Skye said. "So probably. But not that I ever covered."

The committee would do.

I noted that on the board before I turned back to Archie. "What if Miles Marland is into human trafficking?"

Saying it out loud made it sound at once more real and more ridiculous. Why would someone with Marland's money and influence slink into the seediest criminal underbelly there was?

I swept an arm toward the board. "All of these women, except Ramona, have provable ties to something that stops traffickers or helps their victims, right?" I talked faster, my voice picking up speed as the idea gained momentum. "And the paper has a photo of him having dinner with a guy who died while he was having sex with an underage girl. So what if Marland is methodically knocking off obstacles to his depraved side hustle?"

"Why would he be carving them up? Prescott said the woman from the river was drained of blood. If he's just looking at them as collateral damage, like a cost of doing this particular business, what would he have to gain by doing that?"

"Not getting caught, apparently," I said. "If—and I realize it's a big 'if' right this minute—if he killed Officer Hernandez, he murdered a cop and he's gotten away with it for two years. Guys like Marland have egos bigger than their Stetsons. That's a hell of an ego boost. So he gets braver, but he didn't get where he is in business by being stupid. Two years to study this game and choose an MO that looks random unless you know exactly where to look for the connection. How many unsolved serials are sitting in cold case rooms all over the damned country because it's always harder to figure it out when there's not a trail to follow?"

Graham stood. "I don't hate this," he said.

"And the victims were all fighting trafficking, but it's not like they wore capes advertising it. It was a byproduct of the higher-profile jobs they had. Jobs that don't seem all that connected on the surface."

"Lindsey Decker was a volunteer."

"But she was going to school to be a social worker."

"How would Marland know that?" Archie asked.

I shrugged. "Passing conversat—" I clapped a hand over my mouth.

Maggie said she couldn't figure out how Lindsey was paying for school.

The hard look I thought I'd imagined on Emberly Marland's face when I mentioned Lindsey.

"What?" Skye screeched it.

"The kid. She wouldn't tell anyone who his father is," I said. "I thought it might be because she was assaulted, I even ran the little boy's DNA against rape kits, but it didn't get me anywhere. What if it's because his father is Miles Marland?"

33

Making a deal with the devil always pays off in the short term. With the clock ticking louder on Lindsey's life every minute, I didn't have time for the luxury of considering the long term.

We needed an extra person who knew where to dig up dirt, and Skye Morrow was the biggest muckraker south of the Mason-Dixon. She was also invested in this up to her perfectly threaded eyebrows.

"Nothing is more important to men like Miles Marland than their money," I said. "They cheat for it, they steal it in the most technically legal fashion, and some of them might be willing to kill for it. We need to figure out if Miles is losing money somewhere that might have sent him looking for a way to make it back fast."

"Do you know how many mountains of financial records a guy like Marland has?" Archie asked. "And that statement is even predicated on me assuming you can get into them without a warrant, which I don't want to know about if you can."

I wrinkled my nose. "My lips are sealed."

It was late, but adrenaline had my energy level through the roof. We had a focus. I had a lead. For the first time in more than a month, I felt like I was actually doing work that might get us somewhere.

"Skye?" I turned to her. "You in?"

I hadn't looked at her since I called her back into the room. She was pale, hovering in the doorway, trembling head to expensive designer heels. "I did a story last winter," she said. "An exposé on a trafficking ring running out of one of the shopping malls in Round Rock. Cute boys being paid to pick up teenage girls and get compromising video they would use to blackmail them into turning tricks. People think it's all immigrant sex slave labor, which makes it easier for these assholes to hide, sadly. Sometimes it is, but this kind of trafficking young American girls is spreading like wildfire."

"So I've heard. Did your story lead to an investigation?"

"APD brought in three traffickers a week later." Her voice faded to a whisper at the end. "Oh my God, he does want to kill me."

"You're safe here with us," I said. My oath was to protect and serve every Texan. "Want to help?"

She gestured to the files and photos on the table behind her. "You seriously think Miles Marland could be party to something this horrifying?"

I snorted. "Absolutely. But just because I think he could doesn't mean he is. Archie's right. We need proof."

"Can I ask an obvious question?" That was Graham, back in his seat near Archie.

I turned. "Shoot."

"How would a guy like Miles Marland get into this in the first place? These aren't the kind of people you'd think a guy like him would know."

"Marland is a businessman, through and through. If he's in this, he got the idea from his wife's charity. She runs the victims' shelter where Lindsey volunteered. A guy like Marland, seeing all those girls, knowing why they were there—I kind of feel like that would look to him like printing money."

"So is the charity a front? Are people disappearing from there, going back into the trade?" Archie asked.

I hadn't considered that. But Lindsey's dismissal and Emberly's comments about the recipient of the contraband phone swirled up from my memory. "No. The wife was way too earnest. She even knows exactly how many victims they've helped. She sees throwaway people as valuable, healable. If someone went missing from her shelter, I have a feeling she'd track them down. Skye's suburban victims aside, traffickers prey on people society likes to overlook. That's how they thrive. It's not about hiding, it's about choosing victims people don't see."

Skye stepped forward. "If I could have a computer, I can get to work on his financials," she said. "You're not the only one with ethically questionable computer skills."

Archie pointed to a vacant desk. "Knock yourself out. I'll be over here ignoring you."

Skye squared her shoulders, took the seat, and opened the computer.

I turned back to the board. It was decent. But not perfect. There was a victim out of order—Ramona didn't fit the theory. That we'd seen, anyway. I went back to the conference room after my laptop, my phone buzzing a call when I got halfway to the door.

I raised it to my ear. "McClellan," I said.

"It seems your hunches pay off, young lady," Uncle Dan replied. "This report from the phone tracking net has one number at two of the three locations you gave me."

Hot damn. That right there would at least bring someone in for questioning. "Does it say who it belongs to?" I held my breath.

"Not yet, but I requested it. I just saw this, they sent the file right at 5 Pacific time, so it'll be tomorrow, but I'll let you know when I have it. Nice work, Officer."

"Only if it comes through," I said. "Thank you for your help, sir."

"Anytime. We'll talk tomorrow."

I sat down in front of my computer and opened it, not sure tomorrow was good enough. But if we could build a case against Marland and then the warrant put his phone at the dump sites, we'd have him locked up before he could say "easy money."

I opened every file we'd amassed on Ramona Mathers's life.

All her children were grown, her youngest off at college just this past fall and spending the summer studying abroad. Widowed at forty, she'd never remarried. She'd been smart with her husband's life insurance money and hadn't had to return to work.

Nothing that would make her a target with the pattern I had worked out.

I clicked over to Google. Typed in her name.

The fourth result was a website. Click.

"She was a freelance web platform designer." I scrolled down the testimonials. "It looks like since about 2015." It still didn't fit. I clicked to the work samples page. Nothing jumped at me. Clients? Nothing to do with fighting trafficking, law enforcement, or charities. Damn.

I sat back in the chair.

"Nothing?" Archie asked.

"Not anything I can see yet, anyway," I said. "But if it's him, we'll figure her out later—this is spinning wheels we don't have time to spin today. Can we put Marland in Amarillo around the time Officer Hernandez disappeared?"

"Let me see what I can find in credit card activity," Graham said.

"I'll take traffic cams."

"When did she disappear, Archie?" Graham asked.

He rustled papers. "Reported July 7, 2016. She didn't come to work two days in a row, and her partner went to do a welfare check."

I was already logging into the traffic cameras on one window. I opened another and pulled DPS records for cars registered to Marland at that time. There were four.

I copied the first plate number and plugged it in. Watched the wheel spin in the center of my screen.

Nothing.

Next. Nope.

The third one got a hit.

I leaned closer to the screen, the grainy image shittier than normal thanks to night vision. I checked the plate number twice.

"He was there. I have his pickup running a light on Cordova Avenue at just past midnight on July 5."

Archie ambled over. "But you can't see him." He leaned over my shoulder.

"Not in the dark, no."

"Did he report that vehicle stolen at any point?"

I rolled my eyes. "I didn't look."

"A judge is going to," he said. "We have to dot every 'i' here."

"I know." I opened another window and went to statewide auto theft. Entered my DPS credentials. Plate number. VIN number. Owner name. Go.

The wheel spun for what felt like a hundred years before the "no results found" appeared on the screen.

I turned a triumphant grin on Archie. "This is our guy," I said.

"You have nothing concrete yet." He patted my shoulder. "But I'll give you it's not a good look for him."

I took a screenshot of the page and spun my chair to face Graham. "Uncle Dan got a hit. Two of the sites we gave him, same phone. He's calling for registration information tomorrow."

"That sounds like the best news I've heard in a while."

"You're smarter than I would have given you credit for." Skye's voice was quiet but clear as she turned from her screen. "Miles Marland is overextended. Like pulled limb from limb on a rack overextended. Communications from his attorney show that four years ago, he was seriously considering filing Chapter 11. He sold off some property, but that didn't make him enough money to stave it off, from what I can see."

"But he didn't file?"

"Nope. There's a cash influx beginning in November 2015 that has grown steadily and been enough to cover his debt payments, but not pay it down." Skye looked at me. "And he's been writing checks to UT Dallas for three semesters now."

I looked around the room. "Anyone still have objections?"

"It's the surest trail we've found yet," Archie said. "Let's see where it goes."

"If it's his phone, I can have an arrest warrant tomorrow," I said.

Archie stood. "I'd call this an excellent day's effort, ladies and gentlemen. And I'm ready to call it a day."

Skye popped to her feet, alarmed.

I crooked a finger at her. "I'm headed to the Doubletree on South Congress. Why don't you come check in there for the night, too?"

I wasn't sharing a room with her, but I'd stay next door. "You can get the room next to mine. Just until we're sure what's happening here."

Skye's forehead wrinkled as much as the Botox would let it. "Thank you." It was the most subdued I'd ever heard her.

She went to the conference room to retrieve her briefcase and Archie reached for my forehead. "Are you feeling all right?"

"What if it's him?" I murmured. "You heard what she said about the story she did on the suburban thing. Is leaving her at home unguarded any better than just pulling the trigger myself?" I shook my head.

"This is above and beyond, kid." Archie squeezed my arm. "You're a good person."

Archie was the only person breathing who understood how much I loathed Skye Morrow.

He had been at the lake that day, issued the orders that they couldn't move my sister until he arrived on the scene. He had loved Charity as much as he loved me. He knew better than anyone how horrific her death had truly been. Because even Skye Morrow's covertly captured video images of my big sister's shredded, pummeled corpse tossed at the edge of the water like garbage, which the whole fucking world except Graham, apparently, had seen a half-dozen times, had nothing on Archie's memory. Anything for a scoop—Skye should have had that tattooed on her somewhere. I could never forgive her for some of the things she'd put my family through, but it wasn't in me to leave her to the wolves, either.

And if I helped Skye, maybe karma would help me out with Lindsey. I knew by the way Archie's jaw had been tight all day that he felt it, too. We had to save Lindsey. Because we hadn't saved Charity.

34

Jeans and boots still on, I fell into the bed after tucking Skye into her room with instructions to lock every deadbolt.

"This might be the Mondayest Monday ever," I said to the popcorn ceiling.

My phone buzzed on the night table. Not a number I knew.

"McClellan."

"Ranger McClellan, it's Kendra Avery from Rock Harbor Animal Clinic. I'm so sorry about the late hour, I was planning to leave you a message because I just had a chance to sit down and look at these lab results, and... well, I've never seen anything like this."

She said she was going to have labs run from the coyote. I sat up. "You didn't wake me. Thanks for remembering to call."

"Of course," she said. "So, this poor animal you brought me never had a chance. This tissue in her gut died because she was suffering from methemoglobinemia, which is a new one on me. I had to look it up." She paused.

I waited three beats. "I'm afraid it's a new one on me, too."

"Sorry—I was reading this result again." Her words tripped out in a rush. "I...yeah. So, this happens to animals and people when they ingest a large quantity of sodium nitrate. Or a high concentration of it, Google is telling me. It's why her blood was so dark and thick. I know you said your missing woman was feeding her. What was she feeding her?"

"Deli sandwiches. Isn't meat treated with sodium nitrate?"

Her tongue clicked against the roof of her mouth. "Not enough to do this. I'm looking at the content, and even with the blockage, I think her intestine would have ruptured if she'd eaten enough bologna to cause this. Plus, there was nothing in her colon above it."

I closed my eyes, Sebastian's voice whispering in my head. "*Dude digging in the dumpster.*"

I switched the call to speaker and opened Google myself. Three clicks left me staring at my screen. Deli meat wasn't the only thing sodium nitrate was used to preserve.

"Doctor Avery, you're saying the thing you gave me was the last thing this animal ate?" I asked.

"I think so, yes." Papers rustled. "I can't find anything in my notes about other food matter, and I would have noted that."

"Thank you so much for your help," I said. "Nice talking to you again, have a great evening."

I clicked end, my fingers shaking as I touched Jim's name in my favorites list.

No way.

But what if?

"Faith? Is everything okay?" He picked up on the second ring and didn't sound like I'd woken him.

"Please tell me you didn't throw out that specimen I left you." I closed my fingers around Charity's charm bracelet.

"Not mine to throw out," he said. "What's up?"

"I think it is a finger. A mummified one coated in something." It sounded insane even to my ears, but damned if it didn't make perfect sense in the most bizarre way.

"You think what?"

"The vet called. The coyote had some fancy-sounding word for sodium nitrate poisoning. You can use sodium nitrate, a lot of it, to preserve body parts, right?" My breath was coming way too fast.

"You can." Jim coughed. "So you think this animal found and ate a piece of a mummy wearing a ring that someone was just carrying at a shopping mall?"

"You can put the psych ward on hold. I know how it sounds. What I think is that the person who took Lindsey Decker is cutting people's fingers off and preserving them, and he had that one in his pocket or something. The guard said he chased off a dumpster diver a few nights later." I wondered if Officer Hernandez had a ring that was significant.

"And you think it was the kidnapper coming back to look for his gross, mummified body part? That an animal ate."

"Lindsey had been feeding her deli sandwiches, right? So on some level through the rubber it probably smelled like her food, and their noses are pretty keen." The more I talked, the more logical the whole thing sounded.

"You know, as fucked up as this sounds, I can see it, especially after what I had on my table today." Jim sighed. "Okay. What can I do for you?"

"Is there any chance you might be able to get even a partial workable DNA sample from it? We have an in at the governor's office this week if you can just get me something the lab can run."

"Shit, I don't know," Jim said. "I read a journal article a while back about some guys in London pulling ancient DNA, but this is the first mummy I've come across in all my years here. I'll say this, just when you think you've seen every damn thing in this line of work, there's something weirder. I'll give it a shot and let you know in the morning."

"Thanks, Jim."

I dropped the phone back to the table. At least now I knew where their fingers were going. Did Marland just carry them around with him? Because, ew. I shook my head at the little voice that whispered about Lindsey's other ear.

It was after midnight. My alarm was going to go off in what would feel like ten minutes. And we had one hell of a big day coming tomorrow.

* * *

Five. It felt like five minutes later that I awoke to my phone ringing.

"Jim. Why are you already at work?" I said through thick, cottony layers of hard sleep, trying to blink enough to make my eyes work.

"I couldn't sleep, thinking about your nutball theory, so I came to check out the science. I'm not sure I believe I'm saying this, but I figured you'd want to know you were right. This is a preserved human finger. I think I might have figured out how to get a DNA sample out of it, but I won't know if it worked until we get results from the lab. Who do you want me to send it to?"

What was that girl's name?

"Elena," I said, my voice hoarse and still slow. "Send it to Elena at the lab here. I'll get Archie on with the governor. Thank you—you go on home to Sheila and get some rest."

"I have three corpses lined up before lunch," he said. "You think this might help you get this guy?"

If we could get a warrant, it wouldn't hurt.

"I do. You're my hero, Jim." That sounded more normal, the fog in my head clearing a bit.

"Back at you, hon. Sorry I woke you."

"Nah. I need to get my ass in gear. I can sleep after we save the day."

I padded in my bare feet to the coffee maker. When it was burbling caffeine into a little paper cup, I unlocked my door and poked my head into the hallway. Empty. Turning the lock to prop my door open, I went to Skye's. Three sharp raps later, she opened it, though if I hadn't watched her go in the night before, I wouldn't have believed it was her. Her eyes peered out of twin blue-green hollows, her makeup-free face lined and tired. Only her hair looked like TV Skye—blonde and gleaming and practically unruffled at not even 6 a.m.

"Morning," I said. "I'm going to head out shortly. Just making sure you're okay. I would call in from work today and stay here with the doors locked if I were you."

I turned back for my door before the last word was out.

"Thank you," she said. "I know it's too little, too late, but—I'm sorry."

I paused for half a step, nodding. Some things can't be undone. "That's nice to know," I said. "Thank you."

One coffee and a quick shower and change later, I was in my truck headed to Graham's apartment. Miles Marland lurking at the end of a tunnel was all I could focus on. I hadn't liked him when I met him, but I'd met thousands of men just like him and I never liked them. That was how he got past me.

* * *

Graham opened the door in basketball shorts and a bare chest, the first thing that had distracted me from Marland all morning. "Come on in," he said. "Have you eaten?"

The scars on his shoulders and back were horrifying evidence of the evil people could do. I never had a chance to look at them without fear of making him self-conscious, so I took the opportunity.

When my thoughts went from the ridges and whorls on Graham's skin to the way it stretched taut over the hard muscle beneath, I shifted them to the young woman with the charred, disfigured feet, wondering if she might wake up today.

"You never eat worth a damn when you're in the middle of a manhunt." Graham turned back when he got to the refrigerator. "You want some oatmeal, or a banana? That's about the extent of my breakfast buffet, since you won't eat eggs."

"A banana would be great." I pulled a chair out from his Formica-topped table to perch on the edge, setting my coffee on top of today's *Statesman*.

He handed me one from the fruit bowl on the counter and went to the fridge for eggs and cheese. I peeled the banana and took two bites, watching him make himself an omelet. A headline in the teasers at the top of the front page caught my eye: "The Oil Baron's Ball."

I flipped pages as I chewed my banana.

Huge gala at one of Austin's swankiest hotels. Open bar, flowing booze —and Miles and Emberly Marland in half a dozen of the photos.

"It looks like Mr. Marland is even in town this morning." I brandished the paper. "Mighty nice of him to make this convenient." I filled him in on my creepy mummy finger theory. He stared at me so long his fridge started beeping to remind him the door was open.

"Jesus, this guy. But we don't have a warrant yet," Graham said. "And the Supreme Court says we can't go into a hotel room without one, either."

"So we get it while he's sleeping off his Scotch. Speaking of sleep—you get any?"

"Eh. I dreamed about that woman from yesterday." He glanced over his shoulder. "Bad memories, and all that."

"I wish we could talk to her."

"She wouldn't say anything that makes any kind of sense. Trust me."

"I wonder if she's been saying anything at all," I muttered, reaching for my phone and standing as his eggs started to cook. "I'll just be a minute."

I went to the living room and looked up the main switchboard for University Medical Center. The phone menu was long, but ninety seconds in I heard the option for the fourth floor nurses' station.

"BICU, this is Theresa, can I help you?" The nurse's voice was warm honey-infused smoothness, probably damned handy for putting patients in such pain at ease.

"Good morning, Theresa, this is Officer Faith McClellan, Texas Rangers. I'm wondering if there's a doctor on call this morning caring for Britney Teague, the young woman with the badly burned feet who arrived from Waco yesterday."

"Doctor Nash is taking care of her." Her smooth voice dropped lower. "She's in with her now. Can you hold please?"

"Of course."

I tapped my index finger on the arm of a chair in a slow, Morse-code pattern. Short short long. Short short long.

A beep. "This is Dr. Nash."

"Good morning, Doctor." I introduced myself. "I'm wondering if you can tell me when Miss Teague might be able to talk to us about what happened to her. We understand she might have vital information about a missing person's case that's time sensitive, so the sooner we find out what she might know, the better."

The doctor sighed. "She's going to be with us a while, Officer. I'm not sure how many procedures it's going to take to try to repair her feet, or if I can even save them, at this point. How she was upright on them yesterday when the police found her is a testament to the power of adrenaline and fear. I've never seen anyone sustain this much tissue damage and not pass out from the pain, and she got up and ran away? I don't believe I want to know what you're looking for, if it was enough to make her run after an attack like this."

Wait.

What?

"I'm sorry. After what attack? We were under the impression the road burned her feet as she was walking barefoot on the blacktop."

"No. Oh, no no. Pavement wouldn't take it all the way to the bone like that unless...well, I can't give you a scenario for that. She was outside in the sun, and her feet were doused with gasoline, or maybe wrapped in it, and set on fire. Lying on her back, too, from where the sun burned her. I'm not sure how far she walked, but I'd be shocked if it was more than a mile."

Oh, my God. "Thank you, Doctor. Please let me know if her condition changes," I choked out before I pressed the *End* circle and ran for the kitchen.

Less than a mile.

We finally had a place to look.

35

Officer Bolton rang the doorbell while Graham was getting dressed, providing me my second awkward hello of the day before the sun was all the way up.

"Morning," I said.

Graham's footsteps echoed in the hallway behind me, and he shot me an eye roll the rookie couldn't see. I waved him inside. "How's your shoulder?" I asked.

"Fine."

"I'm glad." I craned my neck around the wall and waved a *come on* at Graham, who emerged from his room with his phone pressed to his ear. "Thanks, man. Sorry I woke you."

On the way down to my truck, Graham said he'd called his friend Eddie from Waco to ask for a rough estimate of where they'd picked Britney up the day before.

"The back ass end of nowhere. That's a direct quote," he said as I started the truck. "Apparently they were on their way back from lunch in West."

"Mmmm, kolaches," I said.

Graham laughed. "Better than a banana."

"Better than just about anything," I said. "Approximate isn't super helpful in a search with a radius that big, but it's sure better than we had an hour ago." We had to take it two miles out, just in case the doctor was underestimating our victim. I ignored the sleepy city blurring to life on the other side of the windows, my eyes on the road and my thoughts on Marland. The back ass end of nowhere is sort of fitting for torture, but how was he so confident he wouldn't get caught?

"He sold off some property..." I muttered Skye's words from the night before.

"Huh?" That came from the back seat. The rookie was awake after all.

I swerved onto 35 North and hit the gas. "Tax records. Property. We need to know where Marland owns land, because I'm willing to bet there's something that belongs to him not far from where that woman was found on the freeway."

"The doctor is sure it wasn't the pavement?" Bolton asked. "Her feet, I mean."

I'd been replaying that whole conversation in my head on repeat for almost half an hour. "You know how sometimes a person will say something offhand that sticks with you?" I said slowly.

"Sure." I wasn't positive who said that.

"She said...she said someone might have wrapped this woman's feet in gasoline. It went by me at first, I was too busy wondering what else we assumed wrongly about, but it's stuck in my head rattling around now and I can't unhear it. Wrapped. Like, soaked something in gasoline and wrapped it around her feet and set it on fire. What the actual fuck? Who could do that to another human?"

"A nutcase, that's who. Why did Jeffrey Dahmer eat people? Why did Ted Kaczynski send bombs in the mail? You always have to have a reason, and sometimes there is one, but sometimes you're just dealing with evil, Faith."

I didn't want to accept that. Marland had to be the sicko at the end of this rollercoaster rainbow, and he had a motivation. A selfish reason behind every death. But the torture was something else altogether.

The clock marched on toward the Fourth; less than eighteen hours to go.

We both popped our seatbelts as I turned into the F Company office lot, running for the doors. Graham had identified four properties in the county on his phone, but tax records are notoriously non-mobile-friendly.

I beat him to my desk and plunked my laptop down, flipping it open.

Every page took nine hundred years to load, my foot tapping twice a second as I stared at the screen.

I copied the addresses to a geomapping site. A large home on the lake, an office, a strip mall, and a warehouse.

"There." I pointed. "This warehouse is not far from 35." I pulled out my phone to call Archie.

"We've got him, Arch." I reeled off the details without taking a breath. "Lindsey has to be in that warehouse, and if he's sticking to his holiday theme, our time is almost up. I'm going out there after her."

"By yourself? Like hell you are." I had to hold the phone out away from my head.

"I'm not stupid." I looked around at the empty room. I was also without options, at 7 a.m. on the day before the biggest holiday of the summer. Fine.

I swiveled to Bolton. "You want to come be a hero, rookie?"

"And where will I be?" Graham asked.

"You will be with Archie, arresting Marland the second he puts a toe out of his room at the Driskill." I tossed him my keys. "Take the truck. I'll take a company unit from out back."

Graham looked between me and the door. "I don't think I like this."

"He's not there, Graham," I said. "He's in Austin with a hangover, I saw his pictures in the paper. I have plenty of skills of my own and muscles here going with me besides." I looked up at Bolton. "You'll save me, right, rookie?"

He smirked. "Do my best, ma'am."

"Archie, tell him to come with you." There wasn't a tremor in the words at all, which shocked even myself. "These are your cases. Lindsey is mine. Y'all go get this fucker, and I will find Miss Decker. No judge will fault us when they see what we had, and once we know it was his phone at the dump sites, we're golden. But we can't let him get away. Or get back to this warehouse."

"Where else does he own property, Faith?" Archie asked. "In case you're wrong. Should we dispatch units to other locations?"

I clicked back to the list and widened the search. "Jesus, how many houses does one dude need? House in Highland Park, house in Westover Hills, house out on the lake here, house outside Odessa, house on the beach in Galveston. Oh, and a condo in Houston. Commercial, he has warehouses in all of those cities and strip centers in half of them. How exactly is he losing money?" I kept scrolling. "My gut says she's here, but I'm going to send you these other addresses in Austin and Dallas. See if there are patrol units available for a drive by?"

"Yep. Be careful, kiddo."

"Always am."

I ended the call and sucked in a deep breath. The adrenaline had my Fitbit convinced I was out for a run. I squeezed Graham's hand. "This is it. We've got him. Go."

Before he could protest again, I grabbed Bolton's sleeve, a set of keys off the rack Boone kept by the back door, and a pair of vests from the closet, and took off. Lindsey needed me. And Graham would feel better when I had her and was back in one piece.

36

Holiday traffic wasn't moving yet, only three other cars on the road between my office and the warehouse. I passed it, circled back, and parked a block down.

"What would anyone need with storage out here?" Bolton met me at the front of the cruiser. Flat, brown land spread as far as we could see in every direction, save for one ugly gray corrugated metal building. It was just a bit too far off the freeway to see, and surrounded by a fat lot of nothing.

"Pretty perfect torture chamber, isn't it?" I asked.

He shrugged. "I'm not sure there is such a thing, but I guess I'll take your word for it."

I started for the building, my phone buzzing in my pocket. "McClellan," I half-whispered, putting it to my ear.

"Faith, I have something interesting here I think you're going to want to see," Judge "Uncle Dan" Brinkman said. "Are you free for breakfast this morning, by any chance?"

"I'm afraid I'm not, but it's for a good cause," I said. "It's not even seven in California. How did you get an answer?"

"It seems my son has a friend at Google," he replied. "It just arrived, and knocked me right over when I opened it. Do you know who Miles Marland is?"

I let out a yelp that made Bolton flinch. "Hot damn, we got him," I said. "Yes, sir, I do. He's the chief suspect in this case."

"You need a warrant?"

"Archie Baxter might," I said. "Can I give him your number?"

"Please do. And Faith—I did some reading about recent murders last night. Watch yourself."

"Thank you," I said. "Thank you so much, for your help and for the call, Uncle Dan. I'd love a raincheck on the breakfast when this is over and done with."

"Looking forward to it, young lady."

I sent Archie and Graham a quick text with the judge's number and turned, taking a left around the perimeter of the building. I didn't give one damn about a warrant. I was going in to see what Marland was hiding out here.

Hopefully, Lindsey Decker was still alive for us to save.

* * *

We made it halfway around the outside of the building, Bolton spotting a water well and storm shelter about twenty yards apart in the dirt, before my phone rang again.

Jim.

"Why are you still awake?" I asked.

"I got your DNA. Went over to Travis and ran it myself," he said, triumph coming through thick layers of exhaustion. Jim was pushing retirement, and all-nighters weren't exactly a regular thing for him.

"Excellent, we identified the victim in that case, so Archie will be able to check it against her profile for you," I said. "She was his first kill."

"She?" The way Jim's voice went up at the end of that made me feel a little nauseous.

"Yes. Why?"

Silence.

"Jim?"

"Well, um...pulling a full profile from preserved tissue is impossible, but I got enough to tell you this was a man. A man who probably died about twenty years ago, judging from the half-life I'm getting on this thing."

I stopped walking, the heavy Kevlar vest suddenly making it hard to breathe. "No."

None of that was right. Nothing about it fit. Officer Hernandez would have been in middle school twenty years ago. "How sure are you?" I asked, the tight tremble in my voice drawing Bolton's eyes my way.

"I'm sure enough to call you with it," he said. "There's not an abundance of sample, but I didn't skip a step and the computer only spits out what it sees, not what we want it to see." He paused. "Sounds like I might be screwing up your day. Sorry."

"No worries, Jim. Thanks for taking the extra five miles on this one. And thanks for calling."

I clicked the *End* circle and shook my head.

It might not mean anything. Maybe it wasn't the souvenir we thought it was, maybe he bought it at an occult shop or some bullshit. I was here, we had his phone and his motive, and I wasn't turning around based on a single DNA run on a decades-old sample.

* * *

Heavy brass padlocks held chains on the doors at both ends of the building. On our second lap, I spotted another way in.

"See the window up there?" I pointed to a narrow rectangle of glass about six and a half feet off the ground. "I'm going to pull the car over here, and if we can break it, we can use the car as a step stool to get up there."

"How do we get down on the other side?" Bolton asked.

"We hope it doesn't hurt when we hit the ground. I don't have another option. No matter how cool it looks on TV, shooting at metal in the real world is ill-advised at best and deadly at worst."

"I know that." He rolled his eyes. "But I like my ankles in one piece, too."

I double-timed it back for the car, the Boy Scout motto on Boone's coffee mug flashing through my thoughts.

Nah.

I opened the trunk anyway.

Flares, spare tire, rain gear, shotgun…and bolt cutters.

"I'll be damned," I said. "Thank you, Lieutenant."

I grabbed them and sprinted back, winded by the time I reached Bolton. "Plan B. My boss was an Eagle Scout."

We hurried to the door and I handed him the cutters. Strategy, I could beat him at all day, but for brute force, he was pretty damned handy.

The chain link sliced like butter and fell away. I drew my sidearm just in case, then slid the door back.

Please, God.

37

He was there. She smelled Him before her eyes even came open, curled behind a pile of old tires in a barn she'd spotted in the distance just as the sun sank below the western horizon.

Thirty-eight thousand seven hundred and ninety-two. Her legs shook with fatigue. She knew there would be no food, not tonight, but she could live with that. She found a cracked old garden hose coiled next to the barn and tried the tap, not even waiting for the water to run clear before she started drinking.

She gulped so much that it came back up, the acid it carried along burning her throat as she retched onto the dry, bare dirt, the vomit obscuring the blood leaking from her battered feet with every step.

Slower. Wait.

She raised the hose to her lips, the water still warm, her throat not as greedy this time.

Sip sip sip. Pause. Sip sip sip. Pause.

When the burn was gone, she rinsed her hair and feet and most of her tender, blistering skin. She couldn't reach her back, but the water sluiced over it smooth and cool through her threadbare cotton shirt.

Dark.

Sleep.

So many sleeps, locked away in the dark, with nobody to talk to except other kids who wouldn't live to see next week, in a place where it was a strain to see anything but shadows that would grow and morph into nightmares that threatened her sanity if she let them. But it had given her a gift.

She could smell everything.

The rubber of the tires, the slowly rotting, moldy wood of the barn, the rats burrowing in the stale, sour straw in the loft.

And Him. Even in her sleep.

Especially in her sleep, maybe. Because that's when He was most dangerous.

Musky, thick sweat laced with the booze that practically seeped from His pores was the first thing that hit her nose. Close behind was His breath—stale and sour on the surface, but with sickly-sweet decay mixed in. She could remember the nice lady at the orphanage showing her how to brush her teeth, in another lifetime, and she wondered often in the first months if He even owned a toothbrush. She had. It was pink, with purple flowers on the handle, and the lady smiled at her when she stood at the sink and brushed until the little bell rang on the timer.

"Come out, come out, wherever you are." He made his voice high and whispery. "It's time to go home, tiny spitfire."

That's what He'd called her, since the first day when He'd tried to touch her face with His smelly, greasy finger and she'd spat at Him. She didn't mean to, even. It just happened, without her thinking of it.

She pulled herself to sitting soundlessly, tightening her grip on the railroad tie she hadn't let go of, even as she slept.

"Where are you, spitfire?" He slurred the *S* that time. "I saw the blood, out by the road. Your feet must hurt something awful. Let's get you home. Safe. I can fix 'em."

She shook her head, keeping her breath slow and quiet. One way or another it would end here. They weren't both walking out of this place.

She choked up on the steel club that was almost as heavy as she was. She didn't need to know how she would be able to swing it. She just knew she would.

The tires swayed when He stumbled into them in the dark. He never saw as clearly in the dark as she did, and the barn was as pitch black as her hidey-hole at night.

She planted her feet on the floor, clenching her own rotting teeth together and swallowing screams as she pushed herself to standing on blistered soles.

Both hands on the tie.

His sweat. The grease and heat on His coveralls. His hair goop. His breath.

That was it. When she could smell nothing but His breath, He was close enough.

She clenched her eyes tight and swung for the fences, pain swallowing her right arm into a gaping maw with sharp teeth.

The sound wasn't satisfying the way a crack used to be on a TV baseball game. It was squishy. Soft.

Like a watermelon falling off the counter.

She could see the melon, splattered all over the orphanage's white kitchen floor. She cried. She was sorry.

The nice lady was stern, her smile gone, mouth unforgiving.

The next day, a new lady came to pick her up. Signed some papers and took her "home." The man there wasn't nice, so she ran away. On her fourth night sleeping in the park, He took her "home" to the dark.

She always thought it all happened because she broke the melon. Food wasn't to be wasted, the orphanage lady said.

A half-grunt, and He crumpled.

As she heard Him hit the ground, she figured it was better, imagining His fat, oily head like the crushed-up watermelon guts spilling across the floor.

Not a person.

A thing. A thing that couldn't hurt anyone anymore.

She reached into the top tire for the cutters she'd hidden there when she'd come in. Backup. A surprise weapon she could raise if he took her club.

But he hadn't.

Pulling them down, she knelt, careful to keep her feet out of his blood. She didn't want any part of him mingling with any part of her.

His fingers always smelled like grease and dirt.

She leaned close, moving her head and inhaling until she found what she was looking for.

Grease, dirt, and metal.

She poked him with a finger. Harder.

He rolled, a wet, oozy sound coming from his head. But no breath—she couldn't smell even a hint of it anymore.

She won.

And she wanted her proof.

She found the ring. Raised the cutters.

It took work. Sweat. Twisting and squeezing until her hands and arms ached.

Dark became dim. She kept her eyes on the ring and worked more frantically.

Twist, squeeze, pull.

She fell back to the dirt when it came free. She dropped the cutters, ready for blood, but there was none.

Maybe it had all leaked out already, seeping into the dirt. Down, down, down, away from her.

The ring glinted in the early beams snaking through the slatted wooden walls. Gold. Sharp.

Hers. It wouldn't hurt her ever again.

She closed her fist around it. Found the pocket in her saggy, grungy shorts. Patted the outside.

With the ring in her pocket, she was safe.

She walked carefully around the long end of the tires and let herself out through the wide wood-planked doors.

Back to the road.

Thirty-eight thousand seven hundred and ninety-three. Thirty-eight thousand seven hundred and ninety-four.

At forty thousand one hundred twenty-two, the sun came fully over the edge of the horizon, lighting up a tall cobalt blue pole with a golden ticket at the top.

She didn't know what a Blockbuster Video was, but in the dumpster behind the building she found plastic bags she tied around her blistered, aching feet. And under the bags, she found candy. Boxes and boxes of jujubes and junior mints with crinkled, dented sides. She ripped into one, careful not to stuff her mouth too fast or chew too recklessly. She took three more and surveyed the parking lot.

A car wash. A Walmart. She knew what Walmart was.

She looked down at herself.

Anyone who saw her would call the police.

The police would take her back to an orphanage.

Nope.

She moved as quickly as her blistered feet would allow to the back of the building. Found a corner of an empty dumpster and folded herself into it. When dark came again, she'd slip inside.

Shoes. Food. Soap. Toothbrushes. Walmart had everything, the nice lady used to say before the watermelon fell.

They even had newspapers.

Two days went by before she saw a new one in the rack outside the store, where she sat with a jar and a sign that said she was collecting for a children's charity. She just didn't say it was her.

Local man murdered in abandoned barn, police say. She read the story five times, until she knew it by heart.

No weapon.

No prints.

No suspects.

She cut out the article and wrapped his ring finger carefully in it. It was starting to smell. She'd found a book in the tiny community library about preserving flesh—they were talking about animals, but she figured it couldn't be much different.

It was a bad thing, to kill someone. But she'd make it up. She'd find a way to help people, do penance for sitting silent while he hurt the others.

She watched the business windows on Main Street. Waited for her skin and feet to heal. And went in when she saw a help wanted sign in the saloon.

Was she eighteen? Sure. The man handed her an apron and told her to come back at five.

It took six weeks for the big man in the suit and Stetson to get smitten with her. He told her she was special, and he never tried to hurt her.

When he asked her to go home with him to Dallas, she left Loving County and promised herself she'd never look back.

38

Gasoline. The smell hit me in the face as soon as the door moved, knocking me back a step as my hands flexed around the gun.

Bolton coughed behind me. I shushed him, stepping into the wide, dim room and swinging my Sig in a slow half-circle. My phone buzzed in my pocket.

Not now.

Once my eyes adjusted to the low light, I could make out shelves.

Bolt cutters. Some like the ones we'd used outside, some smaller, some larger. And food. Like, the-zombie-apocalypse-is-coming food—rows and rows of canned vegetables, dried cheese, and enough bottled water to keep a small city hydrated for a year.

"What the hell?" I heard Bolton whisper, and turned just in time to see a shadow behind him. "Stop right there!" I shouted. "Texas Rangers, hands where I can see them!"

Bolton had a small set of branding irons in his hands. But he raised them, anyway.

"Not you, rookie." I stepped around him to the door and found myself looking down at Emberly Marland, considerably shorter without her spike heels.

Her hands went from her hips to her heart, her mouth opening but no sound escaping.

My fingers relaxed on the gun. "Mrs. Marland, what are you doing here?" I asked.

She sucked in several deep breaths, waving one bejeweled hand in front of her face. "The police came into our room at the hotel and took Miles," she said. "I asked what he had done and nobody would tell me, but I heard someone say something about the warehouse in Waco. So I came to see for myself."

I stepped aside to let her in. "Do you know what the meaning of this is?" I asked.

She looked around slowly, shaking her head. "I'm afraid I don't have the first clue," she said. "I didn't even know he owned this building. Miss McClellan, what has my husband done?"

My turn for the deep breath. "He hasn't been convicted of anything. But we arrested him on suspicion of murder. And I think Lindsey Decker might be here somewhere."

Her hands went back to her chest, the color draining from her face. "No. Miles would never, could never."

"Mrs. Marland, can you tell me where the sudden cash flow that saved your husband's financial standing starting in 2015 came from?" I asked.

"What on earth are you talking about? Everyone knows the Marland family is one of the oldest oil lines in Texas. We didn't need saving."

"How involved is your husband with what you do at the shelter?" I asked.

"Hardly at all. He pops in once in a while, but that's my passion."

I nodded. "Ma'am, have you ever heard of an attorney named Daphne Livingston?"

She tipped her head to one side. "I think maybe she worked a case we watched closely, but I can't place the name," she said. "Why is that?"

"Because she was on the governor's special committee to end trafficking, and she's dead. And so are at least two other women who helped trafficking victims."

Emberly shook her head, stepping backward. "You don't think my Miles was..." Her head shook faster. "Not a trafficker. No. He knew how much it meant to me." She stepped back again, her arms flailing like the heel of her shoe had caught in the floor. I lowered my weapon to my side and reached for her, her silk sleeve slipping out of my grasp as she spun, grabbed a pair of bolt cutters half as long as I was, and swung them for my skull like she was playing T-ball.

I ducked, throwing my hands up over my head and sending my Sig flying.

Bolton didn't, catching the sharp tip over his right ear and crumpling instantly, blood spurting from the wound.

My brain didn't want to process what I was seeing, my eyes going back to Emberly as her face twisted and she raised the heavy steel tool for another swing.

I ran, darting between shelves, my boots echoing off the concrete floor and metal walls.

"I can run, too, Ranger," Emberly called. "I'm doing important work here, and you're not going to wreck it for me."

I was five rows deep into the building before I got my head around the fact that she was chasing me. With a weapon. And my gun had clattered to the floor only God knew where.

Great. My hand-to-hand skills and Kevlar vest wouldn't protect my head from getting split like a piñata. At least I knew now why Jim couldn't identify the weapon with certainty.

Her steps slowed before mine did, and I went up on my toes, moving lightly and taking every switchback I could find.

How was a person who ran a shelter for trafficking victims trading in the trafficking arena? Besides the obvious cover, I just didn't get how she could see and talk with and get to know those kids and then send them right back into it.

Not that I was asking right now.

Her footsteps sped again. Closer.

Shit. I took another switchback and stopped.

Seven-foot shelves on either side and a wall.

She'd slowed down not because she was tired. But because she knew she was running me right the hell into a dead end. Smart. It was the first thing on my profile.

I slid my foot backwards and spun around just as Emberly appeared, cutters raised.

"You're smarter than I thought," she said. "But I'm good at cleaning up loose ends, and they already think Miles is guilty."

"So explain to me," I said. "If he's in jail answering questions, how do I die way out here?"

"Lindsey, of course." She shook her head. "After the other one escaped yesterday, she tried to run, too. Caught you both in the head thinking she was attacking Miles when she heard the chains. But you didn't bleed to death before you"—she brandished my gun with a gloved hand—"got off the shot that killed her. It was too late for all three of you by the time I arrived and called frantically for help. Skye will love it."

I backed toward the wall, looking for an opening. She filled the only escape route, and had the only two weapons.

She stepped forward. "I thought you were one of the good ones. So many people who do what you do aren't. I hate to have to do this."

She stepped forward and laid the gun on a shelf, raising the cutters.

39

Emberly liked to talk. It was time to let her.

I threw my arms over my head. "Why?" It came out shrill, loud, ricocheting off the walls like she had me cornered in the Grand Canyon.

It also worked. For a minute. I heard her breath escape on a sigh, her feet going still.

"Why would you do this?" I lowered my arms when I heard her stop. "These women all helped victims, just like you."

"Not at all like me. It takes a village to raise a child, and it takes a village to forget one and leave them to horror, too," she said. "They all liked to smile for cameras and take credit for helping. Just like Miles. But Daphne Livingston signed off on the wrong plea bargain and the judge threw out a case the San Antonio PD spent years building."

"The RICO case was a trafficker?" Anything illegal you could want to buy, Skye had said. And I didn't ask about humans. "But nobody's perfect. If you're going to kill people, why not kill the real evildoers?"

She choked up on her bolt cutters, the urge to gloat and the urge to be done with this warring on her twisting face.

"People like you go after the traffickers. But it took a pastor, two lawyers, a judge, and three social workers to put me into four varieties of abusive foster homes before I ran away and got taken off the streets into a nightmare. And people like you, like Skye Morrow, would go after the man who put me in a cage, the men who beat and raped me...but nobody ever takes the others to task. Their mistakes, their carelessness, their 'just doing my job's' put me there, like Daphne's put other people there." I nodded as she talked, only half hearing, my eyes on the butt of my Sig that was just visible over the edge of the black plastic shelving. Four feet away, maybe. The cutters she held would reach three. Shit. I slid my feet out wide and dropped my center of gravity.

"It was time for them to be punished, too." Emberly swung.

I dove, my arms closing around her calves and bringing her down on top of me. The cutters hit my legs as she fell, opening a gash in the back of my thigh.

"You little bitch," she howled, rolling off, scrambling to her feet. "I have survived things you cannot even imagine."

I ignored the blood soaking the back of my jeans as I pushed off the floor and jumped for the shelf, coming up with my Sig just as she righted the cutters in her hands. I leaned on my good leg and spun, fumbling the gun right side up.

"I'm not losing to you." It was a bona fide snarl, her face twisting into something that didn't even look human.

She rushed forward, howling, cutters raised high.

They were coming toward the crown of my head when my index finger found the trigger.

I squeezed.

Emberly stopped cold. Fell backwards, the metal tool clattering to the ground.

I stood over her, my eyes on the neat little round hole in her forehead and the black pool spreading on the concrete under her.

"You okay?"

I screamed, jumping and raising the gun again.

Bolton shuffled forward, his palm pressed to the cut on the side of his head.

I caught half a dozen breaths, nudging Emberly's limp shoulder with the toe of my boot before I holstered my weapon.

"Nice shot, ma'am." Bolton's words were slurred. "So where's the girl?"

40

We found Lindsey Decker in the storm shelter out behind the warehouse. It took us three tries to get the damned door open thanks to blood loss, and Lindsey, naked and terrified, screamed and shrank into the corner when Bolton was the first down the steps, but I managed to convince her we were the good guys. God, I hoped we were, anyway.

She was dehydrated, malnourished, and had an infection festering in the wound where her ear had been—but she still had all her fingers, and when Mrs. Poway brought Jake into the hospital room, I thought Lindsey might never let him go ever again.

Adam Decker had run from a dealer he owed, a scary-looking dude about 6'7" with thick arms and a face that didn't know how to smile. When the guy figured out he really wasn't getting his money, he had a kid slip Adam some strychnine-spiked dope. Damned lucky he hadn't died. He was finally trying to turn his life around. I hoped he could make it work.

Graham and Archie and I spent the Fourth doing the research we needed to lock down our case.

Miles Marland met his wife in a saloon near the oil fields in Loving County in the spring of 1992. She was waiting tables, he was checking on his fields, and he said it was love at first sight. He thought her clumpy rubber ring holder was funny, and teased her about it until it made her cry one night and she told him the ring had belonged to her father and she liked carrying it around with her. Miles thought the scar on her face was from skin cancer surgery, and he paid to have the best plastic surgeon in Dallas erase it. She also said her parents were dead, which was the only thing that turned out to be true.

A man named Carl Ray Sands found Emberly on the street after she escaped an abusive foster home when she was fourteen. Carl locked Emberly in his basement for more than two years before she got away and ran, leaving him for dead with a bashed-in skull and a missing ring finger in an abandoned barn off Highway 209.

His was the murder I'd found in the paper, the one Sheriff Bud had blamed on outsiders. Once the new sheriff got to digging, it seemed Carl's old back forty was the final resting place for thirteen teenagers he'd picked up in various places and tortured before he killed them. In another universe where Emberly wasn't a murderer, we'd have called her a lucky survivor.

As Lindsey relayed it, Emberly attacked her from behind. When Lindsey came to, Emberly said she wasn't sure Lindsey would've agreed to meet her and couldn't risk the cell phone record of a call to ask, and Lindsey "had to pay."

Once we knew where to look, Emberly's choice of victims made a sort of twisted sense—they were all people who had failed, in her stringent, unforgiving estimation, victims who were like she'd once been. Pastor Allen had allowed a trafficker posing as a reporter to charm her into a tour of her shelter. She'd unknowingly fed half a dozen kids back into the cycle before she figured it out. Ramona designed an online sales platform she sold to a foreign investor who put it up on the dark web and used it to traffic teenage girls through U.S. ports. Ramona never knew that, but Emberly figured it out and she didn't do the forgiveness thing well. Officer Hernandez's falsified evidence let a drug dealer who also dabbled in selling humans walk free, and Lindsey...well... Lindsey did in fact sleep with Emberly's husband, but Emberly knew about that and didn't care. What she did care about was Jeremy, who left Harbor House because Lindsey wasn't there anymore and ended up dead. Regardless of the circumstances surrounding Jeremy's murder, Emberly blamed Lindsey for his death.

But it was Britney Teague that Emberly hated most—the girl with the charred feet was in fact a junkie, and had used her position at CPS to allow several kids to "disappear" out of foster care and into the hands of traffickers in exchange for heroin. Lindsey said Emberly was more hostile and violent after she dumped Britney in the storm shelter. When Britney bolted for daylight while Emberly was busy hacking off Lindsey's ear, Emberly chased her down, set her feet on fire, and left her for dead in the blazing sun—already in an open shallow grave. Britney definitely had some superhuman fight in her to get up and hobble away, and it had saved her life. Hopefully that same determination would get it back on track.

Graham, Archie, and I took Bolton out for drinks at the Work Horse on the fifth, toasting a disaster averted and the memory of the victims we hadn't saved.

There were always the ones we hadn't saved. This made 124 for me. But Lindsey Decker, I got back.

"You're pretty amazing, you know that?" Graham slung his arm around my shoulders, walking me to my truck after we'd had our fill of nachos and margaritas.

I shook my head. "I wish I could save them all," I said. "There was logic there, in an extraordinarily bizarre way, but I keep wondering why Emberly Marland didn't direct her anger at the people who actually deserved it. If you're going to fancy yourself a folk hero vigilante, kill off the scum even we won't really miss."

Graham stopped by the truck, turning me to face him and putting his forearms on my shoulders. "Ever the idealist. Traffickers are like drug lords—well insulated and paranoid about outside attacks. She couldn't get to them. But Emberly Marland had a history with pastors, lawyers, social workers, and cops. They all failed her when her folks died. They let her end up on the streets where Sands could grab her because of bureaucratic bullshit. The guy who was once the newspaper editor out there told Skye Morrow the whole thing, and she's been running it piece by piece all week. She was crazy, Faith. Given the life she had, almost anybody would be. Not her fault, but not society's problem, either. We did a good thing here."

I leaned my forehead against his shoulder. "Thank you. I wouldn't have gotten to her without you. We wouldn't have gotten Lindsey back."

His arms shifted, hands going into my hair, drawing my head back gently. "We make a good team, you and me. Always have."

He held my gaze for half a breath before his lips closed over mine, the sweet, simple kiss melting me faster than the July heat still radiating off the concrete.

"Graham—" I blinked, laying my hands flat on his chest.

"Was that okay?" He tipped his head to the side.

My hands went to his face, pulling it back down to mine.

It was more than okay.

Lindsey was home.

I was kissing Graham Hardin.

And somewhere in the distance, I swear I heard fireworks.

No Sin Unpunished: Faith McClellan #3

When a serial killer leaves a string of victims with political ties, it sends Texas Ranger Faith McClellan into a desperate race to save lives—even the ones she's not sure deserve saving.

While on special assignment to the bank fraud unit, Texas Ranger Faith McClellan accidentally stumbles upon a raging fire consuming the back of a nearby house. When partially-cremated remains are pulled from the ruins, she finds herself back on homicide—and on the trail of a ruthless killer.

As she races to identify the victims, the sadistic murderer strikes again—this time against state politicians with ties to Faith's father, a former governor of Texas. Faith is forced to face shocking and long-buried family secrets as she questions her confidence in the justice system—and those she thinks she knows best.

Soon, Faith and her colleagues realize they're hunting a killer with a personal vendetta, whose ferocious methods of murder are punishment for unimaginable sins of the past.
Everyone is a suspect. The pressure is on. Now Faith must piece together clues from the ashes...before her whole life goes up in flames.

ACKNOWLEDGMENTS

This book marks the tenth anniversary of my headlong dive into writing fiction, and looking back over the last decade, I am so tremendously grateful for so many things, not the least of which is the fact that I ignored the doubting voice in the back of my mind that said I would never be able to write a whole book.

In ten years and nine novels since, I have learned so much and grown as a writer, but no book has ever stretched me the way this one did. I had never written about a missing person's investigation, and as it happened, Faith had never worked one. We learned how to build the case from both sides, Faith and me, and it was a crazy, challenging, fun ride.

As with every book, I owe thanks to so many people who played a part in putting this finished product in your hands.

John Talbot is not only a wonderful agent, but a fantastic friend. Kind and smart and great at talking me through things, Faith wouldn't be here without John's guidance and belief in me.

Randall Klein, who is a truly gifted editor: thank you for your encouragement and insight, but most of all for pushing me and challenging me. This is a much better book for your efforts, and I am so grateful.

Andrew, Amber, Jason, Mo, and Keris, thank you all for your smart and tireless work keeping my books in front of readers and helping me tell the very best stories I can. You are such a joy to work with.

The journalists and law enforcement professionals I worked with during my years as a reporter, my thanks for sharing your wisdom and war stories and teaching me about police procedures and how to get the little things right.

Julie and Sarah, who listen to me whine and tell me I will figure it out when I need it most, thank you for hanging in there all this time. Art, Tara, and Dru Ann, who are fantastic at pep talks, and have superhuman doubt-vanquishing abilities, thank you for being such wonderful friends. Nichole and Aimee, thank you both for checking in to make sure I was getting my words down and patting my head or pushing me forward accordingly.

Justin, my best friend and partner in life and love—thank you for believing in me on the days I don't, for listening to endless versions of every story until I find the right one, and for being the best husband and dad I could imagine.

Avery, Gabe, and Kennedy: you three make me proud every day. I love your kind hearts and adventurous spirits, your inquisitive minds and determination. Keep learning and dreaming, and always step out and go after the hard things that you want in life, remembering that, as Jimmy Dugan said, if it wasn't hard, everyone would do it.

And you, lovely reader—many thanks to those who have been here since the first book was published and those who are just discovering Faith and Nichelle and their adventures. Your time, your reviews, and your kind words mean so much. I read and cherish (and do my very best to answer) every message and email, and I am delighted that you invite my stories and characters to be part of your lives. I hope you'll love this new adventure as much as I do, and I thank you for taking the journey with Faith.

As always, any mistakes you find are mine alone.

ABOUT THE AUTHOR

LynDee Walker is the national bestselling author of two crime fiction series featuring strong heroines and "twisty, absorbing" mysteries. Her first Nichelle Clarke crime thriller, FRONT PAGE FATALITY, was nominated for the Agatha Award for best first novel and is an Amazon Charts Bestseller. In 2018, she introduced readers to Texas Ranger Faith McClellan in FEAR NO TRUTH. Reviews have praised her work as "well-crafted, compelling, and fast-paced," and "an edge-of-your-seat ride" with "a spider web of twists and turns that will keep you reading until the end."

Before she started writing fiction, LynDee was an award-winning journalist who covered everything from ribbon cuttings to high level police corruption, and worked closely with the various law enforcement agencies that she reported on. Her work has appeared in newspapers and magazines across the U.S.

Aside from books, LynDee loves her family, her readers, travel, and coffee. She lives in Richmond, Virginia, where she is working on her next novel when she's not juggling laundry and children's sports schedules.

Sign up for LynDee Walker's reader list at
severnriverbooks.com/authors/lyndee-walker

lyndee@severnriverbooks.com

ACKNOWLEDGMENTS

Much appreciation to three supporters whose early encouragement made all the difference in my love of writing—my mother and high school English teachers, Pat Dannen and Maxine Edwards.

Thanks to all of my instructors and writer friends who have influenced my approach to the craft of writing and also offered countless gems of wisdom and wit, largely for free.

A shout-out to Julie Keefe, photographer extraordinaire! Thank you, friends and family, for your ongoing support—Mary-Beth Baptista, Arlene Blair, Cara Busacker, Vicki Cartwright, Rachel Martin Crocker, Michele Glazer, Ann & Bill Griffin, Kari Guy, Annice Kessler Attoe, Charlie Landis, Sarah Landis, Rosie Locati, Angela M. Sanders, Duane Turner, and Mark Wiggington. An extra special thank-you to Lance Linder for his discerning eye and his appreciation of Maggie Blackthorne.

I also want to thank the team at Severn River Publishing—Andrew Watts, Amber Hudock, Cate Streissguth, Mo Metlen, Keris Sirek, and my fabulous editor, Kate Schomaker.

Tom Griffin-Valade is beta reader, critic, cheerleader, and fan number one. Thanks, babe.

To our children and their partners—Shawn, Amy & Tony, Alexis & Ahmed, and Kai & Hannah—thank you all for believing in me and supporting me. To our grandchildren—Lauren, Logan, Piper, and Zio—thank you for reminding me of what's really important.

ABOUT THE AUTHOR

LaVonne Griffin-Valade was born and raised in the high desert country along the John Day River of eastern Oregon—a place that stoked her imagination and inspired her to become a lifetime writer of short stories, essays, poetry, and novels. She has worn many professional hats: elementary school teacher, mentor, education equity advocate, and serving as the elected Auditor of the City of Portland.

LaVonne has published essays and pieces of fiction in multiple publications, including the *Oregon Humanities Magazine* and the *Clackamas Literary Review*. She earned an MFA from Portland State University in 2017 and was a finalist for the 2018 Fellowship for Emerging Writers at Fishtrap's Writing and the West.

LaVonne lives in Portland, Oregon, and works as a full-time writer. *Dead Point*, *Murderers Creek*, and *Desolation Ridge* are the first three novels in the Maggie Blackthorne series.

Sign up for LaVonne Griffin-Valade's newsletter at
severnriverbooks.com/authors/lavonne-griffin-valade